J

THE *MINNOW* LEADS TO TREASURE

THE MINNOW
LEADS TO TREASURE

by A. Philippa Pearce

Illustrated by Edward Ardizzone

THE WORLD PUBLISHING COMPANY

CLEVELAND AND NEW YORK

Published by THE WORLD PUBLISHING COMPANY

2231 West 110th Street, Cleveland 2, Ohio

Library of Congress Catalog Card Number: 58–5773

WP158

FIRST PUBLISHED IN GREAT BRITAIN IN 1955
UNDER THE TITLE *Minnow on the Say.*

TO

Ernest and Gertrude Pearce

AT THE KING'S MILL

Contents

1. Summer Floods   11
2. Whose Boat?   15
3. Maiden Voyage   20
4. Codlings'   27
5. Scraping and Saving   37
6. The Portrait in the Hall   44
7. A Tale of Treasure   51
8. Over the Bridge   61
9. A Trip to Tea   71
10. Folly Mill and a Ball of String   79
11. One More Try   94
12. "My Wheelbarrow End"   98
13. The Old Channel   108
14. Search by Moonlight   122
15. Old Mr. Codling Laughs   131
16. John Codling Comes Home   139
17. The Board at the Gate   142
18. Pip-squeak   153
19. A Dead End   159
20. Mrs. Perfect Can't Quite Remember   167
21. The Bus to Castleford   179
22. The Smiths at Home   188
23. From Cellar to Roof   200
24. Heigh-ho!   217
25. Treasure for Tea   226
26. Never Tell, David!   241

THE *MINNOW* LEADS TO TREASURE

I

Summer Floods

DAVID MOSS lived with his family in the last house in Jubilee Row. Their house was like all the others, but their garden was something quite out of the ordinary: it ran straight back for the first twenty yards, like all the other gardens. Then, when the others stopped, this took a sudden turn to the right and, in another minute, it had reached an unexpected destination. When the other gardens ended in a hedge, a fence, or a stretch of wire netting, the Mosses' garden was brought to a stop only by the softly flowing waters of the River Say.

"No, Becky, no!" said Mrs. Moss. "You must never play by the river alone. David only goes onto the dock because he's older; if he falls in, he can swim."

The dock was over-grandly named, for nothing and nobody had ever landed there. It had been made by Mr. Moss only so that he could more easily fill his watering can from the river. In the daytime Mr. Moss drove a bus between Castleford and the Barleys; after his day's work, he liked to garden.

David, as well as his father, had uses for the dock, but they were not altogether satisfactory ones. He fished, of course, but he had only a net and jar, and this part of the river was underpopulated with minnows and sticklebacks. He launched boats, but his boats were only toys, carved with a penknife or made of cocked-up paper. He tired even of boat racing—that is, of starting two boats together, and then pedaling round to the bridge over the Say below Little Barley, to see which boat was first at the bridge and downstream toward Castleford. Such occupations—such craft—came to seem unworthy of the solid and spacious dock of Mr. Moss's construction.

One summer, David had been to the dock even less than usual. He had been working hard at school; and besides, the summer had been miserably wet so far. The end of the term came, and David passed his examinations; he would be going to the big school in Castleford next term. He was pleased, but even more pleased because of the long summer holidays ahead. If only it would stop raining! The weather was warm, but the rain fell in torrents.

"Do you think it'll ever stop?" asked David.

"It'll stop," said Mr. Moss. "But not before it batters my sunflowers down. And there'll be floods."

"Bad floods, dear?" said Mrs. Moss.

"Well, floods."

Night after night, David went to sleep with the sound of the rain beating on the roof. Then, one morning, he woke to quietness and sunlight. Out of the window, the sky was a clear, pale blue. Later on in the day the blue would deepen, with heat; there would be no clouds—no more rain.

David dressed and ran downstairs. In the holidays he delivered morning newspapers in the Barleys, to earn pocket money; he always hurried through some porridge before he started out—his mother would not let him cycle on an empty stomach—but he left the rest of his breakfast until his return.

This morning Mr. Moss had already left for his work, and

David was alone at the breakfast table when Becky came in from the garden.

"David! The river's high—so high! Is it floods?"

"You know you're too little to go near the river alone, Becky —Mother says so."

"I didn't go onto the dock," said Becky. "But I'd never seen floods."

"When I come back, I'll take you just to look," promised David. He felt sorry for Becky. It might be several years yet before she was old enough to swim, and so she missed a good deal.

"And will you take me in your boat as well?"

"What would a fat little girl like you do in a paper boat? Or in one of my wooden ones, even?"

"But the lovely big boat you have now, David—will you take me in it?"

"The one nearly six inches long?" said David teasingly.

"The very big one. Will you take me?"

David was in a hurry. He finished the last spoonful of porridge, and ran out to his bicycle.

Becky followed him. "Will you, Davy? Will you?"

"If there's room in any boat of mine, I'll take you in it," David called back as he shot off. Becky seemed content with this, and waved until bicycle and rider were out of sight.

The sun was well up before David got home from his newspaper route. The rest of his breakfast was waiting for him on the table. But the kitchen door was open, and through it he could see the garden door open; beyond that the sun was shining outside on grass and leaves still dark and glossy from the rains. He slipped past the breakfast table and straight out into the garden. He heard Becky call, and her feet coming after him, but he could not wait.

He turned the bend in the garden, and there was the gate to the dock, but the river beyond it—that could hardly be the River Say! The waters were a pale brown, quite without transparency, and curdled here and there into white or yellow froth; they hurried along with a full, rippling motion and with a lipping sound that David had never heard before. The water was higher than he had ever seen it. On the far side of the river it had risen over the bank and moved among the grass blades of the meadow; on his side it had covered part of the dock, and a trickle of water had crept under the gate into the garden itself.

David felt wonderfully excited. He straddled the water on the garden path, and went up to the gate for a better view.

Becky had nearly caught up with him. "Your big boat, Davy —please!"

"Oh, yes, Becky!" he said impatiently.

Then he saw what Becky was talking about. At the dock waited a real boat, a canoe at least ten feet long. It was not made fast anywhere, but the current kept it a prisoner in the angle between the submerged dock and the river bank. Its nose bobbed every now and then against one of the posts of the dock; it reminded David of a dog that wants to be taken out for a walk. The canoe was quite empty.

2

Whose Boat?

THERE WAS the canoe and there was David, and not another
human being in sight. Then Becky arrived at the gate,
panting and crying out, "You can't go without me! You
promised to take me in your boat! You promised!"

"Be quiet, Becky! Who's going in the boat anyway? And
how can I take you in my boat, when this isn't my boat?"

David scowled, and hustled Becky off the dock. She did not
seem to have understood him, for she went back toward the house
really crying now, and gasping out at the same time: "He promised! He promised! He promised!" Her mother came out to see
what the matter was and to call David in to his breakfast.

"He promised," sobbed Becky into her mother's apron, "and
now he won't! He promised!"

"David, you know you can't promise Becky something and
then just break your promise."

"It's not fair," said David. "I said I'd take her in my boat, but of course I haven't one big enough, so I couldn't. But now there's a real boat, but I still can't take her in it, because it isn't my boat."

Mrs. Moss did not follow David's explanation, except for one part, on which she pounced. "Becky isn't to go playing by the river with boats or anything else, even with you, David. Becky, do you hear?" Then she asked, "What is this boat—where is it?"

"At the dock, Mother. It's a canoe."

"Whose is it?"

"I don't know. It must have come from upstream somewhere. There's nothing to show whose it is."

Holding Becky tightly by the hand, Mrs. Moss went with David down the garden path. He was going to open the gate to the dock, but she stopped him, saying, "I can see quite well from here."

Mrs. Moss had always distrusted the river, not for herself, but because she was afraid of her children falling in. The only one who had done so, years ago, was David's elder brother Dick. The falling in had had no special effect upon him, unless perhaps it had given him a taste for water—he was in the navy now.

Mrs. Moss looked over the gate at the river and the canoe as if she disliked them both heartily. "Look," she said, shaking Becky's hand to make her pay more attention, "there's the boat that's not David's to play with. Look how dirty it is inside—you would be dirty all over if you sat in it, and spiders would creep over you. And if you weren't very careful, the boat would go right over, and you'd fall into the cold, wet, dirty water. A canoe is a boat that goes over very easily—the most easily of all—isn't it, David?"

"Well—yes—perhaps."

Becky was crying again for quite a different reason now. "David's not to go into the boat, and fall into the river!"

"No, of course not," said Mrs. Moss. "David's coming in to his breakfast now. David's not going to touch the boat until Father's seen it. David, do you hear what I say? Not until your father comes home."

"Yes, Mother." David looked once more at the canoe, waiting so patiently; then he followed his mother and Becky indoors.

Mr. Moss was not in from his work until tea time. David told him about the canoe at once. After he had had his tea Mr. Moss went to look at it.

"What do you think?" asked David. "I mean, we don't know whose it is—and here it is."

"If you find anything valuable on the road, you take it to the police so that the owner can claim it," said Mr. Moss.

"But I can't carry a canoe to the police station," said David.

"You can tell them about it," said Mr. Moss. "Constable Platt would be the one."

Mr. Moss started gardening, and David set off on his bicycle to Constable Platt's lodgings at the other end of the village. The constable was having tea, but he got out his notebook and wrote down all that David told him about finding the canoe.

"Do you think anyone will claim it?" asked David.

Constable Platt shook his head doubtfully. "If it came from upstream—as it may well have done," he said, "then it came from that Great Barley." (Constable Platt, like David, lived in Little Barley.) "Now, I won't be taken up in what I say, but some of those Great Barley people have more money than they know how to look after. Maybe they won't think of asking after a lost canoe for a long time."

"Then will *you* ask *them*?"

Constable Platt looked reprovingly at David. "I've more to do than go chattering about canoes all day. Besides, I'd have to know whose grounds go down to the river—or who has permission to keep a boat on the river from someone else's grounds."

"Then you don't think——?"

The constable snapped a rubber band round his notebook, and reached for the pot of jam. "Before we can say the boat's unclaimed, we must wait. We may"—he paused, while he kept a strawberry from falling off the jam spoon—"have to wait a long time."

Waiting a long time, with a full-sized boat bobbing at your own dock—it was very hard. David thought he could not bear it. He wanted to prove quickly what he felt in his bones: that no one owned the boat, that no one had the right to claim it from him.

He went home and onto the dock again, to stare at the canoe. He bent down to put the flat of his hand on its nose; he pressed downward slightly, and felt how strongly and bravely the vessel rode the water.

While David was still bent over the canoe, his father came to fill the watering can.

"Well, what did Platt say?"

"Nothing much. He thought it might belong to some rich person in Great Barley, who wouldn't bother to report the loss at once."

"That I don't believe," said Mr. Moss. "If Jim Platt saw the boat—why, you've only to look at it to see it's not a rich man's boat—unless he's forgotten it for a score of years. The varnish is half rubbed off, and look at the cobwebs inside. And I'll lay it leaks." Mr. Moss pressed heavily on the side of the boat so that it tilted sideways. Water that must have been hidden under the floor boards flooded out and over the cobwebs in the bottom. "There!"

"That might be just rain water," said David.

"I'll lay it leaks," repeated Mr. Moss. He looked at the boat very thoughtfully. Then he said, "There's an important clue if Platt were interested in clues."

"Where? Where?"

Mr. Moss pointed to the piece of thick string that had been used for tying up the canoe. One end of it was fastened to a metal ring in the nose of the boat; the other end was tied to a short piece of wood that floated in the water.

"You can see plainly what happened," said Mr. Moss. "The canoe was tied to a post somewhere, but the wood of the post was rotten—look, you can see it is. Then, maybe with the extra strong current of these floods, and the canoe pulling hard on the cord, the post snapped and the canoe was carried away, down to us."

"But that still doesn't tell us where the canoe comes from," said David.

"It could," said his father. "I mean, if you could find a post or stump by the river bank that had been recently broken, and that this piece of wood fits—then you'd have found where the canoe was moored. When I say 'you,' I mean someone—anyone— Constable Platt if he'd ever trust himself to the water."

"Do you think it would be unsafe to go out in this canoe?"

"Not it. It'll only have a slow leak, like a slow puncture, that's all. You could bale the water out, or haul her up onto the bank a bit, tip her half over, and empty her like that. She's light enough. A boy like you could do it. Mind you"—Mr. Moss looked sidelong at his son—"your mother wouldn't like you to go in a boat." He picked up his watering can, filled it, and went back to his gardening without another look or word to David.

"David! David!" called his mother from the house. "It's time you came to bed."

David hesitated. Then he sighed, "I'm coming, Mother."

3

Maiden Voyage

IN THE MIDDLE of the next morning Constable Platt called to see the canoe. Like Mrs. Moss, the constable did not offer to go onto the dock, although by now the flood waters had gone down enough to leave it fairly dry. He looked over the gate at the canoe, and then wrote in his notebook.

"A canoe," he wrote, "made of wood, about ten feet long, or more. Two narrow seats"—he looked puzzled, but went on writing—"two very narrow seats."

David did not correct him, but it was clear that Constable Platt knew nothing about canoes. If paddlers sat on the slender crosspieces that the constable called seats, then the balance of the boat would be quite wrong, and the crew would soon be overset and go into the water. David knew that the paddlers sat on the floor boards, the two forward paddlers leaning against the two crosspieces, and the third one leaning against the stern piece of the canoe.

The constable looked searchingly at the canoe again, and David waited, in silence, to see whether he would notice the things his father had picked out as clues. After a few seconds Constable

Platt closed the notebook and put it away. "The main thing is," he said, "it's a boat. I'll let that be known about a bit, and perhaps we shall hear something. If not—well, of course . . ." He looked at David thoughtfully in a way that set David's heart beating fast. Then, noticing David's eager expression, he went on, "Mind you, the boat has to be more than just unclaimed: we must leave no stone unturned, in every avenue we explore, to establish ownership."

After Constable Platt had gone, David went back to the canoe. He was thinking about the position of a paddler, that the constable had misunderstood. Surely, it would be very uncomfortable, with the crosspiece biting into the paddler's back. David found a piece of flat wood and propped it up in the stern of the canoe so that the paddler there might have something to lean back against. He put it in the stern because if there were only one paddler in the canoe, he would, of course, sit there to steer better.

Next, David began to wonder what the canoe was called. There was no name painted on her anywhere. Perhaps she was called *Beauty*, or better still, the *Water Vole*. She was brown like a water vole, and he felt almost certain that she would move through the water with the same quickness and quietness.

David was unusually silent over his midday dinner, still turning over in his mind possible names for the canoe. Mrs. Moss knew that he had spent most of the morning at the dock, and Becky was still fussing that he should not go in the nasty boat and fall into the river. As Mrs. Moss cleared away the dinner dishes she said, a little crossly, "Do be quiet now, Becky. I wish this business of the boat were cleared up! Now, David, why don't you forget it for a bit? Why not go a long cycle ride this afternoon? Look —here's sixpence for buns for your tea."

"Thank you." David took the sixpence, but when his mother was not looking he slipped it into the ornament on the mantelpiece, where she kept loose change for the milkman. Then, while his mother was in the scullery, and Becky with her, he went out to the dock to look at the canoe again. He tested its weight by lifting it a little by one end. He found that, as his father had said, it was not too heavy even for him to manage. So he took out the wooden back that he had set in the stern, and hauled the canoe a little way up onto the dock, and tilted it almost over, so that the water in it rushed out into the river. Then he tilted the canoe back onto an even keel, lowered it into the water again, and put the wooden back into place again. Then he stared into the canoe. The floor boards at the stern seat were splashed now from the water that had been emptied out, but the hot sun was beginning to dry them already.

David's eyes moved next to what his father had called the important clue—the lump of rotten wood at the end of the mooring rope. If anyone went upstream as far as he could go, looking really carefully as he went, and nowhere found the stump from which that had been torn—"Well," said David aloud, "then I should have missed finding the owner in that way. If Constable Platt failed in his way too, and if no one claimed it of their own accord . . ."

He left his thinking aloud unfinished while he went back into the garden to the little tool shed. He could not at first find the kind of thing he wanted among the seed boxes and oddments of wood. Then he came to his father's wheelbarrow; it had a slat of strong wood which fitted across one end, but which could be taken out if necessary. Mr. Moss had made it himself and found it very useful. David hesitated; then he took the wooden slat from its place and carried it back to the dock again.

He moved quietly and quickly now, without any hesitation. He drew the canoe exactly level to the dock, stepped into the stern seat, and sat down. He leaned back against the wooden support, grasped the wheelbarrow end firmly, and pushed off with it. He was afloat.

The strength of the river current had dwindled with the floods' going down. David found he could drive the canoe against it quite easily with deep, short, strong strokes of his piece of wood used as a paddle. The canoe went forward, quickly, cleanly—

like a fish in water, David thought. She was not as portly as a trout, kinder than a pike. What fish was she?

"I shall call her the *Minnow*," said David softly, digging deeply with his paddle. The canoe shot forward as if in answer to her name.

Paddling the *Minnow* upstream was like being able to go right into some familiar picture. At first, David knew the scenery well, for sometimes in hot weather he had swum short distances upstream and downstream from the dock. But soon it grew strange, with a special strangeness that came from his seeing close at hand what before he had seen only in the distance.

David was covering the open stretch of the river between Great and Little Barley. Water meadows came down to the river on either side, with pollarded willows scattered along the banks. At one place was a kind of bay where cows strolled down to drink, and several were standing in the poached mud as David came past. They stared at him in amazement until the *Minnow* was level with them; then they seemed all to feel panic together and in a clumsy rush turned their hindquarters on the river and jostled up the bank. David was alarmed for a moment by the suddenness of their movement, and dropped his paddle into the water. He set the canoe violently rocking with the lunge he made in grabbing it back. He realized then how delicately the *Minnow* was balanced.

The first that David saw of Great Barley was the spire of the parish church, poking above some distant trees. Then there were two people on the river bank: a young man lying face upward to the sun, fast asleep, and a girl—the girl from Great Barley post office—leaning against him as though he were a bolster. She was picking daisies and tossing them over her shoulder, sprinkling his body with white. She stopped when she saw David in the canoe, and laughed and called to him to beware of a very dangerous weir just round the bend. He thanked her and went on rather cautiously, but there was no weir round the corner; nor did he ever find later that there was any weir on the River Say in this part of the country.

Now the houses of Great Barley began. Some of their gardens came right down to the river and then the river bank would be planted with rambler roses and irises. Often the grass was cut, and, once, on a square of lawn stood a deck chair and beside it a book dropped face downward on the grass. Nowhere in the gardens was there anybody about, perhaps because it was now nearly tea time. Only one person seemed to have thought of keeping any kind of boat on the river, and that was only a punt.

All the way upstream between the meadows David had been looking out on both sides for a stump of wood to which the *Minnow* might once have been tied. Now, between the gardens, he found the search more difficult, for there were so many stumps and posts to be examined. He decided to look on the left bank of the river as he went upstream, and then on the right bank when he came back. So far he had seen nothing.

The Great Barley stretch of the river was much more wooded than lower down. At one place the woodland was overgrown and the trees neglected; a great tree had fallen right across the water, making a natural bridge from one side to the other. It had not fallen too low, however, for David and the *Minnow* to find a way under, brushing through a hanging tangle of dead ivy. That stretch of overgrown woodland seemed to mark the end of Great Barley. Now there came more meadowlands again, and round a bend David saw ahead what must be Folly Mill. This was the end of the voyage upstream, for the mill was built right over the river, and there was certainly no way through for the *Minnow* to have come, even during the height of the floods.

Below the mill the current flowed swiftly. David let it twirl the canoe round and set her off again downstream. The current was with her now, and there was very little paddling to do. David was glad of that, for his arms and shoulders had begun to ache, and his paddle was raising a blister in the palm of one hand.

After all, it had been shaped for use on a wheelbarrow, not in a canoe.

On the expedition downstream, it was the turn of the right-hand bank to be examined for broken stumps. When David reached the fallen tree, however, he decided to take the *Minnow* over to the left bank to go through the gap already made in the ivy. The current was flowing fairly strongly here; David shipped his paddle, and, catching hold of a trail of ivy, began to ease the canoe through. The ivy was like a curtain over the entrance of a cave, dividing the brilliant sunshine of one side from the gloom of the tree-overgrown banks on the other. As the boat nosed through the curtain, a voice suddenly came out strangely from the gloom and quietness.

"I see you!"

Still clinging to his ivy strand, David peered into the dimness. He could see nothing—nobody.

He let go of the ivy, and at once the canoe began to slip forward.

"Hey!" called the voice, and again, "Hey! Hey!"

David's eyes were by now accustomed to the green half light, and he saw who had called. A boy, bigger than he was, stood on the right bank. He had dark-red hair and a pale face. David was too surprised to realize how quickly the current was carrying him by, but the boy on the bank saw, and it seemed to throw him into a frenzy of anger.

"Stop!" he shouted. "Stop!" Then at once he stooped and picked up something—a stone or a lump of wood—and threw it. He evidently did not mean to hit the boat, but to make a splash that would drench David.

In a swift confusion of alarm, anger, and excitement David twisted round in his seat to face the attacker. As he did so he felt his paddle slipping overboard. He swung round again and flung himself forward to catch it. The *Minnow* seemed to lose her head completely, and David, from a half-kneeling position, toppled wildly, and fell into the water.

He came up gasping just beside the canoe, which, provokingly, now rode perfectly evenly again without a passenger. The wheel-barrow end was already out of reach, floating downstream.

The boy on the bank had never stopped shouting, and now David began to understand what it was about.

"You rotten thief!" shouted the boy. "That's my canoe! It was you stole my canoe!"

David would not in the least have minded falling into the river but for the complicated miseries he now foresaw. He had lost the *Minnow* to her rightful and unpleasant owner; he would have to go ashore and fight the owner for calling him a thief, and, as he was the smaller boy, he would probably be beaten. He would then have somehow to make his way home and present himself to his mother in clothes still dripping from the river. He would have to confess to his father that he had taken and lost his wheel-barrow end.

David treaded water and, raising his arm, gave the canoe a strong push toward the boy on the bank. Then he himself floundered toward the same bank. It was difficult enough to land: the bank crumbled and slid slimily from under his clawing fingers. Suddenly he felt a strong arm under his—an arm that hooked him out of the water as if it were landing a fish. The red-haired boy had not helped him; he was still bending and murmuring over his canoe. David's arm was held by an untidy-looking elderly woman, with a beaky nose. She dropped his arm, and then took his hand between hers and, raising it, pressed it softly.

"Why," she said, "what a delightful surprise! You, of course, are kind David Moss!"

4

Codlings'

THEY STOOD together on the river bank, hand clasped in hand. David gazed at the woman, and she at him; her gaze was searching, his a stupefied stare. She went on speaking; he kept silence.

"I'm Miss Codling," she said, "and Adam—Adam!—is my nephew. Adam!" she called again, and the boy by the canoe raised his face toward her. "Adam, dear, I've not had a moment to tell you before. When the postman came this afternoon, he said the constable had told him that a canoe had been found, and was being kept safely." She turned back to David. "Your name is David Moss, isn't it?"

Miss Codling had to repeat her question before David answered, "Yes."

The boy, still crouching by the canoe, said softly, "When I saw him, he wasn't keeping it safe; he was in it."

That stung David at last. "I was looking for something," he said. "I had a clue."

"A clue?"

"Yes," David almost shouted. "Look at the mooring rope. It's tied to half a stump of wood. I knew that if I found the other half, I should know where she belonged."

The other boy did not answer, but he took a pace toward David, pulling the canoe after him. Then he bent down, with the broken piece of mooring wood in his hand. He fitted it to the top of a stump that David had not noticed before. The two pieces fitted together and made one stump—the stump to which the *Minnow* had been tied.

The boy looked sidelong at David again, and then at the mooring stump. Then he said, "It was a pity you fell into the river. I'm sorry."

"Goodness! Into the river!" cried Miss Codling, as though she had quite forgotten whence she had drawn David. "The boy's soaked. You'll catch a cold—pneumonia. Come along now! Adam, tie the canoe up, and come and help."

Miss Codling, still talking, led David away from the river bank. They took an overgrown path that soon brought them out of the woodland onto a tousled lawn before a big house. Here, in the open, there was sunshine, and the heat of it reassured Miss Codling a little.

"There!" she said, halting and drawing away from David to look at him. "You are in a mess! I really think it would be best if you changed out here on the lawn. It doesn't matter your dripping here, and it's warmer outside in the sun. Adam!"

"Yes, Aunt Dinah?"

"Go and get a bucket of warm water, and the watering can with the rose. I'll get towels and clothes. Perhaps there are some things Adam has outgrown or that have shrunk that would fit you, David. Wait here."

Miss Codling went into the house, and Adam Codling after her. David was left on the lawn, staring at the house. "So this is what they call Codlings'," he thought. He delivered newspapers to Codlings', but he left the papers in a box at the very top of the long drive. He had only ever had a glimpse of the front of the house through the trees. This was the house from the back, he supposed. It was gaunt and shabby, with paint peeling off the door and window frames. The garden door stood wide open, and he could see right into the house, to the hall, and at the farther end of it, to a front door with deep panels of glass.

The house looked quite deserted now that Adam Codling and his aunt had disappeared into it. Everything seemed very quiet. Then a harsh voice from inside the house called, "Dinah!" There was no answer. A door opened somewhere, and David saw the figure of a tall, thin man in the hall, silhouetted against the light from the front door. He came down the hall to the garden door, on the threshold of which he stopped, blinking into the sunlight. He was very old, and wore a flimsy, faded-blue dressing gown dragged closely round him. His hair was the mingled color of rust and cobwebs; his head was bald on top, and the sun beat upon it now. With a bony hand he drew a blue-spotted handkerchief from one of his pockets and began to tie a knot in each of the four corners. He fumbled because he was not looking at what he was doing. His eyes seemed to fix themselves upon David. When he had tied the knots, the old man set the hand-kerchief on his head as a protection against the sun; then he sank his hands into his dressing gown pockets, and peered even more intently across the lawn. David stood quite still—there was no movement about him but the steady drip of the dank river water from his clothes. He felt afraid to move under such a stare; he was not sure whether he was being looked at or looked through.

At last the old man withdrew his gaze and turned back into the house. At that moment, Miss Codling appeared, hurrying along the hall, with a pile of stuff over her arm. "Were you calling me, Father?"

"Yes." He said no more, but laid a detaining hand on the crook of her elbow. She waited patiently. After a while he said, "You know, Dinah, I've just had an interesting experience. I've just seen a drowned boy, and one in quite modern-seeming dress. I don't remember any boy being drowned in the Say in recent years."

"But, Father——" began Miss Codling.

"I know my memory has grown worse," said the old man humbly. Miss Codling did not go on with what she was about to say. There was a pause. Then he said, "It has escaped me, too, Dinah, what I wanted you for. I'm sorry." His hand dropped from her arm, and he moved indoors and turned into one of the rooms.

Miss Codling came quickly down the steps from the porch to David. "Here are towels," she said, "to use when you're clean. And here are some clothes that may do."

Adam came behind her, staggering lopsidedly with a bucket of gently steaming water.

"That's it," said Miss Codling. She put the towels and the clothes on the grass, and looked at the two boys. "I wonder," she said hesitantly, "if I might leave you two to do what is necessary, and get back to my hoeing?"

Adam said, "It'll be all right, Aunt." David nodded, although he was still a little nervous at being left alone with Adam Codling.

Miss Codling went off to her hoeing, and David began to strip off his clothes, while Adam fetched the watering can and fitted a rose sprinkler to its spout. When David was naked, Adam began to wash him down with warm water from the can. David turned round slowly, while Adam aimed his spray of water. They began to talk.

"I'm an orphan," said Adam, "with no brothers and sisters."

"I've a brother and a sister," said David. He nearly added that he had a mother and father too, but changed his mind.

"You'd better shut your eyes," said Adam, "while I water your head. You've rotten leaves and scum in your hair."

David shut his eyes and held his nose while the warm water streamed over his head and neck and shoulders. When he could speak he said, "Can you swim?"

"Yes," said Adam.

"So can I."

"I saw you could. You dog-paddled ashore after you fell in."

"I can do breast stroke, too, only I didn't feel like it, then."

"I can do lifesaving."

The conversation went on while Adam helped David to dry himself and get into clean clothes. Adam carried the dirty clothes indoors. He said his aunt would wash them later.

Then, together, they walked round the big, untidy garden. Parts of it were neglected, as though all hope of cultivation had been given up: briar roses and blackberry bushes arched themselves across paths where grass grew lank and high. Other parts were more carefully tended, with rows of vegetables, and beds of flowers in bloom.

Adam led the way to a high south wall, where espalier fruit trees sunned themselves. The early plums were ready to eat, and wasps moved drunkenly over the ripest. Adam picked the best of the unspoiled ones, handing some back to David and then filling his own pockets. They sauntered on, eating, spitting out plum stones, talking.

"It was my birthday last holidays," said Adam, and paused.

"What did you have?" asked David.

"My cousins in Birmingham sent me some money, and I asked Aunt Dinah to put some more to it." Again he paused.

"What did you buy with it?"

"Varnish."

"Varnish?"

But Adam slithered off the subject onto another. "I may have to go and live with my cousins in Birmingham after this summer."

"Wouldn't you like that?"

"No. My cousins have children, but they're girls—younger than me, too."

"I've a sister much younger than me."

"There are four of these girls, and I'd rather live here than in Birmingham."

They came to the end of the south walk, where the path turned a corner. Here stood an old wooden summerhouse that was collapsing partly from age, and partly under the weight of a great honeysuckle that leaned and crept all over its walls and roof. Adam went half inside and felt under one of the seats. He came back and held up something for David to see. "This is my varnish."

The tin was new and covered with instructions in tiny print that could not be read at a glance. But two words, in capital letters, seemed to leap to David's eyes and into his understanding: BOAT VARNISH.

"It's expensive stuff," said Adam, "but the man in Castleford said it was well worth it. He told me how to use it."

He hid the varnish under the seat again. David said, "So it's boat varnish."

"Yes."

David said hesitantly, "Were you thinking—I mean, had you planned—?"

At that moment, walking on, they rounded the corner of the path and saw Miss Codling, bent over one of the flower beds. She had descended from hoeing to a savage hand weeding. At the sound of the boys' approach she straightened herself and gazed at them in surprise.

"Why!" she said, "you have been quick. Do you want tea yet?"

"It's quite late, Aunt Dinah."

Miss Codling wiped two earthy fingers on her sacking smock, felt in the folds of her skirt, and pulled out a watch.

"No," she cried, "it can't be! It's far later than I thought—it's really too late for tea."

David's hopes fell, but Miss Codling went on, "It will have to be a high tea, and we must be quick. We'll have boiled eggs and cheese and blackberries—" She broke off to stare at David.

"Those clothes! Where are the dirty ones? I ought to have washed them at once."

"I put them in the bucket in the bathroom," said Adam.

"I'll wash them while you begin getting the tea. We'll have it outside," she called back to them as she went.

Adam set David to gathering the blackberries, while he went to find three new-laid eggs and boil them. By the time David came back to the kitchen with his colander full, Adam was carrying the tea things outside. David waited in the kitchen, looking timidly into the hall. It was empty—there was no sign of old Mr. Codling. The hall was paved, with threadbare rugs along it. The walls had been papered long ago with a heavily patterned red damask paper, which had faded to an uneven pink. There was nothing in the hall except the rugs and, on one of the walls, a portrait in a carved oval frame. The colors of the portrait were very dark, but David could see a pale face and dark-red hair.

"Is that a picture of your father?" he asked Adam.

"What, that? Goodness, no! Go and see what's written at the bottom of it."

David went closer to the picture until he could read the straggling letters and figures at the bottom. "A.D. 1585," he read.

"That's my ancestor," said Adam. "Jonathan Codling."

David studied him. The man in the portrait wore a closefitting, dark tunic with little gilt buttons down the front and a white pleated collar at the neck. On one thumb he wore a ring with a dark-red stone in it; the stone was held in place by silver work that, David could just see, represented foliage. In the same hand the man held a single red rose. To David he had the look of a fop and a dandy—except for his face; that was plain, hard, almost secretive.

"He looks knowing," said David, "clever."

"Too clever by a long chalk," said Adam, shortly. "Here, lend me a hand with the cups and saucers."

David had expected the Codlings to have old and precious china and silver tea knives, but there was nothing like that. The knives were ordinary dinner knives and the cups and saucers were of thick, white ware, often chipped. Then Adam brought one cup and saucer and plate that were different: they were of such fine china that David could see the light through it, and on their surface delicately painted ladies moved among painted flowers. Even so, the cup was cracked.

The table was laid, the eggs boiled, the tea brewed, by the time Miss Codling came out of the house.

"They're washed," she said to David, "and they'll be dry, ironed, and aired for tomorrow afternoon if you could call for them."

David said, "Yes, I can call for them."

"Good. Pour out, Adam dear," said Miss Codling. She began to cut and spread a slice of bread and butter so thin that David expected to see it crumble between her fingers. She laid it carefully on the fine china plate. Adam had already filled the cup with tea.

"There," said Miss Codling.

Adam took the tea and the bread and butter indoors. He came back a few moments later carrying the bread and butter. "He said he didn't want anything to eat."

Miss Codling sighed. "I wish he had more appetite. Never mind. You two divide this between you. And start your egg, David. It must be getting cold."

They had eggs and bread and butter, followed by bread and jam or bread and cheese, and blackberries with sugar and the top of the milk. There was no cake, for which Miss Codling apologized.

After tea, the two boys cleared away and helped Miss Codling to wash up. Then she went into the garden, and David said, "I ought to be going, I suppose."

"I'll come with you to the top of the drive," offered Adam.

They walked together in silence until they reached the two stone pillars that guarded the gateway.

"Well," said David.

"See you tomorrow afternoon," said Adam.

"Yes."

"Will you be in a hurry then?"

"I don't think so."

"We might have a look at the canoe," said Adam. "It's been laid away ever since my father died, and that's more than ten years ago. It needs a lot doing to it before it can really be used on the river."

"My father thought it had a slow leak somewhere."

"Did he? The man in Castleford said it would need two coats of varnish to stop leaks and so on. We'd have to clean it up first, of course, and scrape off all the old varnish and rub the surface smooth with glass paper. Aunt Dinah has some glass paper, and we might be able to scrape with ordinary knives if we were careful."

"My father has a special scraper for that kind of job," said David.

"I say! Could you bring it tomorrow afternoon? Could you?"

"All right." As David spoke he remembered his father's lost wheelbarrow end, but he repeated, with more boldness than he felt, "Yes, I'll bring it."

"Good. I was afraid that with a knife we'd be gouging bits out of the wood."

David had gone on from remembering the wheelbarrow end to wondering what his family were thinking and saying about him now.

"I ought to go," he said.

"So long, then," and Adam turned back blithely to Codlings'.

David, without his bicycle, had to walk all the way home. It was almost dusk by the time he reached Jubilee Row. Lights were on all along the Row, and curtains drawn. Only old Mr. Barncroft was still leaning over his gate, smoking.

"So you're back," he said to David.

"Yes," said David. "Good night." He wondered uneasily why Mr. Barncroft had said that, but he did not wait to ask.

As he pushed open his own garden gate he saw something

white moving against the upstairs window. A casement opened, and Becky's voice came down to him: "Oh, Davy! You're not drowned after all!"

The window closed discreetly again as the front door swung wide open, and his mother came running out to meet him.

"David!" Her arms came round him and held him in a clasp of iron, pressing him against her, while she stormed over him. "You naughty boy! You wicked boy! Disobedient! Thoughtless! I shall never forgive you—never—never!" She repeatedly kissed the tips of his ears—the rest of his face was buried—and then pushed him away from her to look at him. She still held him tightly by the shoulders, at arm's length. "Why," she cried, in fresh alarm, "why are you wearing those clothes, David?"

"And what have you done with my wheelbarrow end?" asked Mr. Moss. He had been repeating this question for some time, but his voice had not been audible above his wife's.

5

Scraping and Saving

MR. AND MRS. MOSS had guessed where David had gone
when they had found his bicycle still in its place and
the canoe vanished. Since then Mrs. Moss had not had
a moment's peace of mind as all the Row came to know. Mr. Moss
had been calmer, until he discovered the loss of his wheelbarrow
end.

Now that David was home he was made to explain himself.
The story of his afternoon's adventure held the full attention of
his parents. Except that his mother cried out when she heard of
his falling into the river, they listened in silence.

"And did you see poor old Mr. Codling?" asked his father.

"Yes," said David.

"He's been queer in the head ever since his son died, long ago.
Did he speak to you?"

"No." David said no more.

"And they gave you a good tea," said Mrs. Moss. "That was
kind."

"Especially as they're as poor as church mice," said Mr. Moss.

"They say you rarely meet Miss Codling about the village because she's ashamed of being seen dressed as she is."

"She didn't seem ashamed of anything," said David.

"Nor do I believe it," said Mr. Moss, quite severely. "The Codlings have always lived in Great Barley and never had anything to be ashamed of, for being poor isn't that."

"David didn't say it was, dear."

"Maybe not," said Mr. Moss, but unrelentingly. "And what about my wheelbarrow end, floating downstream goodness knows where?"

There seemed no answer to that, and the moment was certainly the worst possible for asking to borrow the scraper. David was relieved for once to be sent upstairs to bed. Mrs. Moss began to make herself a late cup of tea, which, she said, was all she needed now.

Next morning, David came in from delivering his papers to find that his father was not at the breakfast table.

"Oh," he said, "has he gone, Becky?"

"No. He's in the garden looking at his roses for a minute."

Mrs. Moss, who was in the scullery where she could overhear the conversation called: "David, will you go and ask for one of his best rosees? I want it to set in a vase in the front window."

"All right." David hesitated. "Mother, has Father said any more about the wheelbarrow end?"

"I don't think so. Why?"

"I wanted to ask him to lend me one of his tools. But he may not like to."

"You can but try. And remember my rose, David."

David went out into the garden, where Mr. Moss, like a bee after honey, was visiting each bloom on his rose bed.

David came and stood by him. "Father, could you lend me that scraper of yours? I promise I'd be very careful with it."

Mr. Moss examined a rose tree thoroughly for green fly, and then said, "What did you say?"

"Could you lend us your scraper—for scraping the old varnish off the Codlings' canoe?"

Mr. Moss passed on to another rose tree, without straightening up and without looking up. "You promise you'd be careful with it," he said scornfully. "Where's my wheelbarrow end?"

He said no more, and David turned back abruptly into the house. He tried to imagine himself, this afternoon, telling Adam that he hadn't the scraper after all.

At the garden door he met his mother. "Well, did you get it?" she asked.

"No. He said, what about his wheelbarrow end."

"When you asked him for a rose?" said Mrs. Moss, amazed.

"Oh, no, I forgot that. I'm sorry. I was asking him to lend us his scraper. He wouldn't."

Mrs. Moss went outside to her husband, still by his rose bed. David, watching out of the window, could see them talking together—he could even hear the murmur of their voices. Mrs. Moss touched rose after rose with the tips of her fingers; finally, over one, she paused long and at last Mr. Moss cut it and gave it to her. Still they talked together, Mrs. Moss holding her rose up to her face and sniffing at it. Suddenly, in answer to something that his wife had said, Mr. Moss spoke with great force. In the raised tones of anger, the words "my wheelbarrow end" came to David clearly. He turned away from the window in despair.

His mother came indoors, humming, and went to put her rose into water. Then his father came in, in a hurry now to be off to his day's work.

"David, where's my lunch basket?"

"Here, Father."

"David"—Mr. Moss was already opening the front door—"you can borrow the scraper." As David poured forth his thanks his father hesitated and then added firmly, "And don't let it go the way of the wheelbarrow end." Then he was gone.

David was so happy that he spent all the morning helping his mother or playing with Becky. As soon as he had finished his midday dinner he mounted his bicycle, with Adam's clothes in a parcel tied onto the handle bars, and cycled over to Codlings'.

Adam was waiting for him. "I say, you've got a bicycle."

"Yes," said David.

"Did you remember the scraper?"

"Oh, yes," said David.

They went at once down to the river bank. Adam had pulled the canoe half out of the water.

"It's funny," he said, "when you first begin lifting her, when she's still partly in the water, it seems so easy. But the more she gets on land, the heavier and clumsier she seems to get."

"That's because she's a real water creature," said David.

"Yes," said Adam. "Anyway, I thought I'd wait for you to help me."

"Where shall we put her?"

"Well, I found two old trestles, and I thought we could lay her on them upside down. That's how they work on boats in the Castleford boat yard. I saw them when I was getting the varnish there."

Between them they carried the canoe to Adam's trestles, which he had set up under some trees. There they laid the canoe upside down and set to work. First they scrubbed down the outside with soap and warm water. Then they wiped it with a clean cloth. When the surface was dry, they were ready to begin scraping off the old, blistered, half-perished varnish.

They took turns with Mr. Moss's scraper. It was hard work, for the scraper had to be dragged slowly along the surface, being pressed down very hard at the same time. As they grew more skillful in the use of the scraper the boys found that the old varnish curled and flaked away beneath the cutting edge. But it was always slow going.

The scraper, working at its best, gave out a prolonged squeak. Miss Codling appeared suddenly round the trees to ask them if they could possibly keep it on a lower note.

"It sets my teeth on edge," she said.

"We have to make that noise, Aunt Dinah, if we're to do the job properly."

"And when will the job be finished?"

"Well, it's taking longer than expected. Tomorrow, don't you think, David?"

"It looks like it."

"Why don't you break from work and have some tea now?" said Miss Codling, looking mostly at David.

"Well, really," said David reluctantly, "I don't think I ought to stay, thank you. Yesterday my mother rather wondered where I was when I didn't turn up until late."

"But she knows you're here today?"

"Yes, but I didn't say I wouldn't be back for tea."

"When you come tomorrow you must warn her," said Miss Codling, and turned away again. She never seemed to like to waste time in standing and talking. Now she had to come back again to say that David's clothes, washed and ironed, were waiting for him on the steps of the porch.

The boys worked a little longer at their scraping, and then David said he really must go. They picked up David's clean clothes, in exchange for Adam's, and went up the drive together. David let Adam try out his bicycle.

When they reached the gateway David said, "Do you know, I come here every morning. I deliver your newspaper into this box."

"Do you really? And I come here while Aunt Dinah is making the breakfast and collect it. Do you like delivering papers?"

"It's quite easy. And Mr. Ellum pays me something. I bought a stamp album with the newspaper money last Christmas."

Adam looked thoughtful. "Does he ever take new delivery boys on?"

"Oh, yes."

"I mean, I wonder if I could earn some money that way?"

"Well, you could. Only I don't see how you'd manage a newspaper route without a bicycle."

"Oh, well," said Adam, as though he didn't care—as though he despised himself for a money grubber; but then he added, "Anyway, I really need to earn more money than that. You see, Aunt Dinah says I shall just have to live with the Birmingham cousins after this summer, because there's not enough money for clothes and things."

David kept silence, and Adam seemed to feel encouraged to go on. He showed David the length of his arm and the shortness of the sleeve striving to cover it. "I go on growing—I can't stop. Aunt Dinah says she wants me to go on, but it worries her all the same. It means I'm awfully expensive in food and clothes."

"And would just you go to Birmingham?"

"Yes. There's still enough money from Grandfather's pension for the other two here. Besides, Grandfather just couldn't live anywhere else, so that's that. And I don't believe Aunt Dinah could, really. And I don't believe I—" He stopped abruptly, afraid of making some claim that might seem too great. "Aunt Dinah's made up her mind about me, because of my growing so much, and I shall have to do what she says. But I don't want to live anywhere but here. I like living here." He spoke emphatically, to explain his preference for the gaunt, shabby house with the half-wilderness half-garden that surrounded it. "And the river . . ."

"I should think you do like living here," said David warmly, "with the river."

"What I need—what Grandfather and Aunt Dinah need—is more money. That's why I want us to get the old canoe done up and on the water again."

"I don't quite see—" began David. All he could see in his imagination was a picture of their taking people for canoe trips on the Say, and that somehow did not look at all likely.

"It's a long story. I'll explain some time," said Adam. "But that's why I wanted you to help now with the canoe. And later too if you're free. We could work together."

"Of course," said David, "but I still don't see——"

"And I've an idea," said Adam. "You deliver newspapers here, and I collect them from this box. Right. This is an ideal place for leaving secret messages to each other."

"But I can come and see you, without any messages."

"You never know, for the future." As he spoke Adam picked a hawthorn leaf, held it up, and dropped it into the box. "A privet leaf means 'today.' And a hawthorn leaf means 'tomorrow.' Blades of grass for the hours." He picked three, one of which he tore across. He dropped the two-and-a-half blades into the box. David looked in.

"A hawthorn leaf and two-and-a-half blades of grass: tomorrow at half past two, I'm to come."

"That's it."

"All the same," said David, "I don't see that we shall need secret messages, whatever we do."

Adam did not reply, and the expression on his face warned David of the uselessness of asking questions now. They spoke of other things, until at last David mounted his bicycle and started for home. He turned in the saddle for a last look back. Adam's hand was raised in farewell. His head, with its dark-red hair and pale face, was more than ever like that of the man in the oval picture. He had the same look of secrecy and determination.

6

The Portrait in the Hall

EVERY DAY now David spent his afternoon with Adam Codling working on the canoe. Every afternoon he stayed to tea with Adam, until Mrs. Moss grew quite worried.

"Why don't you ask him to tea here, David? It's hard on Miss Codling to be always giving you tea—I know your appetite."

"But we can't work on the canoe here, Mother," said David.

"That canoe!" sighed Mrs. Moss.

The work on the canoe was going well, but there were setbacks. After the first coat of varnish had been put on and brushed well into the crevices, David picked up the remains of the varnish in its container and felt its weight anxiously.

"We've used much more than half," he said to Adam.

"Well?"

"I mean, we haven't as much varnish left for the second coat as we've used for the first."

They had hardly been extravagant in using the varnish, but there would just not be sufficient for a second coat; nor had they money enough to buy more. They stared at each other for some seconds. Then Adam struck his hands together. "Money!" he cried angrily. "Money!"

David was not yet in despair. "Mr. Ellum pays me my newspaper money at the end of this month. Perhaps he'd pay me for as much delivery as I've done so far."

Mr. Ellum, when the difficulty had been twice explained to him, agreed to the arrangement David suggested. The money from Mr. Ellum, together with what very little Adam and David already had, was given to Mr. Moss on one of his trips to Castleford. He visited the boat yards in his dinner hour and brought back to David the container quite filled.

"I say," said Adam, when he saw it, "that's more than I expected for the money."

"Is it?" said David, puzzled. "My father just said, 'Here's your varnish.' It's the right kind, I know."

"Anyway," said Adam, "we've so much, we ought to be able to put the second coat on outside, and one inside as well. At Castleford they said it wasn't absolutely necessary to varnish inside, but it would be a very good thing."

When the second outside coat was on, the boys stood back from the canoe in admiration.

"She looks just wonderful," said Adam. "We shall have to think what to call her."

David had foreseen this moment when the *Minnow* must be known by another name, for she had never really been his to name. He could not bear to speak.

"What name do you think?" asked Adam.

"I don't know."

"Come on."

"After all, it's your canoe," said David, with an effort.

"No, it isn't. She was my father's, and now we're doing her up together, and you've paid for half the varnish. She's as much yours as mine."

"Oh, all right," said David, as though badgered into something he did not care for.

"So what shall we call her? You said the other day she was really a water creature. What about calling her the *Moorhen*? Or the *Water Vole*? She's brown like a vole."

"I think she belongs to the water even more than that," said David. "I mean, like a fish."

"A fish . . ." Adam became thoughtful. "There's the *Eel*, or the *Trout*, or the *Pike* . . . None of them are quite right, really."

David decided to be bold. "Of course, any fresh-water fish is too small, anyway. But for quickness in the water what about the *Minnow*?"

Adam frowned. "The *Minnow* . . . the *Minnow* . . . A minnow's really very small."

"Much too small."

"But, on the other hand, for quickness—should we call her the *Minnow*?"

"What about the *Water Vole*?"

"I'd really rather have the *Minnow*, for quickness."

"Just as you like," said David, "the *Minnow*." He managed to speak with apparent indifference, but he was so happy that, forgetful of the new varnish, he gave the *Minnow* a friendly slap of the hand. No real harm was done, but his hand left its impression on the still sticky surface: the side of the *Minnow* forever bore the five fingerprints of David Moss.

Now, when the name was settled and accepted, Adam said slyly, "Or, of course, we could have called her the *Fortune Seeker*." David's eyes stared; his mouth opened for an eager question. "But I like the *Minnow* much better as a name, really," said Adam hastily, "and the other would only make people ask awkward questions." After such a hint, questioning was impossible. Besides, Adam at once turned the conversation back to the subject of canoe varnishing.

While they waited for the *Minnow's* second coat of varnish to dry, the boys occupied themselves with looking out the old canoe paddles and wooden backrests. They found as well some canoe cushions—very lumpy, very faded, and with holes from which clothes moths fluttered in indignation. Nevertheless, the cushions were heavily embroidered in silk, with the initials J. C. worked in their corners. Adam's father had been John Codling.

The varnishing of the canoe inside and out was the work of some days altogether, and, in spite of all their other preparations, there were times when Adam and David seemed to have nothing to do but to visit the *Minnow* again and again, to feel whether her surface were still sticky. These were the times when David hoped that Adam might allow himself to reveal his plans for the future.

One afternoon, after they had for the third time felt the *Minnow's* coat of varnish, Adam led the way indoors. It seemed early for tea, and Adam did not go at once to the kitchen. He halted under the portrait of Jonathan Codling.

"He had plenty of money—at least, he was rich. He could make our fortune now, too."

"How do you mean?" said David. "If you sold him?"

But that was not it. Adam explained that the curator of the Castleford Museum had come over to see the picture at Miss Codling's invitation. He had, it was true, been very interested. He had pored long over the background to the head, which he said seemed to include local scenery.

"Scenery?" David peered into the dark, variegated blur behind Jonathan Codling.

"There are some trees—there, I think; and there's a bridge with two arches—that white thing there."

"And are you going to sell the picture, then?"

Adam shook his head. "The museum man said Aunt Dinah could sell it easily, but not for very much. The artist isn't famous, he said, and Jonathan Codling isn't famous. Selling the picture couldn't make our fortune."

"But you said—" David spoke quietly and slowly. He was near exasperation, but he knew that he must not rush Adam if he wanted to have the secret. "You said just now that the picture could make a fortune."

"I didn't. I said *he* could—Jonathan Codling. And even then it must be Jonathan Codling and the canoe together."

"How, then?"

Adam opened his mouth and shut it again as if even now he could not speak out plainly. David waited. Surely the moment had come. "Well," said Adam, "it's like this." He drew a deep, slow breath. While it sighed its way in, the kitchen door opened and Miss Codling looked out.

"I thought I heard someone talking. Do you want tea yet?"

"No, no," said David, and then added ill-advisedly, "Adam only brought me in to show me the picture."

"Oh," said Miss Codling in an altered tone of voice. She looked at them watchfully. "What were you two talking about exactly?"

"What the museum man said about the picture, Aunt."

"Only that? Well . . ."

Miss Codling seemed unwilling to leave them there together. She waited a moment and then, as neither boy stirred, she said, "For once, we'll have an early tea. You can start getting it ready."

"I'll help Adam outside with the table and chairs," said David.

"No, he can do that by himself quite well. Adam, you go outside. And you come into the kitchen, David, and help me to chop lettuce. We're having lettuce sandwiches, as there's no cake again."

Miss Codling as successfully prevented Adam's confidential talk with David as if she had forbidden it with all her authority. The boys were not left alone together again until after tea, and by then Adam seemed to have repented of the little he had already said. He ignored David's attempts to reopen the subject of

Jonathan Codling, the canoe, and the fortune. They parted almost coldly.

Yet that very evening David heard the secret, although not from Adam Codling. When he got home, Mrs. Moss was in the middle of baking cakes. The day before she had had the courage to send a message by David to Miss Codling asking whether she might make a cake for the boys' tea. Miss Codling had sent back a message that she much appreciated Mrs. Moss's kind suggestion, especially as she herself was an infrequent cake maker. She would be delighted to have a cake from Mrs. Moss. The next afternoon —she chose the afternoon because her husband liked something fresh from the oven for his tea—Mrs. Moss set to work. When David walked in she was just opening the oven door to take the cakes out.

David sat down gloomily on a corner of the kitchen table. The smell and sight of the majestic plum cake, freshly and especially made to celebrate his friendship with Adam, only irritated him. His mother's pride and pleasure seemed heartless.

"There!" said Mrs. Moss. "There! That's something for you and your friend to eat through!"

Mr. Moss, drawn into the kitchen by the smell, said, "Now that's a cake of a sensible size."

"Not for you, Bob," said Mrs. Moss. "It's for David to take to Miss Codling's for their tea."

Mr. Moss was not downcast, but sat on the corner of the table opposite to David, watching his wife. Presently she took from the oven a batch of rock buns.

"Ah!" said Mr. Moss, knowing they must be for him. Mrs. Moss began to turn the buns out of their little tins, and as she did so Mr. Moss swept together the hot crumbs into the palm of his hand. He lingered over the eating of them.

"Old Mr. Codling never tasted better, even in his heyday," he said, tasting slowly.

"What was he like in his heyday?" asked David, roused a little by curiosity.

"I've seen him score his century, when he was captain of the Great Barley eleven," said Mr. Moss. "And then he played tennis —not flashily, but he'd last—he'd last. And my father said he'd never seen a prettier hand at bowls."

"We found an old set of bowls in the summerhouse at Codlings'," said David. "They were in a box inlaid with ivory and ebony, and it had been lined with velvet."

"He liked to do himself proud, and everyone else too." Mr. Moss shook his head. "That's the way the money goes."

"Used he to be very rich?"

"Rich enough. But he spent when he was young, and his son —that's your Adam's father—was like him."

"They might get rich again, some day," said David, and thought sadly, "but not with my help."

"Not with old Mr. Codling as he is, and Miss Codling a woman, and your Adam just a boy." Mr. Moss was almost at the end of his crumbs; he shook them together one last time in the palm of his hand and prepared to open his mouth for the final throw. "Not unless they find their hidden treasure." And he threw the crumbs faultlessly into his mouth and turned to the tea tray that Mrs. Moss had just set by him.

"Hidden treasure?" cried David. "What treasure? When was it hidden? Where was it hidden?"

"If Mr. Codling had known that, he'd be a rich man now," said Mr. Moss. "All I know—and it's no more than the old talk of the Barleys—is that there was a treasure lost to them long ago."

"Is there no clue to where it might be?"

"Clue? Oh, yes, they used to say the Codlings had a clue all right, but it never helped them to the treasure."

"What is the clue?"

"That's more than I know. You'd better ask your friend Adam that." Mr. Moss started his tea and closed the subject by reaching for one of the newly made rock buns.

7

A Tale of Treasure

DAVID CAME to a decision. He would ask Adam point-blank about the treasure, for, if he were to help, Adam must surely take him into his confidence. What reason could there be for withholding any secret? He was Adam's friend and joint master of the *Minnow*.

He cycled over to Codlings' next day, full of this resolution. He freewheeled down the drive and round the corner of the house, and found himself at once the audience of an unexpected scene. Old Mr. Codling had ventured right out of the house onto the lawn and there he stood, holding Adam by his shirt collar— perhaps by the scruff of his neck. He was shaking him in emphasis of his speech.

"You are," said Mr. Codling, "the idlest gardener's boy we have ever employed. I don't know how much my daughter pays you weekly, but the wage cannot but be far too much. I have watched you. I see, from my study window, the state of the flower borders, and I see you idling your time away playing round

51

my son's canoe. I can tell you that when my son comes home
he will put a stop to all that. When my son comes home you will
be sent packing unless you mend your ways. My son is expected
home any day—I warn you."

With a final shake, Mr. Codling shook Adam from him and
went indoors, muttering angrily to himself. Adam did not seem
at all put out at what had happened, until, turning, he saw David
within view and within earshot; then he went scarlet.

"My grandfather is an awfully clever man," he said, moving
toward David almost threateningly. "In his study he reads all
kinds of books other people never think of reading—history and
books by philosophers and books in foreign languages. That makes
him different from other people. His head's full of things other
people aren't clever enough to think of."

David only stared wonderingly, and Adam went on more
calmly, "What you heard just now doesn't really mean anything's
strange about my grandfather. Aunt Dinah says so. It's all quite
easily explained. You see, when I was going to be born, my father
had been away at the war a long time, and Grandfather was
expecting him back—there were going to be all kinds of celebrations. And then, when my father was on the way home, he was
killed, and the news came suddenly to Grandfather and made
him very ill. My mother was made very ill too, and she died soon
after, when I was born. Grandfather recovered, but he seemed
to have forgotten that he'd ever heard the news of my father's
death, and he wouldn't let anyone tell him again—he wouldn't
listen. He'd never let them explain that my father was really
dead. He went on expecting him to come home—he still expects
him. You heard what he said."

"But your father died all those years ago."

"I know. But Aunt Dinah says that, though he's so clever in
other ways, Grandfather's got all muddled about time. He still
thinks it's the time before my father died, so of course he still
expects him to come back. Sometimes he thinks it's longer ago
still, and that my father is a boy and going to come back from

his boarding school for the holidays. Sometimes he thinks it's the past and present together—it's very confusing for him."

David remembered fleetingly how Mr. Codling had thought he was a drowned boy—the ghost of a drowned boy, he supposed; but his mind was working on another consequence of Adam's explanation. "Your grandfather always thinks it's the time before your father died."

"Yes, I said so," said Adam a little impatiently.

"And you were born after your father died?"

"Yes."

"Then your grandfather doesn't know you're his grandson—he can't know who you are?"

"No. And, you see, I happen not even to be like my father in looks. My father had very fair hair, Aunt Dinah says. Grandfather doesn't know who I am, and mostly he just doesn't bother about it at all; but today he was upset—Aunt Dinah's worried that he's not quite as well as usual—and he decided I must be the gardener's boy. Of course, there hasn't been a gardener here for years and years.

"It's all quite logical," Adam concluded. "Grandfather's not a bit queer in the head—only with that confusion about the time."

"I see," said David sympathetically.

David had left his bicycle, and they were walking toward the house now. Adam seemed to have some new purpose in mind, although he went on speaking of the same subject. "Grandfather's often been clever when other people—even Aunt Dinah—have been stupid. Grandfather believed in the treasure"—David almost jumped—"and was looking for it nearly up to the time that my father died. Now, Aunt Dinah won't hear of looking for the treasure. She says it's a waste of time and a cause of discontent. She says that if the Codlings in the past had worked harder to make money, as other people have to, instead of trying to find it, we shouldn't be so poor now. She doesn't want me to begin looking for the treasure, because of that. But I shan't be able to make money until I grow up, whereas I can look for the treasure now. And it's now we need to make a fortune for Aunt Dinah."

"Are you and I going to look for the treasure?"

"Yes," said Adam, "but without letting Aunt Dinah know. She wouldn't approve."

By now they were in the hall, under the picture of Jonathan Codling again.

"And the treasure has to do with the picture?" asked David, growing bolder.

"Yes. Jonathan Codling owned the treasure and hid it, and left—well, not exactly instructions——"

"A clue," breathed David.

"A clue so that the treasure might be found again. The clue's a written one—you must see it, of course, before we begin the search. We'll have to ask Aunt Dinah to let us see it: it's very old, and she keeps it safe. I think she'll show it to us all right if she's sure we want to see it just from curiosity, and not for the beginning of the search. Of course, it'll be tricky to deceive Aunt Dinah."

David went pale as he thought of trying to deceive Miss Codling. "It doesn't seem quite—" he began slowly.

"It's for her own good. She needs the treasure, and we'll find it for her; but in the meantime she mustn't suspect anything." Adam looked hard at David. "Are you curious about the picture, David?"

"Yes," said David.

"Do you want to know all about Jonathan Codling?"

"Yes," said David.

Adam pushed open the door of the kitchen where Miss Codling was at work. "Aunt Dinah, David's curious about the picture in the hall. He wants to know the story of Jonathan Codling."

Miss Codling came out of the kitchen wiping her arms on her apron. She looked at Adam; Adam gazed back unflinchingly. She looked at David and into his eyes; David began to hold his breath and to count. When he reached seven, he felt his eyes screw up and his nose begin to tickle, and he sneezed. It wasn't quite a natural sneeze, but it was good enough; he could avoid Miss Codling's gaze.

"Well," said Miss Codling, relaxing, "it makes quite a good story—the life and end of Jonathan Codling." She leaned against the jamb of the kitchen door and began in a leisurely way.

"Jonathan Codling lived in Barley at the time of the great Queen Elizabeth. He lived in a fine house—the house has gone, of course, but it probably stood where this house stands, and was even larger. He was very well off indeed. He owned most of the land in both the Barleys and round about. He had traveled abroad, too, and served the Queen, and had friends like Sir Francis Drake. Because of that, he was wealthy in ways unusual for just a country gentleman: he had gold and silver, beautifully worked, and rings and necklaces set with precious stones, and other things. All this is not written down, but it has always been known in our family.

"Now, in the year 1588—perhaps you know what happened in 1588?"

"The Spanish Armada," said David confidently.

"Yes," said Miss Codling. "In the year 1588, King Philip of Spain sent his great fleet—his Spanish Armada—against England, to conquer her. For years English people had been expecting and fearing the coming of the Armada. Well, in the summer of that year the Armada was sighted off the coast of Cornwall, and the alarm was spread. By sea, English ships made ready to fight the Spanish; and, on land, Englishmen armed themselves and gathered into camps as soldiers prepared to resist invasion.

"Jonathan Codling was one of those who rode off to join the Queen's Armed Forces in camp."

"What happened next?" asked David.

"Nothing," said Miss Codling, "as far as Jonathan Codling was concerned. The Spaniards were beaten at sea, and there was never any fighting on land. Jonathan Codling was free to come peacefully home."

So far the story was puzzlingly dull, and David wondered whether Miss Codling meant, after all, to hold back the secret of the treasure itself. "Is that all?" he asked guardedly.

Miss Codling took a little key from a chain that hung round her neck, and held it out to Adam. "Adam," she said, "the box from the bureau."

Adam was gone without a word, as though he had been waiting for his orders. He was back in a moment with the box—an old box made of thin wood and still smelling faintly of the cigars that Mr. Codling had smoked from it long ago. Miss Codling untied the piece of black ribbon that was round it, raised the lid, and lifted out a silk handkerchief that lay on top. Underneath were two sheets of paper, folded separately. One was stiff and yellow and breaking away at the edges, and was covered with a hand-writing, the ink of which had faded to the palest brown. Miss Codling unfolded it and showed it to David. "This is the story, as it is told by Jonathan Codling's wife," she said.

David advanced his eyes slowly to within a few inches of the writing. "I can't read it."

"It's not surprising. This is not very good handwriting of over four hundred years ago; only scholars can read it easily. But my father was something of a scholar, and he was interested in searching"—she corrected herself—"was interested in the story of the treasure. He mastered the handwriting and made a fair copy of it, word for word the same, except that he made the spelling and punctuation modern."

She put the first paper carefully back, and took out the second. It was a sheet of ordinary white paper, written over in a hand that was old-fashioned, but so bold and clear that David could read it easily.

The paper was headed:

THE NARRATIVE OF JUDITH CODLING

In the month of July, in the year of Our Lord one thousand five hundred and eighty eight, Jonathan Codling, of this parish of

Great Barley, gentleman, took leave of his wife and his children and all his household, being summoned to take up arms against the Spaniards, which did then most devilishly threaten this Kingdom. And, forasmuch as none knew what might be the end of these wars, Jonathan Codling would have hidden away in a secret place some of his treasure, that it might be a comfort to his wife and family in any time of distress that God might send. Therefore he laid together many of his most precious things, as rings and chains of gold, and bracelets and other things, among them being the silver necklace, with pearls hanging thereby like tears, that was brought but lately from Italy, that he gave to Sarah, being our eldest child.

All these he laid together, and, going forth from the house, took with him, and went out through the herb garden, and after that none knows where, it being night. He was away a clear hour, and came back empty-handed and spoke not of where he had been, but called for clean hosen, for that his were wet through. Then, said he, would he to horse and away. But first I prayed him to tell me where he had hidden the treasure, else were it of little avail to us, if ill befell us. But he said me nay, crying that I was too loose of tongue to keep a secret, which God knoweth to be false. Yet, said he, he would teach the secret to our daughter Sarah, being then eleven years of age, for that she had a good memory and a silent tongue. He took her from her bed, where she then was, and woke her, and spoke with her privily and long, and thereafter bade that no one should question her after his going. Then he took horse and rode away.

Now, when, by the will of God, the danger to this Kingdom was ended, then did Jonathan Codling and other loyal gentlemen of these parts freely leave their camps, purposing to come home again. They rode forth and reached Castleford at nightfall, and there would lie that night, and so come home the next day. Jonathan Codling, being ever an impatient man, would not lie so near home and yet from home, so that, for all his friends could say, he rode on alone at night toward Great Barley.

Now, in the morning, I had word that my husband's horse was cropping of the grass outside the house, but with no rider. Fearing some ill, I sent servants back along the way to Castleford, looking on all sides as they went; yet saw they nothing of their master, and so met his friends coming on from Castleford, nor knew they anything.

While yet we questioned what might have befallen him, came a shepherd of Little Barley who, driving his sheep to market, had chanced to look over the bridge, and saw a man lying in the river below. This man was Jonathan Codling, and he was dead. There was no mark of foul violence upon him, save a bruise upon his brow, and how he came there none could guess. For his horse knew the way well and was of great steadiness, and the night was moonlit; nor was the rider either drunken or ailing when he left Castleford that night.

After the death of my husband, I sought to recover the treasure he had hidden. Wherefore I asked my daughter Sarah to repeat what he had told her. Then she repeated an empty rhyme, saying this was all he had taught her. When I beat her soundly, she only wept, and cried that indeed this was all her father had taught her, taking great pains that she should have it by heart, word for word, and breath for breath, as he would have it said. Nor could I ever beat more sense or memory into her.

Through the folly of my daughter I do believe our family hath lost a treasure as great as any in these parts. For this foolish rhyme is all that she remembers of what her father told her:

"There's no rhyme," said David.

"No," said Miss Codling, "it was torn off my father's copy years ago. But the original is still here, of course." She unfolded the first paper again and pointed to the bottom of it. David found that he could just read the crabbed writing of the rhyme. At the same time he heard the voices of Miss Codling and Adam saying the words softly and slowly.

"Whan Philip came to the single Rose
Ouer the water
The tresor was taken where no one knows
None but my daughter."

"I don't understand it," said David. "What does it mean exactly?"

"That's what Jonathan Codling's widow, and others after her have asked," said Miss Codling. "Some of the meaning is quite plain. Philip, of course, is King Philip of Spain. The single rose is probably Queen Elizabeth: her badge was the Tudor rose, and she was single, either because she was unmarried, or because she was the wonder of her time—unique—single. So the first two lines seem to give the date—1588, when King Philip sent his fleet over the water against Queen Elizabeth. The rest of the rhyme simply says that, at that time, Jonathan Codling hid his treasure and only told its whereabouts to his daughter."

"But," objected David, "the rhyme doesn't tell at all where he hid the treasure, at that rate. It only says he told his daughter where he hid it."

"It's certainly a puzzle," said Miss Codling. "Judith Codling clearly thought that, besides being taught this verse, Sarah had been told exactly where the treasure was. So she beat her well to try to make her remember."

"Poor Sarah!" said David. "What happened to her in the end?"

"A few years afterward she was married off into a family by the name of Ashworthy, away up in Cumberland. It's my belief that Judith Codling determined that, if poor Sarah couldn't remember the secret for her own family, she had best be sent as far away as possible where no one else could worm the secret out of her and profit from it."

"I wonder if the Ashworthys beat her, too, to make her tell," mused Adam.

"No one knows," said Miss Codling. She had put the papers back, replaced the silk handkerchief, and tied the box up again.

She seemed about to take it back to the bureau. "That's the story of the man in the portrait that you asked about, David."

"Thank you very much."

"It's a queer old story," said Miss Codling, "but it's nothing more. I mean, it oughtn't to send anyone off on a wild-goose chase after hidden treasure."

"I suppose not."

Miss Codling fixed David with her eyes. "I hope you and Adam won't go off on any such wild-goose chase."

David looked at her, speechless. Miss Codling, after waiting in vain for an answer, became insistent. "I want you to promise, David, not to go treasure hunting." David continued desperately silent, and Miss Codling fortunately misinterpreted his silence as one of bewilderment, rather than as a kind of humble defiance. She softened her tone to coaxing, and phrased the same demand, as she thought, differently and more easily. "You've plenty of other things to do, after all. You've had a good time revarnishing the canoe. Now I want you to spend all your time going voyages in her."

David, looking past Miss Codling's face, saw Adam's; it was moving very slightly up and down in an unmistakable nod.

"Yes," said David, "we'll spend our time going about in the canoe."

"And," said Adam, "exploring over the tree bridge—I want to show David that."

"Certainly," said Miss Codling. She sighed with relief. "Really, I never expected you'd both be so sensible about leaving that wretched treasure alone. I'm glad Jonathan Codling's story is told, and done with, and put right out of mind."

Miss Codling smiled upon them and turned away. Released from her gaze, David looked boldly at Adam, and watched with fascination one eyelid slowly drooping and as slowly rising again, in the enjoyment of a leisurely and pronounced wink.

8

Over the Bridge

WELL AWAY from the house and his aunt, Adam turned to David. "I'll explain."

"Yes," said David, with a little indignation.

"We've not promised not to look for the treasure, but we have promised to spend our time going expeditions in the *Minnow*, and going over the tree bridge." He waved his hands impatiently as David opened his mouth to speak. "I'll explain about the bridge and show it you, in a minute.

"Well, we promised to do those two things because, I hope, they'll be the very things that'll help us to the treasure. That is, if the clue is really in the rhyme, as I believe it is. After all," he said earnestly, "Sarah Codling wasn't likely to have forgotten anything else she was told, or to have made a silly mistake. Her father trusted her more than he did her mother, and she was a sensible age—eleven."

"That's true," said David, "after all, I'm eleven."

"There you are. So let's say, as Sarah said, that the only clue is in the rhyme."

"Yet there just isn't one there."

"Unless everyone has missed it so far."

"You mean a code?"

Adam shook his head. "You can't make up a code in a hurry, in the middle of the night, with your wife nagging you. No, I was thinking of something different. Punctuation—commas and so on."

"Commas?" said David hesitantly. "I don't remember seeing any commas in the rhyme."

"That's just it: there aren't any."

"Well, then——"

"But when you say the verse, you have to put the punctuation in, in the way you say it. I mean, you have to pause where you think there should be a comma."

"Well, of course."

"It's obvious, but it leads to things much less obvious. For instance, the Narrative said that Jonathan Codling taught Sarah not just the words of the rhyme, but how to say them—where to breathe and pause. That is, he taught her the punctuation."

"Go on."

"But why did he bother, unless the punctuation—the pausing —were unusual?"

"Go on."

"But all that's just the kind of thing that gets easily overlooked. And if Judith Codling were upset and worried and cross——"

"And stupid," said David, caught up into the excitement.

". . . and stupid, it's just the kind of thing she'd overlook. She'd hear the words said by Sarah, but she wouldn't hear the way they were said. And very soon the way they were said would be lost."

"Oh, what was the verse? I can't remember it!" David cried in impatience and despair.

"I can. I'll say it with the comma-pause where Aunt Dinah puts it—where Judith Codling almost certainly put it, and where

Sarah—I think—almost certainly didn't put it—that is, at least, until she was bullied and beaten out of her common sense." Adam cleared his throat, and recited:

> *"When Philip came to the single rose*
> *Over the water,*
> *The treasure was taken where no one knows*
> *None but my daughter."*

"To move the comma," said David very thoughtfully.

"Suppose," said Adam, "you put it after the first line, instead of after the second."

David, who now knew the rhyme for himself, began:

> *"When Philip came to the single rose,*
> *Over the water*
> *The treasure was taken . . ."*

At this point, Adam interrupted him to repeat in a loud, emphatic whisper the new and surprising message: "OVER THE WATER THE TREASURE WAS TAKEN."

David was excited, but still doubtful. "Was it just a bluff, then, his going out to hide it that night? Did he get it overseas somewhere, later? But then, he didn't go over the water at all. Your aunt said he was going to fight the Spaniards on land, not on sea."

Adam was enjoying every stage of David's reasoning that he himself had traveled through not so long ago. When David paused, puzzled and at a loss, Adam prompted him.

"But the sea isn't the only water. It wasn't the water nearest to Jonathan Codling the night he took the treasure from the house."

"The river!" cried David, his whole face lighted with joy. "The River Say at the bottom of his garden!"

"And remember those wet stockings that he came back with and had to change."

"And, of course, they'd have a boat."

"He went out in the boat, secretly, with the treasure——"

"And hid it 'over the water'—somewhere on the far bank of the river!"

The boys gazed at each other, beaming mutual congratulations. David was stirred by so deep an excitement that he stood as in a trance of feeling: he felt the warmth of the sun on his neck; he heard the soft humming of the bees; he smelled the leaves of the apple mint that had strayed over the neglected path and been trodden and crushed under foot. Adam stretched out his hand and took his, and began leading him, almost ceremoniously, toward the river. "This," he said, "is the beginning of our treasure seeking."

They went down to the river bank and to the fallen tree, through whose ivy trails David had had to force a way on his first voyage in the *Minnow*.

"This is the tree bridge," said Adam. "I've explored over it already, of course, but we ought to go again, so that you know as much as I do. Then we work on together."

The tree bridge joined the Codlings' piece of woodland with an even drearier, damper-looking piece on the far side of the river. "That bit of the far bank used to belong to Grandfather and Aunt Dinah," said Adam. "It was the last bit on the far bank that did. I remember Aunt Dinah's selling it to Mr. Nunn, who farms the land behind. He thought it might be useful for getting at the river for his cattle. But he's never cleared it or used it."

"And you still go into it?" asked David.

"Mr. Nunn doesn't mind," said Adam. "Aunt Dinah asked him, and he said we could go in as we liked. Aunt Dinah goes over in the early summer, because there's a special wood orchis that grows there. She says she hopes and prays Mr. Nunn will never clear the ground, because of the orchis."

David tried to imagine Miss Codling creeping over the tree bridge that now faced him. His imagination failed; and yet, equally, he could not imagine her being baffled for one moment if she really wanted to reach the other side.

The climb across was slow and uncomfortable rather than dangerous. Sharp twigs and the bristly stems of ivy poked and grazed their hands and knees; tree dust and splinters of dry wood and fragments of dead leaf flew into their eyes and mouths and lodged irritatingly in their hair. Adam led the way, giving the advice of one well used to a difficult road.

"Mind how you get off the tree!" he warned. "The bank on the Nunn side is boggy. Tread on the tussocks."

The far bank for perhaps ten feet from the river was almost under water. Then the ground rose slightly but sharply, and became much drier. Except on the marshy river bank, ivy grew everywhere over the ground in tangling snares. David had one shoe filled with bog water, and had tripped painfully twice, before he stood side by side with Adam on safe, dry land.

"I've been over every inch of this," said Adam—"except, of course, for the boggy bit—with a garden fork. I don't mean actually digging, but driving the prongs in over and over again, expecting them to strike against something—a box—a chest—a casket."

"The treasure."

"Yes. But I found nothing."

They walked directly away from the river, until they found themselves, in a few minutes, at the end of the woodland. A corn-field lay before them, and in the distance on the far side of the field the red roofs of a farmhouse.

"That's Mr. Nunn's," said Adam. "This is his field. I stopped using the fork here."

"Why?"

"Forking for treasure is pretty hard work," said Adam. "Besides, you can't start doing it all over a person's crops."

David acknowledged the justness of these remarks, yet he could not help wondering privately whether Jonathan Codling's limit for hiding might have been not at all the same as Adam's limit for searching. Even if Jonathan Codling had wanted a hiding place on his own land, he had, according to Miss Codling, the whole of the two Barleys to choose from. No consideration of crops need have stopped him.

All the boys had seen of any interest so far were several small slabs of stone, lying half hidden under the ivy.

"They're graves," said Adam, "graves of dogs that my father and my grandfather owned." He stooped and tore the ivy away from one of them until David could read the letters: TOBY.

"I remember his dying," said Adam. "Aunt Dinah and I carried him over in a piece of sacking, and buried him. He was really Grandfather's dog. He was an awfully good sort, Toby. He was the last dog. Aunt Dinah said we just couldn't afford a dog's keep after that."

David cleared his throat awkwardly. "I suppose," he said, and hesitated, "I suppose—I mean, I don't expect you used the fork—"

"No. The treasure was buried over four hundred years ago; the burial of dogs here was only begun by my grandfather— that's only about fifty years ago. So there was no need for me to disturb their bones."

They walked back in silence to the fallen tree. David found the little damp wood sad. While he was in it he felt his excitement and hopes ebbing away from him. As soon as he reached the tree bridge he started back across it eagerly, ahead of Adam.

David was halfway across when he felt one of his ankles gripped tightly from behind, and Adam's voice said, in a warning whisper: "Wait! Someone's coming!"

David at once crouched down until chin, chest, stomach, and legs lay along the tree trunk, and his whole body was concealed among the ivy; Adam would be behind him in the same position. To hide at once seemed natural, although Mr. Nunn had given a general permission to the Codlings to use his bank, and although Miss Codling knew they were going over the tree bridge. Whoever it was, however, was coming neither from the Nunn side nor from the Codling side but up the river itself. Peering through the ivy leaves, David saw a punt moving upstream toward the fallen tree. A stout woman with glasses sat in the middle. She would have had a comfortable, gentle look, except for the peevish expression now on her face, and the over-intent way in which she was knitting. Behind her an elderly, bald-headed man stood and punted.

The punt came right up to the fallen tree, and then, as though the end of the voyage were reached, turned completely. But, instead of allowing it to go downstream again, the punter maneuvered his boat until it was almost underneath the tree, and there held it. From his position, David could not see the man at all, but he could see the woman—the top of her head and the flashing ends of her knitting needles.

David was torn by curiosity at what the man might be doing, and the desire to giggle at the sight of the top of the woman's head so directly—so temptingly—beneath him. He felt laughter beginning to shake him, and then felt Adam's hand tighten warningly on his ankle. He choked down his laughter, but as a necessary relief, moved his fingers quietly and skillfully so that a dead ivy leaf detached itself and floated down upon the bun of graying hair beneath him. The woman defended herself at once with a nervous sideways cut of her knitting needle.

"Andrew," she cried, "this is a most disagreeable place. A spider has just dropped on me."

"Not a spider, dear—a leaf," replied Andrew tranquilly. They were silent again, and now David felt only the burnings of his curiosity. He still could not see Andrew at all, and still could not imagine what he was doing. Suddenly the woman in the punt spoke again, revealing that even while being able to see Andrew she shared David's curiosity.

"Andrew!" she cried, with a kind of timid exasperation, as she dropped her knitting into her lap. "Will you tell me what you're doing?"

"Looking."

"At what?"

"Just at the Codlings' place."

David caught his breath, both at what he had heard and at the sudden pain of Adam's nails digging into the flesh of his ankle. More startling still was the woman's next remark.

"Once—yes; twice, even—I could understand it. But again and again, every summer, to punt your way up here and then just to stop and stare—there can be no sense in it, surely."

"Sense? Sense?" David could hear from the man's voice that he was quite undisturbed in his reverie by this criticism. After a pause, David heard him sigh and whisper to himself, "There might be sense in it, some day, somehow."

There was the sound of effort in his voice on the last word. The punt pole had been brought into use again, and the punt moved forward downstream. The woman was looking at her knitting again, the man was still gazing into the Codlings' woodland; neither looked back to the fallen tree, where, from the dull brown and green of the ivy, rounded eyes stared out, until the punt and its occupants were beyond sight.

Adam and David did not speak until they were both on their own bank again. Even then, there was at first a long and thoughtful silence.

"I saw that punt when I first came up in the *Minnow*," said David at last. "The people weren't in her then."

"They live in one of the houses with gardens that go down to the river."

"Who are they?"

"Their name is Smith—at least, they say it is."

"What do you mean, 'say it is'?"

"It's probably false. Smith is only a name people assume, to escape the police."

David thought deeply. His curiosity and distrust had been fully aroused by the scrap of conversation they had overheard, but he could not go as far as Adam in suspicion. "Smith must sometimes be a real name," he said. "There are several Smiths in the Barleys. There's Timmy Smith in our Row—he plays with Becky. His name's his own all right."

"How do you know?"

"Well, his father's Mr. Smith."

"And how do you know *his* name's not false?"

David was not prepared for such unrelenting questioning. His head whirled with wild new doubts, and he said no more.

Adam said, "We'll talk to Aunt Dinah. I'll bring the conversation very casually round to the Smiths, and find out what she knows."

Miss Codling was quite willing to tell the little she knew about the Smiths on hearing only so much as that they had been seen in a punt. She said that the Smiths had come to Great Barley about five years ago and settled in one of the riverside houses. They had called upon her in a very friendly way on their first arrival, but Miss Codling had had neither the time nor the inclination to continue the acquaintance. She had never returned the visit, nor been revisited. The Smiths were, by all accounts, well-off. Mr. Smith worked in London, and traveled to and fro every day by train, which few businessmen could afford to do; besides, he and his wife were often away for weeks on end, staying in London. When they were in Barley they lived alone; Miss Codling believed that there was a daughter, but she had never been seen. There information came to an end.

When they were alone again, David said to Adam, "I don't really think the Smiths are a threat. They seem well enough off anyway, without looking for treasure."

"But what were they doing, then? What did their conversation mean?"

"I don't know."

"And why should anyone disguise himself under the name of Smith?"

This last question remained with David on his way home that evening. A rosy-cheeked little boy was perched on one of the front gates of the Row as he came slowly past.

"Hello, David!" he cried.

"Hello, Timmy," David answered absently.

Behind Timmy, there was a sudden commotion as Timmy's

father heaved his bulk up from his gardening. "Hello, David!" he said, good-naturedly. "How are your father's sunflowers?"

David was about to answer that they had never really recovered from the rains, when it suddenly occurred to him that the smile on Mr. Smith's face was too broad to be quite natural; and Mr. Smith's eyes were certainly so bright as to be almost glittering.

"How are they?" repeated Mr. Smith, in real or well-feigned surprise at David's hesitation.

"Quite well, thank you," said David, in confusion. He began to move homeward again quickly. "Good night, Mr.—Mr.—" The name stuck in his throat; he could not say it. He left Mr. Smith gazing after him with a look of the plainest astonishment on his simple, red face.

9

A Trip to Tea

ADAM'S AND DAVID'S thoughts were now dedicated to the hidden treasure. The tree bridge drooped across the river for no other purpose than to lead the search into Mr. Nunn's land. The *Minnow's* mission was to take them further in the quest; even the Smiths were only interesting as they might be perhaps in rivalry for the treasure. Yet, in spite of all this, there was a whole afternoon when both seekers lapsed almost entirely from their singleness of purpose.

The *Minnow's* varnish was perfectly dry, and they had carried her down to the river and lowered her into the water. Adam had put into her bow one of his aunt's garden forks; the wooden backs were in position, and the paddles ready.

"Our first voyage for the treasure," said Adam, with a solemn enthusiasm, and stepped in and settled himself in the stern—it was his turn there after David's maiden voyage upstream. David sat in the middle.

They had not made any detailed plans of where they should go first to begin the search. This was the moment to decide; yet they both sat perfectly silent, staring trancedly ahead of them. Adam began to dip one finger after another into the water. At length he said, in a faraway voice: "David, let's go fast."

Without a word and without turning his head, David helped to shove off from the bank, and they began to paddle downstream. At first they paddled together clumsily, sending the canoe on an irregular and jerky course. Then they caught a common rhythm, and at the same time began to find the best and strongest stroke for speed. Their paddles flashed upward together, streaming from the river, and then went down again in evenly-powered strokes that sped the *Minnow* over the water as though she rejoiced in her element. Faster they went, and still faster, until David gave a breathless little laugh, and Adam cried, "I'm done! Let's rest!" And even then, with paddles shipped, the *Minnow* bore them on with effortless speed.

"We'd forgotten the treasure," Adam said.

"Not really," said David brazenly. "I think it's rather a good idea to make a general survey of the far bank all along, and see what's most hopeful, for a beginning."

"Which way shall we go, then?"

"Downstream—go on downstream," said David quickly, and then blushed to think that Adam might ask him his reason. An occasional convenience of canoe conversation, however, is that the talkers never face each other. Adam accepted David's opinion, without his curiosity being roused by the sight of David's red face.

They went on downstream past the riverside houses of Great Barley. All these houses had been built long after Jonathan Codling's time, and David wondered whether, deep under a lawn or a flower bed, the treasure might be lying waiting, even now. If so, what daring and lawlessness would be needed for either of them to go digging for it there?

"This must be the Smiths' land," said Adam. The punt, now empty, lay chained to a mooring post. As the canoe drifted past, the boys looked up the garden to the house. It all looked as different as possible from Codlings': the garden was perfectly kept, with close-cropped grass, weedless paths, and beds neat even to their flowers being arranged in geometrical patterns of color. The house was smaller than Codlings', but every window was clean and polished and draped with curtains, and window frames and doors gleamed with white paint.

"Look!" said David as his eye caught sight of some moving shape behind one of the windows. It was the only sign of life that they saw.

"I wonder . . ." said Adam.

When they had passed the last of the Great Barley houses and were in the open country, all lingering thoughts of the treasure left them. They tested the *Minnow* and tested their own skill and strength in her. They back-paddled, they forward-paddled; they sent her twirling in circles; they raced a squawking family of tame ducks, clapping their paddles fiercely into the water to an abrupt chorus of "One—two! One—two!" Then they changed their methods altogether, and saw how stealthily they could go. They grudged the soft whisper of water against the prow of the canoe; they slid their paddles soundlessly into the water and, as they drew them slowly out at the end of each stroke, held them so that the drops from the paddles had only a finger's breadth to fall before they were united to the river again. Their care was unexpectedly rewarded, for as they stole round a bend of the river, they surprised a great gray bird that rose and wheeled with slowly flapping wings, its legs trailing behind it, still shining wet from the river.

"A heron," whispered Adam. "They often fish in the Say, Aunt Dinah says. Only you don't often see them. They choose lonely places."

Below the heron's fishing ground the boys explored a branch of the river—hardly more than a side ditch—that David had only noticed in passing on his first voyage. The side stream was very narrow where it left the Say, and grew still narrower farther on, from the growth of reed banks on either side. Adam and David struggled on, however, using their paddles to push against the bottom; there was no room to use paddles properly. Their effort was worthwhile, for the stream widened again, so that passage became easier. They reached a low bridge of iron girdering over which ran a railway line. As they passed under it, David stretched up one hand and touched the ironwork overhead.

"Why!" he cried, in surprise, "it trembles! Feel it, Adam."

Adam felt it too. "It's very slight," he said, "but it's growing more distinct; and I can hear something—it's a train coming!"

There was a faraway whistle, and a muffled drumming in the air that grew nearer and heavier. Then, in only a few minutes, the Castleford-to-London express was on top of them, thundering, roaring, rattling over their heads, until they shuddered and pressed their hands to their ears in an unaccustomed mingling of delight and terror. Then it had passed with a farewell whistle.

They paddled out from under the bridge, to continue their exploration; but now the stream narrowed again quickly, and this time the reeds blocked the way entirely. David waded ashore through them and tried to help the *Minnow* by hauling on the mooring rope, while Adam, abandoning the use of his paddle altogether, pulled on the reeds. They advanced only a few inches in as many minutes, and David, from the bank, reported that downstream as far as he could see the channel was choked. There was nothing for it but to turn back.

"Anyway," said Adam, "it's pretty certain that Jonathan Codling never came along here on a dark night in a hurry."

There was no room to turn a canoe, so the boys changed their positions and now sat facing the other way. As the *Minnow* was shaped exactly alike at both ends, there was neither inconvenience nor humiliation in this rearrangement.

When they came into the main river again the Great Barley church clock was striking four.

"There's at least an hour before we need be back," said Adam. "What shall we do?"

"Go on downstream. As a matter of fact," David added, "we shall be up to my father's dock soon."

"We might pay your family a surprise visit," Adam remarked lightly. David said nothing in reply, but redoubled the strength of his paddling. As he had said, they were quite soon at the dock. They brought themselves smartly alongside, and Adam held the canoe steady by his grasp on one of the corner posts, while David prepared to get out. He had half raised himself, when he saw his father in the garden, attending to one of the fruit trees.

"Father!" he called.

Mr. Moss turned and looked in the general direction from which the voice had come, but evidently saw nobody. He turned slowly in a complete circle, still looking carefully, and ended by facing the dock again, the picture of a man amazed.

"Father!"

This time Mr. Moss was not taken by surprise, but started at once toward the spot from which he was sure the voice had come. He soon had a view of his son's head and shoulders just above the level of the dock.

"Well!" he said, leaning over the gate and gazing at Adam— at whom he nodded, by way of introduction—and David and the canoe. The boys waited for him to say more.

"Well," said Mr. Moss, "she certainly looks different from the day when she drifted up against here on the floods."

"Two coats of varnish outside and one in," said David, beaming at the sensation caused by their arrival: this was what he had hoped for.

"And thank you for getting us the last lot of varnish, and for the loan of the scraper," said Adam.

Mr. Moss said nothing, nor did he smile; but David knew from a certain delicate rearrangement of the lines of his face that he was pleased. Still pleased, he looked into the canoe and noticed the fork in the bow. "What's that?" he asked, in the way he had of suggesting a questioning mind rather than any precise query.

Adam, in confusion, answered him literally: "It's my aunt's garden fork."

"Oh," said Mr. Moss. He disliked answering questions himself, and did not expect others to be any more obliging. Nevertheless, he had not quite finished with the subject of the fork. "If that fell in, it'd sink to the bottom," he said. He glanced along at David. "Not being all of wood," he said, "that wouldn't go floating away downstream."

At that moment Mrs. Moss's voice was heard from the house. "Bob!"

"There's your mother ready with the tea, David," said Mr. Moss. "You'd better bring Adam along indoors. Your mother and I would have been alone—Becky's out somewhere."

Mr. Moss started back toward the house, and Adam prepared to follow him at once.

"But I say," said David, "what about your aunt? She was expecting us back to tea, wasn't she?"

"Not until five or after. Come on! Don't you see," Adam said emphatically, "we can have two teas if we're quick!"

By the time the boys reached the house, they found Mr. Moss announcing the visit to his wife. From David she had already heard, with sympathy, many stories of Adam Codling; on the other hand, she had never lost her distrust of the canoe that had come from him. Now, she repeated after Mr. Moss, but in an entirely different tone—one of disapproval—his explanation, "Came in the canoe."

Mrs. Moss turned to meet Adam for the first time, and David felt suddenly chilled as he realized the misfortune of the meeting. Not only was Adam straight from the canoe, but he was looking exactly as, according to Mrs. Moss, a boy should not look. How many times, as Mrs. Moss tidied David in exasperation, had she told him she could not endure a boy with a dirty face, with dust in his hair, with a button missing off his shirt, and so on! All these Adam had—and more, for invisibly to Mrs. Moss as yet his shirt was hanging out of his trousers at the back.

Adam advanced confidently toward Mrs. Moss with his hand outstretched. Her expression remained one of reserve as her hand went out to meet his. Then, abruptly, her expression changed, and her hand, instead of taking his, gripped the wrist above it.

"Oh!" cried Mrs. Moss. "What a terrible hand—how did it get like that?"

Adam tried to remember. "I think the reeds must have cut it when I was pulling on them. But it's all right, Mrs. Moss, really."

"Nonsense! Not with that horrible river water and river mud all over it! Come straight upstairs to the bathroom, and I'll clean it and put something on it." Holding Adam by the wrist, she led him away with her.

When Adam came down again, not only was his hand bandaged, but his face was clean and his hair combed, and Mrs. Moss, who came immediately behind him, was tucking his shirt tail in as he went, with only a kindly resignation in the clicking of her tongue.

The tea was a very good one—the kind that Mrs. Moss provided on the rare occasions when her husband was back from work in the early afternoon. Both the boys ate well, but they had hardly finished when Adam glanced at the clock and said that they ought to be getting back.

"Won't you stay here, now you are here, David?" said Mrs. Moss.

"His bicycle is with us, Mrs. Moss," said Adam quickly, and smiled meaningly at David. He plainly meant that David should not be cheated out of his second tea. The thought of another voyage in the *Minnow* attracted David much more than the thought of another tea; he positively did not want any more to eat, and felt surprised at Adam's wolfish hurry. Yet he had already noticed that Adam always seemed hungry; he had to crush the unpleasant idea that he was greedy.

Both boys got back into the canoe and set off on the journey upstream. Mr. and Mrs. Moss, arm in arm, leaned over the gate of the dock and watched them go. It was David's turn to sit at the back. Knowing that he was being watched, he sat very erect, raised his paddle very high, dug it in very deeply and strongly, and altogether paddled with great style.

"I suppose he's safe," said Mrs. Moss.

"Of course, he is," said Mr. Moss. "And I like the lad with him."

"Yes. He somehow reminds me a little of Dick, just before he went to sea." This, for Mrs. Moss, was the highest compliment that could be paid.

"But not at all so well filled out," said Mr. Moss.

"No. He's thin."

They watched the canoe growing smaller and smaller. "He ate more than I've ever seen Dick eat at tea," said Mrs. Moss.

"Boys are hungry."

"Not as much as that. Didn't you say the Codlings were poor?"

"Yes—as church mice."

"That's what I mean."

Mr. Moss turned and looked carefully at his wife as if he would understand from her expression something he could not from her words. "That's what you mean?"

"I mean," said Mrs. Moss sadly, "I don't believe they can afford enough to eat at home." She shook her head. "Poor boy!"

10

Folly Mill and a Ball of String

ADAM AND DAVID made up for their first outing with the *Minnow* by many afternoons of work in close search for the treasure. Their beat was that part of the river bank which stretched upstream from Mr. Nunn's land. By starting there, they shelved the problem of how to carry the search into the prim riverside gardens of Great Barley. Upstream, between Mr. Nunn's land and Folly Mill, there were only open meadows.

Every afternoon, to Miss Codling's satisfaction, Adam and David set out on a voyage in the *Minnow*. Miss Codling was not aware, however, that her garden fork always went with them on their expeditions, together with a length of string and some wooden pegs. For Adam had determined that the search should be systematic. As soon as they landed, he marked off with string and pegs a plot about ten feet square and having the river as one of its four boundaries. Then, he and David took turns in forking over this space. When they had probed every inch of ground, the string and pegs were moved to enclose the next plot. So they moved slowly up the far bank, examining as they went.

The work had to be slow in order to be thorough, and it was

also unexpectedly tiring. The fork had to be stabbed in, each time, with enough force to drive its prongs to their full length into the close, matted turf. Then it had to be withdrawn with a strong upward pull and twist. Before long, David's arms began to ache, then his shoulders, and then his whole body. He did not complain—neither did Adam, but David suspected that he suffered in the same way.

The work was slow, tiring, monotonous, and disappointing. Every so often the prongs of the fork would strike against something hard, and then whichever boy was at work would dig the obstacle up. Nearly always it was a stone; once it was a rusted piece of metal—possibly part of a plowshare; once it was an old iron saucepan, which they carefully emptied, but its contents were only earth and worms.

They quickly lost count of turns of work, of plots of land, of the unhopeful afternoons. One afternoon seemed no different from those before it. David, as usual, said, "Fifty! It's your turn!" and, leaving the fork still upright in the earth, flung himself onto the river bank, with his aching shoulders to the ground. Adam took over without a word, and began the stabbing and heaving. "Ten," he grunted presently; and David shut his eyes against the blue of the heavens and tried, by relaxing every muscle, to rest himself in preparation for his next exertion. After a while, "Twenty!" said Adam. And David tried to forget what the fork felt like and what it would so soon feel like again, in his hands. "Thirty!" said Adam, and then, it seemed almost immediately, "Forty!"

"Adam!" said David, opening his eyes and sitting up.

"Yes?" Adam paused, and rested on the fork.

"We get down about nine inches every time—that's the length of the fork prongs, isn't it?"

"Yes."

"But how do you know Jonathan Codling didn't hide the treasure more than nine inches deep?"

Adam did not answer.

"And," went on David, "we go over a strip ten feet back from the river bank; but how do you know Jonathan didn't bury the treasure farther away from the river than that?"

It seemed as if Adam were going to remain silent, but at last he said, "What do you suggest, then?"

"I don't know."

"Do you want us to give up?" He was fierce now.

"No, of course not."

"Well, then?" Adam calmed himself a little. "Don't you see? We have to find the treasure—we just have to find it. If we begin saying it may be more than nine inches deep, or more than ten feet away from the bank—well, we might as well say it's a hopeless job to look for it at all; we should never find it; we should just have to give up. Don't you see?"

"Yes," said David, and then, "isn't it my turn with the fork, now?"

"No, I've nine more jabs to do." But Adam still leaned on the fork, brooding. "If only there were anywhere besides the ground on this far side of the river where he might have hidden it. . . ."

"There are the trees," said David, "but none of them round here are the kind that lives hundreds and hundreds of years."

"No," agreed Adam, "it would have to be a building—a very old building. If only there were some really ancient ruins!"

There were no ruins of any kind in either of the Barleys. Both the parish churches were very old, and probably some of the thatched cottages, but all these were on the wrong side of the river and well away from it at that. On the side in which the boys were interested there were only the modern riverside houses of Great Barley, and in Little Barley, the Council houses, the shops built for them, and the bus shelter—all new. Even Mr. Nunn's house was not old.

Adam and David went through all the possibilities. Then David said, "Of course, there's Folly Mill—that's pretty old. The trouble is, Jonathan Codling was only away an **hour** when he went to hide the treasure. I don't think anyone could get up to Folly Mill and back to Codlings' in an hour."

Adam considered. "In a 'clear hour,' Sarah Codling said. Perhaps it might be done. On the other hand, are we sure that Folly Mill's as old as all that, anyway?"

"No," said David. "But then we're not sure that the treasure's buried only nine inches down, or that it's buried within ten feet from the bank. Or," he said with defiance, "that it's buried at all."

Adam flung the fork savagely down. "Let's have a change from this. Let's go up to Folly Mill."

Once they were in the canoe, their spirits began to return to them; it was impossible not to respond to the *Minnow's* buoyancy and grace. They paddled away gladly from the hated, over-familiar bank, with its pegs and string and garden fork, and went upstream to Folly Mill.

The day's work was just over when they reached the mill. A big green truck, with "Mark Tey, Flour Miller and Corn Merchant" on its side, was being driven into its shed. Presently the driver came out and, in company with two or three other men, all in dusty coats, mounted his bicycle and rode away. The mill door still stood open, however, and a big man with a bald head and a bushy black beard stood in the doorway. He seemed to be absorbed in examining a sample of corn that he tipped slowly from the palm of one hand to the other.

"I think that's Mr. Tey," said David in a whisper. "He owns Folly Mill."

They paddled quietly into the shadow of the mill bridge where they felt themselves comfortably invisible from the miller's eye. Here the *Minnow* chose to turn round, but they still kept her underneath as far as possible; only her bow poked forward from under the bridge and into the sunlight.

"Where shall we look first?" said David. He spoke in a whisper, but the echoes under the bridge took his whisper and threw it eerily to and fro.

"Well," said Adam, "we're searching on the left bank—the far bank, so I suppose the place to search here is on the left side of the arch. I must say it looks hopeless, though."

He put out his hand to the brickwork, which was smooth and dank and almost green, being covered with something between slime and fine moss. As Adam touched it a voice started the echoes again—a voice that was neither his nor David's: "Are you looking for treasure?"

Looking upward and outward, Adam and David saw a face that seemed to hang from the top of the arch of the bridge, gazing at them: it appeared to have a remarkably wide and horribly shining chin, and to have a head of extraordinarily upward-growing and spreading black hair. With a cry of alarm, David, who sat in the stern of the *Minnow*, pushed off with his paddle so violently that the canoe shot forward and out from under the bridge altogether. They passed directly under the apparition, unharmed.

Now, gazing back, the boys realized that the face they had seen was quite normally attached to a body; its strangeness had been due to its having been viewed upside down. Mr. Tey, noticing the bow of the canoe from the bridge, had had the curiosity to lean right over and peer underneath. From below, his beaver beard had seemed at the top, and his bald, shiny head at the bottom of his face. The vision had been appalling.

Rather ashamed of their recent panic, Adam and David turned the canoe a little way from the bridge and steadied her to face the mill and the miller.

"Are you looking for hidden treasure?" called Mr. Tey.

"What makes you think we might be?"

"I think I recognize that canoe. Your grandfather came up in her once, years ago, on the same search."

"My grandfather?"

Mr. Tey laughed. "I'm sure of the hair, even if I'm not sure of the canoe. That's Codling hair you have. It's your grandfather's, to the exact shade."

"I am Adam Codling," admitted Adam. There was no opportunity to consult privately with David, so on his own responsibility he took the chance he saw. "And we are looking for the hidden treasure."

"Secretly," put in David, thinking uneasily of Miss Codling.

"Yes," said Adam. "So could we perhaps come ashore and have a look?"

"Certainly."

The boys grounded the canoe in a muddy little bay and made their way up through banks of nettles to where Mr. Tey stood. He, meanwhile, had turned his gaze from Adam to David, whom he considered very carefully. When David came within reach, he took him by the ear, not violently, nor impertinently, but reflectively—almost reminiscently. "Your name, of course, is Jordan," he said.

Adam was surprised at the silence before David spoke in contradiction. "No, it isn't; it's Moss."

"Moss?" cried Mr. Tey. "With those ears? You're a Jordan. Surely," he pleaded, "you're a Jordan."

"Well," said David reluctantly, "well, my mother's name was Jordan, before she married—Alice Jordan."

"Ha!" cried Mr. Tey. "I said so! Alice Jordan—now, whose child was she? Herbert Jordan's? Or maybe daughter to Nathaniel Jordan, the blacksmith?"

"Grandfather was a blacksmith."

"And she married a Moss?"

"Yes. My father is Robert Moss."

"Not Bad Bobbie Moss, that was?"

"Oh, no," said David, startled. He had never heard of such a person.

"Bad Bobbie Moss—the terror of both the Barleys," said Mr. Tey. "The only boy that's ever climbed Sam Truelove's orchard wall. He had to get back in a hurry. He fell and cut his head open so badly, they took him off to Castleford hospital and put stitches in. He was lucky not to lose his right eye, they said. He'll bear the mark of that till his dying day if I know anything."

David's mouth fell open. Then, with a gulp, he shut it and said, "How could it be the same Moss? My father drives the county buses and grows prize roses."

"Ah, well," said Mr. Tey amiably, letting the subject drop, "no doubt there are other Mosses."

Adam took the opportunity of a break in the conversation to edge the talk round to the treasure again. "Did you know my grandfather well, Mr. Tey?"

"Well? We sat on the Great Barley parish council for two and twenty years. He was chairman all that time."

"No wonder he trusted you with the secret of the treasure," said Adam.

"It was never much secret that the Codlings had lost a treasure and wouldn't be above finding it," said Mr. Tey. "I remember the day your grandfather came up here in that canoe. As soon as he saw me, he shouted at the top of his voice. 'Hi!' he said. 'I've come up especially to see you.'

" 'Why,' I said, 'why trail up in a boat, when we meet this evening in the village hall?'

" 'Ah,' he said, 'this is different. I've come over the water because I'm searching for the hidden treasure.' "

"Are you sure?" asked David.

"Sure?"

"I mean, that he said that."

"Word for word he said it. 'This isn't at all the same thing,' he said. 'I'm on the lookout for lost treasure,' he said, 'and that's why I've come over the water by canoe.'

" 'Well,' said I, 'if you think the treasure may be hidden here, you're welcome to come and look.' Out he got and in he came."

So saying, Mr. Tey turned from the river and, a boy on either side of him, faced the mill. As he looked up at it David had the impression of a pale face against one of the dust-covered upper windows. Then, it was withdrawn. Neither of the other two seemed to have seen it. Mr. Tey said, "Work's stopped and everyone's gone home. It's a good time to look over."

They passed into the mill. Outside, the setting of the sun was leaving light without brightness; inside, it was already dusk. There were naked electric bulbs hanging from the rafters, but Mr. Tey did not trouble to switch any light on; he knew his way too well. "Mind your heads!" he said as a general warning and then, "And the floors are a bit uneven too." David, who came last, unashamedly held a pinch of Adam's shirt tail between his fingers as a guide. His eyes were almost better shut than open. He felt dust-laden cobwebs brush against his face and softly shed their burden upon him. The air was thick with the rich, dry smell of corn and flour—of flour that had gone to make loaves long since baked and eaten.

Mr. Tey suddenly stopped. "Tiddly widdly widdly!" he called enticingly. A white phantom appeared on top of a pile of sacks, and, the next moment, was at his feet, sliding round and round his leg, purring.

"She has kittens, somewhere," said Mr. Tey. "They'll be white like their mother—they always are—and famous ratters." He stooped to touch her, but the cat glided away and ahead of them. She kept her distance ahead during all the rest of the tour of the mill.

Mr. Tey was clearly determined to take them everywhere and show them everything, but he was thinking of flour milling rather than of hidden treasure.

"White bread's poison to the stomach," he said. "You want to eat bread made from wholemeal brown flour." He made them feel its roughness between finger and thumb, as though they were silk fanciers. "And brown flour that's been stone ground is the best of all." And he showed them his great millstones—two in position for grinding, and one leaning against the wall waiting to have its surface renewed.

Up and down stairs they were led, past cliffs of bulging flour sacks, under low-beamed arches, through obscurities in which even the white cat ahead of them seemed an uncertain moving blur. Only once did Mr. Tey refer to old Mr. Codling and the treasure. "Now your grandfather was very interested in this part of the mill," he said to Adam, "but he didn't find any treasure here." They were standing in a narrow passageway. Looking down, David saw, through the cracks in the flooring, an inkiness that seemed faintly to be moving. He realized that they were standing immediately over the River Say, and shuddered to think that its waters could ever wear that appearance. What had attracted Mr. Codling's interest to such a spot?

"And lastly," said Mr. Tey as they mounted more stairs, "I'll show you the carpenter's workshop." They turned sharply into a kind of room, with windows all along one side above a long workbench strewn with chips and shavings of wood, ends of string, boxes of nails, and tools. It was lighter here than elsewhere in Folly Mill, but even so, they would not at first have noticed that the workshop had an occupant, but that the cat ran forward with an eager mewing sound. She jumped into the lap of a little old man who sat cross-legged on a pile of empty sacks. He had been straining sideways to the window for the last of the light, mending old sacks with string and a tool that was halfway between a stiletto and a needle curved wickedly at its pointed end. The cat on his knees prevented his work. He pushed feebly at her, but she took no notice. Then he looked up and saw Mr. Tey.

"It's that overcast," said the old man peevishly. "I can't see to work."

"But, Squeak," said Mr. Tey, "it's not overcast; it's evening coming on. Didn't you know the time? Didn't you notice the mill had stopped? Everyone else has knocked off and gone home long ago."

Squeak said nothing in reply, but shook the cat off him, and began very slowly to stack his work away.

"You'll be late home again, and then your daughter will have something to say," warned Mr. Tey.

This threat speeded Squeak's movement, and he was just

sidling past Mr. Tey and the two boys when he happened to raise his shortsighted eyes to Adam's face. "Oh!" he whispered, and fell back.

"Yes," said Mr. Tey, who seemed almost to have been hoping for this, "he's like his grandfather, old Mr. Codling, isn't he?"

"Yes," said Squeak faintly.

"Squeak Wilson knew your grandfather well," Mr. Tey said to Adam. "Didn't you, Squeak?" There was no answer. "You worked for him for years, didn't you, Squeak?" There was still no answer. "Come, Squeak," said Mr. Tey, who seemed to be enjoying some private joke, "where's your tongue—where are your manners?"

"How is your grandpa?" stammered the old man.

"Quite well, thank you," said Adam.

"And how is your aunt?" asked Squeak, gaining a little confidence. "She always put in a good word for poor Squeak Wilson."

"Quite well, thank you."

This interchange gave Squeak Wilson so much courage that he began again to edge his way out. He had already reached the door when Mr. Tey called after him: "Hurry home, Squeak, and remember—no sips of homemade wine on the way."

Squeak gave a little cry and made a rush through the door. Then they heard the frightened scrabbling of his feet on the stairway, fading. Mr. Tey was convulsed with silent laughter at the effect of his advice; his body bent over until his great beard almost swept his knees, and his arms swung to and fro, helplessly. When he had straightened himself and begun wiping his eyes, Adam asked, "Why is he called Squeak?" But Mr. Tey was too preoccupied with his own thoughts to answer him. "I ought not to have chaffed him so, perhaps," he said, "but it was a temptation. He's a poor thing—jack of all trades and master of none. Your grandfather used to employ him as odd-job man, but there was—well, there was some trouble, and he left. I give him sack mending to do when I can. He's a poor thing, in all conscience." Mr. Tey so affected himself that he started downstairs after Squeak Wil-

son, calling repentantly, "Squeak! Wait a minute there, Squeak!"
But when he reached the ground floor, with the other two at
his heels, Squeak was not there. When they got outside, Squeak
Wilson was already on his tricycle and several hundred yards
away—his little body taut with the effort of escaping as fast as
possible.

Mr. Tey locked the mill door behind him and pocketed the
key: the tour was over.

"If you like to come again when the kittens are older, you can
have one each," he said.

"Oh, yes, please," said David. Only the other day, his mother
had remarked that Becky was too young for them to have a dog
yet, but that a kitten would be a different matter.

"Bring a basket then in a few weeks," said Mr. Tey. He looked
at Adam. "One for you, too?"

"How much food does a cat have to be given?" asked Adam.

"It depends how many mice and rats there are about—if it's a
sporting cat, that is. Of course, a kitten can't hunt; you have to
start it on milk—quite a deal of milk."

"No," said Adam, "I won't have one of the kittens. But thank
you very much."

At that moment a voice, sharp and thin as a needle, called from
the direction of the mill house: "Mark!"

"Ah, well," said Mr. Tey, preparing, in rather a flurried way, to
take his leave, "you've looked for your treasure in the mill, anyway."

"Yes," said David, detaining him, "but what we were wondering was how old is Folly Mill?"

"Oh, pretty old."

"But how old exactly?"

"Well, it goes back a good bit, I should say."

"Four hundred years?"

"Oh," said Mr. Tey, taken aback, "I couldn't say as to that at
all. All I know is that my grandfather used to tell about the building of it, but whether that was in his lifetime . . ."

"But if he told you about the building," insisted **Adam**, "surely, he told you when it happened."

"Mark! Tea is waiting!" called the voice, nearer this time. Mr. Tey fidgeted, torn between his impulse to obey and his desire to remain and instruct. But he could not resist the opening Adam had given him.

"The story my grandfather told was of why the mill was built, not when. And it concerns one of your forebears."

"Mine?" said Adam, in surprise.

"Yes—Darius Codling—'King' Darius, he was called about here, because of his highhanded ways. He ruled both the Barleys, all right, but once he quarreled with some gentry below Little Barley, toward Castleford, and they wouldn't give in to him. They were using the river for their own water mill and for some fishponds. Darius Codling decided to spite them by taking their water from them. He cut a new channel for the river, that by-passed them and stole their water power."

"But could he do that?" asked Adam, shocked. Living by the river, he knew something of river laws.

"Right against the law," said Mr. Tey, "but what did he care!"

"And wasn't it terribly expensive?" asked David.

"It was," said Mr. Tey. "Moreover, the new channel he cut had to by-pass not only his enemies' mill, but his own mill in the parish of Little Barley. So he had to let that go, and build an entirely new mill farther upstream. This is it; and that's why it's called Folly Milly."

"You mean," said David, "his folly?"

"That's it," said Mr. Tey. "His obstinacy—his waste of money—his waste of time—"

Adam began to feel uncomfortable, hating the sound of what was so like a warning sermon from Aunt Dinah on the family weaknesses. When he most longed for an interruption, it came. The owner of the sharp voice, Mrs. Tey, came round the corner of the mill. She was small enough for her husband to have held her up by one hand, but she had a face and eyes that made nothing of differences in size. "Mark!" she said. "I've called you twice." Then her gaze moved to Adam and David. "Boys!" she said to herself, quietly, but with a lifetime of dislike in her voice.

Mr. Tey flourished his hand and spoke so loudly and suddenly to Adam and David that they jumped. "Be off!" he cried. "I can't have you pestering me like this. Off with you!" Without waiting to see them go, he turned and followed his wife back to the mill house and tea.

"Well!" said Adam resentfully. But David, who perhaps had more opportunity, in the Row, of observing married life, said, "Poor Mr. Tey!"

They launched the *Minnow* again, and set off home. They had seen and heard enough that afternoon to give them plenty to think about.

"It didn't somehow sound as if Folly Mill were old enough," said Adam.

"No," agreed David; but he was thinking of Squeak Wilson as well as of the treasure. Mr. Tey's face upside down had appeared peculiar by a trick of vision, and only for a few moments at that. But Squeak Wilson had been odd from that first appearance at the window to the escape on a tricycle. Most odd of all was his name. "I wonder why exactly he's called Squeak," said David. "I should hate to be saddled with a nickname like that."

"Like being called Telltale Moss."

"Worse, really—more like Treachery Codling."

On their way downstream, they called for the pegs and string and garden fork. They were all as the boys had left them; nobody visited this part of the river bank. As he stowed them into the bow of the canoe Adam sighed. "Going upstream didn't really help us as far as plans for the future go."

"I wonder if you noticed at the time," said David hesitantly, "what Mr. Tey said your grandfather said—I mean, when your grandfather was coming upstream in the canoe." David had had this subject in his mind ever since they had left Folly Mill, but had not dared to open it to Adam; it would make the use of string and pegs and garden fork seem more futile than ever.

"Well," said Adam, "I noticed that Grandfather had said he'd come up specially by boat because he was searching for the treasure. It looks as if he'd made some of the deductions we did. He thought Jonathan Codling had gone by boat that night, and Grandfather wanted to test whether he might have got as far up as Folly Mill, and then back, in the 'clear hour.' "

"Yes," agreed David, "I should think all that's true, although it doesn't make much difference to us. But I was thinking of something else. Your grandfather used the words 'over the water'—you know, the words in the rhyme—when he spoke to Mr. Tey. And he used them with a new meaning—a meaning we've never thought of."

"A new meaning to 'over the water'?"

"Yes. Your grandfather said he'd come 'over the water.' He didn't at all mean 'across the water,' from bank to bank, as we've been understanding it, but 'along the water'—by water."

There was silence for a while, and then Adam said, "That alters everything."

"I'm afraid so."

"If the treasure were just taken by river, instead of across the river, then it may have been hidden on the right bank just as much as on the left bank: it may be absolutely anywhere."

David tried to soothe Adam's rising bitterness. "Except," he said, "that the treasure's unlikely to have been hidden very far from the river, at least on the near bank, else Jonathan Codling would have found it quicker to go by road in the ordinary way. And then, there's still the time limit. He was only away a 'clear hour'; that is, he couldn't have got farther upstream than, say, Folly Mill, and downstream—well, we don't really know about downstream yet."

"The search has become so wide," insisted Adam, "that it's practically hopeless."

David could not agree with this conclusion. He did not answer, however. He was engrossed in the enjoyment of a daydream. It had suddenly become possible that the treasure was hidden, after all, on the near bank—the bank on which Jubilee Row stood—the bank where David lived. Suppose, he thought, with a thrilling in his body—suppose the treasure lay under some undug part of the Mosses' garden—under a garden path, or under the rough ground where his mother hung out the washing. . . . Or suppose, his imagination went on, unkindly, it had been buried under what were now the foundations of Jubilee Row. Then, there could be no hope of recovering it.

At the very moment when David's fanciful hopes faded, Adam's irritation and disappointment had grown to uncontrollable strength. They were in the canoe by now, and, with a sudden exclamation, Adam reached forward to the now useless ball of string and the pegs and flung them violently overboard into the river.

"Oh!" gasped David, who had provided some of the string and knew that the rest must be Miss Codling's gardening twine. The pegs were of no particular value, but the string—thirty feet of it—was a real loss. There was no hope of rescuing it, for the ball had been hurled far from the canoe, and it was already becoming soaked with river water and beginning to sink. As he watched it David remembered Mr. Tey's story of "King" Darius and his folly: Adam seemed to have inherited some of the family's temper. It was lucky, perhaps, that Adam had not laid hold of his aunt's garden fork in his present fury. The fork might have ended its service at the bottom of the River Say as Mr. Moss had half prophesied.

11

One More Try

THE LOSS of her gardening twine was no light matter to Miss
Codling. She knew that Adam and David had borrowed
it for their own purposes, and she had not asked what their
purposes were; nor did she now. She did, however, expect to
know how the twine came to be lost. "Lost," she pointed out, was
such a general description. Then Adam had to tell her that he
had thrown the ball into the river quite deliberately—in a fit of
anger.

Miss Codling's temper was perhaps a little shorter than usual—
she had been worrying recently about her father, who was sleeping badly at night. She spoke very forcefully and at length to
Adam about what she called "the wicked waste" of twine. She
pointed out that, as the loser, she had a right to compensation of
some kind; and, in these special circumstances, she intended to

exact it. Adam was already spending most of his mornings helping her in the house or the garden. It was only fair, now, that he
should give up at least one afternoon to the same work.

When David next visited Codlings' he did not find Adam
waiting for him by the *Minnow*. He walked back toward the
house looking for him. He did not like to call Adam's name, for
he could see old Mr. Codling in a deck chair on the garden porch,
his blue-spotted handkerchief over his face. David stole by him
round the house to the kitchen door.

In the kitchen Miss Codling had been going through the milk
account, and had dozed off as she sat at the table. David's entry
woke her with a start.

"Oh," she cried, in the bewilderment of leaving sleep, "where's
Father? Oh, David, it's you! Did you see Mr. Codling on the
porch?"

"Yes, he's asleep."

Miss Codling relaxed, and picked up the milk book again. "Did
you want something?" she asked, giving David only half her
attention.

"I wondered where Adam was."

"Oh." Miss Codling put down the milk book again, and
looked at him rather severely. "Adam's at the henhouse."

"Could I go there?" asked David. Somehow he knew that permission was necessary.

"Certainly, if you like. He's cleaning the henhouse and repair-
ing it. It's a job that will probably take him more than one afternoon. If you go and talk to him and interrupt him, it will take
him longer still. That's all."

She picked up the milk book and frowned at it. "I wish milk
weren't so expensive."

"Could I help with the henhouse?"

Miss Codling put down the milk book once more, and looked
at David.

"It's a nasty job—a henhouse," she said at last. "But—oh, yes,
you can go and help him. If between the two of you you get the

job done more quickly, well—good luck to you." Unexpectedly, she had begun smiling. "You can tell Adam that, too. The henhouse—you know where it is? By the ash tree at the bottom of the garden."

David left the kitchen and made his way out to where the Codlings' fowls were kept. There was no sign of Adam, but all the hens were huddled together at the end of the run as far as they could get from their henhouse; the henhouse itself was shaking as if possessed.

"Hello!" called David.

"Hello!" came the answer from inside the henhouse. "Hens are about the dirtiest things I know." As he said this Adam crawled down a hen ladder and out of the low entrance. He was dressed protectively in a kind of smock made out of old sacks. "I've cleared the worst away," he said, "and now I've got to clean it all down thoroughly, and nail up some loose boards, and so on. It'll take me some time, I'm afraid. I shan't be free for a bit."

"Your aunt said I could help you—she wished us good luck with the job."

Adam brightened. "Did she? She didn't say anything like that when I last saw her."

David began to take off his jacket. "But it's not really your job," said Adam. "I mean—well, I lost the gardening twine."

David brushed this argument aside. "That's not the point. The sooner this job is done, the sooner we can start looking for the treasure again."

David saw Adam's expression change. "I don't know that it's any use starting again," he muttered.

David stared at him—at Adam, the last of the Codlings, the descendant of the resourceful Jonathan, the inheritor of a clue to hidden treasure. "Adam!" he cried. "You can't do that! Listen—!" David protested, argued, almost threatened, while Adam fidgeted, picking hens' feathers off his sacking.

Only when David, with the last of his breath, had reached the subject of Adam's exile to Birmingham did Adam say: "All right, then. We go one more voyage of search—one more."

"Downstream," said David, "because we never really gave downstream a chance last time. We only went as far as our dock."

"One more voyage, then," repeated Adam, "and downstream."

Their agreement made, they began on the henhouse with an energy that made the hens, even at the other end of the run, quite distraught with fears for the outcome.

In only two afternoons the henhouse was clean, neat, and well repaired—ready for reoccupation. The hens clustered round the door, anxious and inquisitive, fussily encouraging each other to go in. Adam and David, however, were not there to watch their re-entry, for as soon as they were free they were off to the *Minnow*. They and the *Minnow* were to have one more chance in the search for the hidden treasure.

12

"My Wheelbarrow End"

ADAM AND DAVID came out onto the river bank at the place
where the *Minnow* was moored, just as a boat was passing
on its way downstream. At least, that is what they would
have thought if the boat had not been Mr. Smith's punt, poled
along by Mr. Smith. He waved his hand at them as though he
wanted to be friendly, but neither boy responded; they did not
move or speak until the punt was out of sight, round the bend of
the river. Then Adam said, "He looked as if he just happened
to be passing. Really, he came up only as far as here—as he did
the other day, and then stopped—as he did then. When he heard
us coming, he set off again downstream as though he were on his
way down there all the time."

"Oh, I don't know," said David. "It's just possible he went
upstream farther than here, and was coming down again, inno-
cently."

"Did he look to you as if he'd had to push his way through the
ivy under the tree bridge?" asked Adam. It was true that Mr.

Smith had had not a speck of dirt on his white pullover, not a streak of dust on his bald head.

"Even supposing you're right," said David, "what can we do about it?"

"Nothing. It seems to me that we can never do anything about anything."

This was the mood—the Birmingham mood, David called it to himself—in which Adam had entered upon the voyage. He was allowing himself to hope for nothing. Although he felt none of David's enthusiasm, however, at least he shared in his painstaking labors. He had brought with him the Codlings' alarm clock, in order to time the "clear hour" they might allow themselves for the whole voyage. And, so as not to confuse their timing, he and David paddled steadily downstream, without stopping or slowing down.

The afternoon was made for dawdling. The sun was hot upon their backs, and the drops of water that flicked over their arms were cool and enticing. They glided over clear, weedless depths where they could have stripped and dived and swum, and they never lingered. They drove before them shoals of darting fish in the shallows, and David thought of jam jars and nets, but without pausing in his paddling. They passed the side stream that led under the railway bridge, without a glance. They passed the Mosses' dock, and now they were in country new to them. They looked from side to side as they went. The banks were almost exactly as they had been toward Folly Mill—water meadows and willows, and not an ancient ruin to be seen. Bend after bend of the river, and now they were in sight of the Little Barley bridge and the main road over it. One or two cyclists passed, and a car, and one of the big red buses that David's father drove.

David at last paused in his paddling. "Which arch do we go under?"

"It doesn't matter, does it?"

"Well, it might, because Jonathan Codling might have chosen this bridge for his hiding place."

"Any more than anywhere else?" asked Adam, in the tone that David had used for the same kind of doubting question on their last expedition. "Besides, I don't think the bridge looks as much as four hundred years old. And where could we start looking for a secret hiding place in this stonework?"

The bridge was built in a graceful but very plain style, with no kind of decoration or irregularity. Stone fitted to stone as closely and smoothly as if they had grown together. There seemed no place for secret hiding holes.

Nevertheless, David insisted on their examining all the lower stonework, taking the *Minnow* backward and forward through the three arches. There was nothing of significance to be found.

They left the bridge and set off again downstream. They had not gone far when the alarm clock in Adam's pocket went off with a sudden rattle that made David jump.

"Goodness! Why did you let it do that?"

"I set it to go off exactly half an hour after we left home. We've taken half an hour to get here, and we shall take more than half an hour to get home, because of paddling back against the current. That means we shall have done a voyage of more than an hour altogether. We're due to go back now, and we've seen nothing."

David had to plead. "Let's go just a bit farther. We wasted five or ten minutes at the bridge. We ought to go a bit farther."

They went on again, David paddling especially hard and looking from bank to bank with a desperate hope. They had still seen nothing when Adam said, "We've been eleven minutes by the clock."

David had no arguments or excuses left. He stopped paddling, with something like a moan.

"Turn her," said Adam.

The *Minnow*, under their direction, slewed round, until her bow pointed upstream again. They were paddling into the sun now; sunlight reflected dazzlingly from the water. David, who was sitting in the stern, suddenly saw something of quite unexpected interest. His arm shot over Adam's shoulder, his forefinger pointing. "Look!"

There was such a trembling excitement in his voice that Adam's heart leaped in response. "Where?" he cried. He stared until his eyes watered; the sunlight on the river's surface threw a glittering as of gold and silver and precious stones up into his eyes, blinding him for a moment.

"Look! There—there!" cried David again. Adam's vision cleared as he looked along David's rigid finger toward the bank. But all he could see was the muddy outlet of a meadow drain, across which someone had laid a piece of driftwood as a kind of makeshift bridge.

"Look!" cried David. "It's my father's wheelbarrow end!"

"Is it?" There was a sudden deadness in Adam's voice, but David did not notice it.

They paddled across to the ditch, and David took the piece of wood aboard, disentangling it from the dried river weed that was wrapped round it. Then he stowed it at the bottom of the canoe, under his knees, and they began paddling upstream again. Their course was not as even as it should have been, for their strokes were ill matched now. David paddled strongly and eagerly, humming in time to his strokes; Adam paddled irregularly and almost feebly—as if wearily.

They came in sight of the Mosses' dock just as Mr. Moss was leaving it, having come to fill his watering can. David called to him to wait, and he did so.

"We've something for you," said David as the canoe glided up to the dock.

"Oh?"

"Guess what it is."

Mr. Moss shook his head, but David had already reached under his knees and brought out the wheelbarrow end. He held it up. His father stared at it, advancing his fingers very slowly to touch it, as though he could hardly believe it was real.

"My wheelbarrow end!" he said at last, and took it in both

hands and turned it over and over, rubbing the palm of his hand over its surface.

"That's oak for you," said Mr. Moss. "It seemed wasteful at the time to make it of oak—even of an odd bit of oak. But—ah! —you can't beat oak. Water can never harm it."

"It hadn't been in the water all the time," said David. "Someone had fished it out onto the bank."

Mr. Moss, getting more used to his possession again, began to remember how it had been lost in the first place, and how he had felt then. "I've missed it sorely," he said, frowning at David.

"I'm sorry," said David humbly.

Mr. Moss shook his head. "I don't know what boys are coming to—no sense of right and wrong, nowadays. Let this be a lesson to you." He included Adam in this warning. Adam, however, had too recently suffered for his own wrongdoing to accept further reproof. He felt stung to some retort, and ventured a shot in the dark.

"Well, Mr. Moss," he said, perfectly politely, but rather slowly, "it's no worse, say, than robbing orchards." He looked up sharply as he spoke. Mr. Moss's expression had not changed by the slightest movement of a muscle, but perhaps his color had deepened. At any rate, Adam saw clearly what he had never noticed before: a scar, white against the red of the rest of Mr. Moss's skin. It was on Mr. Moss's temple, just against his right eye.

"Orchards are quite different from wheelbarrow ends." He turned back, composedly, to David. "Where did you say you found it?"

"Below Little Barley altogether. Someone had picked it out of the river and jammed it across a ditch."

"Mr. Moss!" persisted Adam. But Mr. Moss was determined to talk about wheelbarrow ends, not orchards.

"Ah!" he said to David. "No doubt. Like a bridge over the water."

"Over the water . . ." Mr. Moss's words abruptly deflected

Adam, as nothing else could have done, from his chosen subject of conversation. "Over the water . . ." Both boys, to Mr. Moss's amazement, were repeating his phrase after him in a whisper, and not once only: "Like a bridge over the water . . ."

"Aye," said Mr. Moss, "a bridge over the water. I don't see why you——"

"Turn her!" With a threshing of paddles, the *Minnow* was turned, and began to drive downstream.

"But tea's ready!" called Mr. Moss. "Where are you off to? Hi!" He was as completely ignored as if the paddlers were not still within a few yards of him, and within range of his shout. As they drew well away, Mr. Moss shook his head slowly. "Boys!" he murmured in wonder. With the back of his hand, he rubbed the scar on his brow, and smiled reminiscently. "Boys!" Still smiling, he carried the wheelbarrow end and the can back into the garden.

Already almost out of sight downstream, the boys had only breath for gasping conversation.

"Idiots that we were!" jerked out David. "Over the water— of course, a bridge is over the water!"

"The bridge—the bridge is the place," agreed Adam.

By the time that they were actually within sight of the Little Barley bridge, David had thought of another reason for supposing it to be Jonathan Codling's chosen hiding place.

"I say!" he panted. "That's perhaps why Jonathan Codling had the bridge painted into the picture of himself: it could be a kind of extra clue, somehow."

With a cry, Adam stopped paddling. "Then there's something wrong somewhere! The bridge in the picture isn't the same as this bridge—look at it!"

David stopped paddling too, to gaze at the bridge ahead. "I don't remember the bridge in the picture," he said uncertainly.

"They haven't the same number of arches."

"Are you sure?" David closed his eyes, trying to make them

remember nothing but the portrait of Jonathan Codling. He saw again the dark hair and the pale face and the red rose, and, behind the red rose, a white shape in the background—a bridge. He peered at it in his imagination, and in his imagination, Jonathan Codling, with a gesture of ironic politeness, moved the hand that held the rose so that he could see more clearly: the bridge in the picture had two arches.

David opened his eyes and gazed ahead: the Little Barley bridge had three arches.

"And yet," said Adam, "we can't be wrong. The bridge is over the water in the way nothing else is; it must have something to do with the rhyme and the hiding of the treasure."

"We can't be wrong," David agreed stubbornly.

They paddled up to the bridge and examined it again. The stonework was as smooth and close and discouraging as ever. High over the middle arch, however, under some strands of ivy Adam's eye caught sight of something—marks of some kind. They were so high that he could only lift the ivy from them by using the tip of his paddle, held at arm's length above his head.

"I'll hold the ivy away, and you see whether there's anything underneath."

"Yes, there's faint carving—writing."

"Ah!"

There was a silence while David looked, and then Adam had to lower his paddle and ease his aching muscles.

"Well, what did it say?"

David seemed at a loss. "It didn't say anything. At least, it didn't spell anything. There were just a lot of capital letters."

"Perhaps it's some kind of direction in code. I'll poke the ivy away again, and you write the letters down, and then we can work on them."

Adam had a pencil stub in his pocket. Neither boy had any paper, but David could write on the handle of his paddle.

Again Adam held the ivy clear while David looked and wrote.

When the operation was finished they had the message—if it were a message—copied, capital letter by capital letter, before them. This is what it said:

ADMDCCCVDC

"I'm not as good at solving codes as I am at making them up," David confessed after a while.

"I don't believe this is a code," said Adam. "Were there any dots between the letters?"

"Dots?"

"Periods."

"I didn't notice. I don't think you could have seen—the ivy had speckled everything."

"Well, supposing there were periods after the first and second letters, then this might be a date, beginning A.D.—Anno Domini —In the year of the Lord. I suppose it would be the date when the bridge was built."

"But there are no figures," said David, not fully understanding.

"Ah! This would be a date written in Roman figures—we've done them in Latin at school. M is the first letter of the Latin word that means a thousand, so M stands for a thousand; D stands for five hundred——"

"In the year of the Lord, fifteen hundred and something!" cried David excitedly. "That's going to be about right for Jonathan Codling and the Spanish Armada."

"Wait!" warned Adam. "We've to add a lot more to fifteen hundred. C stands for a hundred, and there are three C's, so you have to add three hundred to fifteen hundred."

"Eighteen hundred," said David, cast down again.

"And V is five." Adam paused as if deeply puzzled.

"Eighteen hundred and five," said David, "and then D again— you said that was five hundred."

"But you don't write Roman numbers like that," said Adam. "I mean, when they've got down to the fives and so on, they don't go back to the five hundreds again."

"These Roman numbers do," said David, obstinately, "so what does it matter?"

"But even if they do, the date doesn't make sense. The D and C at the end would make six hundred together, and if you add that to what went before—well, it makes a date right in the future."

There was a long silence this time. Then Adam shook his head and said, "No, I don't think the six hundred at the end can belong to the rest."

"Listen," said David slowly. "The date, A.D. 1805, means that the bridge has been rebuilt since Jonathan Codling's time. Very well. If the treasure were hidden in the old bridge, then it must have been found by the people who pulled it down in order to rebuild. Perhaps they hid the treasure again, six hundred paces or something from the bridge, and carved this message."

David looked at Adam, not very hopefully. Adam shook his head again. "Why should they hide it a second time?"

"I don't know."

"Just supposing you're right," said Adam. "The six hundred isn't much of a clue. Six hundred what? Paces? Or feet? Or inches? In which direction?"

David's theory was full of weaknesses, and he himself had no confidence in it. Yet nothing better occurred to either of them.

They examined the bridge once more, and then began to paddle back the way they had come in such a hurry. When they reached the dock David got out, and then held the canoe in to the side for Adam to do the same.

"Would your mother mind if I didn't come to tea after all?" said Adam. "It's getting very late, and Aunt Dinah fidgets nowadays if I'm much longer away than I've said. I think it's her worrying about Grandfather just now."

"I'll explain to Mother," David reassured him. "It won't matter."

"Your bicycle's with us. You'll have to walk round tomorrow —but you will come?"

"I'll come."

They said good-by, and the *Minnow* started upstream again. David, watching from the dock, noticed that Adam had changed paddles; he was now using the one on which had been penciled the inscription from the bridge. Adam missed a stroke every now and then in order to study the paddle handle and its message. He still, after all, held interest and faith in a quest that seemed to be growing more and more hopelessly mysterious. David reflected, with some satisfaction, that Adam had not again spoken of their agreement that this recent expedition if not immediately successful was to have been their last.

13

The Old Channel

B EFORE he visited Codlings' the next day, David had worked
out no less than six different theories to explain the inscription on the bridge and its connection with the treasure.
He could not decide which theory he preferred—or, rather, which
he found the least unlikely.

Adam, on the other hand, had worked out one theory and was
impatiently waiting for David's appearance to expound it. He was
sitting on the steps to the front door, nursing a large magnifying
glass, when David arrived.

"I thought you were never coming," he said, his hand already
on the doorknob. "Come inside—but come quietly: Grandfather's
lying down upstairs, and we're not to disturb him."

Adam led the way indoors, and David followed on anxious
tiptoe. He was shutting the door behind him with the same
smooth discretion when he was taken unaware by its peculiarity

of old age; in the last stages of being closed it gave out a low grinding sound, and caught with a loud crack.

"Who's that?" called old Mr. Codling's voice, rather muffled, from some distant bedroom.

Adam put his finger to his lips; they stood perfectly still, listening. There was no further sound from upstairs, and after a while the boys moved down the hall until they stood underneath the portrait of Jonathan Codling. Here Adam had already placed a kitchen chair in readiness. Still holding the magnifying glass, he mounted the chair and laid hold of the frame of the picture. "The paper showing our family tree is kept on the back of this picture," he explained in a low voice. "Grandfather found it, long ago, and brought it up to date and pasted it here. Grandfather—"

Behind his speech, and almost unnoticeably, had come the sound of a door opening softly upstairs. Then Mr. Codling's voice came again, sharply and loudly this time, from the landing above them: "Ah! There is somebody—I knew it!"

Mr. Codling, in his dressing gown as usual, leaned on the bannisters and looked down into the hall. David thought that his face looked thinner than ever—or perhaps his eyes were larger and more brilliant. The quick eagerness of his first expression vanished as he saw who was below.

"Only boys!" he said. He paid no attention to the magnifying glass and the kitchen chair, but addressed Adam and David at once. "You're sure my son didn't come in with you?" Adam shook his head. "I'm expecting him daily now. Are you sure you haven't seen him? I say, have you seen him?"

"No, sir," said Adam.

Mr. Codling looked at David. "Why do you not answer? Are you hiding something? Have you seen him—seen him on the way here, perhaps?"

David tried twice to answer, but his throat had suddenly gone dry. Mr. Codling, fixing him with a deeply suspicious gaze, had just put his foot on the first step going downstairs when Miss Codling appeared behind him. She looked very tired; her face was white, with dark shadings under the eyes. She laid a hand on Mr. Codling's shoulder. "Father, dear!"

He stopped at once and turned to her. "Dinah, are those boys holding anything back from me? Why doesn't John come? I feel sure he's coming soon; and yet he doesn't come."

"Father, dear"—Miss Codling sounded weary, but without any impatience—"that's only Adam and his friend."

"They know nothing about John's coming?"

"No, indeed. Come back to rest, Father—you had no sleep last night. You shall be told if anyone comes for you; I've promised you that."

"But I want to be the first to meet John—to be standing out on the steps to welcome him in when he comes. Can you be sure to call me in time to do that?"

"The moment anyone comes for you I will call you. I promise."

Mr. Codling seemed as satisfied as was possible. He turned back toward his bedroom, leaning on his daughter's arm. "I wonder, Dinah, if you would care to come and read to me? You read well; it is very soothing."

"Of course, Father."

They passed out of sight down the passage, murmuring together. In a minute, Miss Codling called down to Adam: "Adam, will you fetch your grandfather's book from his study—a little book, he says, red, with gold lettering. It will be on the table by the window."

"All right, Aunt."

Adam made as if to go off, then turned and thrust the magnifying glass into David's hands. "Be having a look while I'm away," he said. Then he was gone on his errand.

David mounted the chair and carefully twisted the picture on its cord until it lay with its face to the wall. On the back, as Adam had said, was a diagram of the Codlings' family descent for the last few hundred years, showing who was whose child and who married whom. The space was crowded with names and dates; the writing had had to be so small that David saw at once the usefulness of the magnifying glass. Through it he studied the tangled growth of the family. The name of Jonathan Codling occurred almost at the beginning of the chart, and in capital letters: he had evidently founded the family's prosperity and notability. There was the name of his wife, Judith; and the only name that David knew among his children—Sarah Codling. Of her the tree said: "b. 1577; d. 1630; m. A. Ashworthy Esq." There was no note of the birth of any Ashworthy children, but David realized that the draftsman of the diagram had not had room to record the children of any but the eldest Codling son in each generation, tracing only the main line of descent. David was soon tired of following even that and skipped to the end of it —again to names that he knew. He supposed that Bertram Arthur was old Mr. Codling, for his children were Dinah Mary and John Arthur. There were notes of their dates of birth and a note of John Arthur's marriage. There was no note of his death, nor of the birth of his son, Adam.

David was pondering this omission of Mr. Codling's when Adam came downstairs again. "Well," he asked, "have you made the discovery?"

"I didn't know what to look for."

"For D. C., of course," said Adam. "We were so busy turning those letters on the bridge into Roman numbers that we never thought of the last two being really letters—initial letters of a name."

"D. C.," mused David. "C standing for Codling, that is?"

"Yes. And D—well, I could only think of one D."

"David?"

Adam was taken aback. "I never thought of that. Anyway, there doesn't seem to have been a David Codling. I went through the whole family tree, and there was only one man's name beginning with D." His finger reached up to a name about halfway down the diagram. David applied his magnifying glass to it and read: "Darius Codling. b. 1744; d. 1818."

"The dates fit," said Adam. "The date on the bridge was 1805 —during Darius Codling's lifetime."

"So he's probably the D. C. who rebuilt the bridge," murmured David. He carried the magnifying glass over the tree, searching. "He seems to be the only Darius. He must be Mr. Tey's Darius— 'King' Darius."

"And just because he's 'King' Darius," said Adam, "there's every chance that he never rebuilt the bridge at all." He seemed elated, rather than cast down, by this thought.

"What?" said David, in confusion.

"He couldn't rebuild it," said Adam, "because there never was a bridge there before his—so I believe. He built it for the first time. Don't you remember what Mr. Tey said about 'King' Darius?"

David thought back to the details of Mr. Tey's story. Then he understood. Darius Codling, because of his quarrel, had made a new channel for the River Say over part of its length, somewhere between Folly Mill and the Castleford reaches. The new channel would still have had to cut across the Barley-to-Castleford high-road; if so, a new bridge must have been built—the bridge whose date was 1805.

"Yes," said David, "yes—I see. The bridge at Little Barley."

"That's Darius Codling's new bridge over his new channel—at least it seems to fit. What about the old channel? And"—Adam could not resist sinking his voice and slowing his speech—"what about the old bridge over it? The two-arch bridge? Jonathan Codling's bridge?"

"There isn't another bridge on that road," said David positively.

"There must be," insisted Adam.

"There just isn't."

"Remember," said Adam, "that the old channel may have dried right up in all those years. It would be a bridge perhaps without any river under it, so you might not notice it as a bridge."

"It's just possible," said David slowly. "The road from Castleford through Little Barley and on is very humpy in places. And sometimes you can't see much besides the road because of hedges and things. It is just possible."

"It must be so," said Adam. "It's just a question of finding the old bridge."

"I tell you what: I'll take my bicycle and go really carefully along that road and make a search."

Adam was unenthusiastic. "Do you think that's the best way, really? I mean, if the hedgerows are as thick as all that, and—well, other things . . ."

"It's a pity you haven't a bicycle, too," said David.

"Yes," said Adam.

David tacitly gave up his claim to play a lone hand in the game.

"I wondered," said Adam after a pause, "if we should try going by the *Minnow*—both of us—as far as the Little Barley bridge, then striking along by the road from there."

"Adam," said David, with a strange quietness, "what about following the side stream that goes under the railway bridge—the one we found on our first day out?"

"But we couldn't take the *Minnow* up it very far. We got stuck that day—don't you remember?"

"You don't see what I mean," said David. "That side stream is either an ordinary side stream, or else it might be—it just might be—what's left of the channel of the old river. Then it would lead us straight to Jonathan Codling's bridge."

There seemed no undue agitation in Adam's voice as he called up to his aunt to say that he and David were just going out in the canoe. Yet their going was in such haste that they left Jonathan Codling's face still turned toward the wall, and within five minutes they were in the *Minnow* and paddling fast.

"You're in a hurry," called Mr. Smith. He was stepping into his punt as they went by.

"Yes," said Adam briefly. When they were well past, he

paused in his paddling for the first time. "David, look back, and see if he's following us."

"No, he's going upstream."

"Ah!" The exclamation seemed to mean both "Good!" and "I suspected as much!"

The boys paddled on swiftly in silence. Soon they were looking on the left bank for the outlet they had decided might be the old channel. When they reached it they drove the *Minnow* down it, under the iron railway bridge, and beyond. Then, when the boat was prevented by the growth of reeds as well from drifting back as from going forward, both boys waded to the bank and climbed onto dry land.

There was some slight rise and fall of ground ahead which, together with the crisscrossing of meadow hedgerows, hid the view; in particular, there was as yet no sign of the main Castleford road.

They decided to follow the course of the channel closely as their only guide. It dwindled as they followed it, until it was no more than the narrowest ditch, overgrown and overhung with vegetation. They could still pick out its course, however, by the deeper green of the grass at its edge, and the marsh plants that grew along it—kingcups and water forget-me-nots and brooklime.

Suddenly the watercourse disappeared into a large patch of nettles into which the boys hesitated to follow. They began skirting the nettles, casting about like hounds, to recover the track at the point where it must come into the open again. The ground here was uneven, and the boys both stumbled more than once. Then, David, who happened at the time to be ahead, tripped and fell, with a cry of pain.

"Bad luck!" said Adam as he passed him.

David was up again, but before he went on, looked to see exactly what had caused his fall. "Adam!" he called in a tone that brought Adam back to him at once.

"I thought you were all right. I thought you just tripped."

"I did. But look what I tripped over." With his foot he held the grass and nettles away from a great stone that lay almost buried. "It's part of a millstone—like the ones Mr. Tey showed us in his mill. And if you look, there are some bricks lying about, and there are probably plenty more under the nettles. I believe this place is where the old mill stood—the mill that Darius Codling had to replace with Folly Mill."

"If this is the site of the old mill, then this must be the channel of the old river, and it must—it must lead to the bridge," said Adam. They were awestruck with their own detective powers.

Off they went again. They found their water track once more, and followed its every turn and twist; they dared allow themselves to look at nothing else. Suddenly a toot, some way ahead of them, made them lift their heads and stare. Before them, the faintly marked channel curved and slid away to a high hedgerow of bushes and trees. Above these, like the enormous hat of a passerby, was traveling the red roof of a bus.

It was the Castleford road ahead, without a doubt.

Adam and David made for the point at which the watercourse appeared to strike into the trees and bushes to meet the main road. Before they had reached that point, they could see through branches and leaves an archway of stonework. Side by side, they parted the bushes and gazed at the way—the only possible way—their dank serpent of a stream escaped under the highway. There was a bridge—not a big bridge, nor a very elegant one, but one which had once served its purpose. The bridge had two arches.

Now that they had it before them, the feeling of anxiety and hurry left them. This was Jonathan Codling's bridge, and nothing could take that certainty from them.

"This is where the shepherd looked over and saw Jonathan Codling, lying dead," said Adam. "And I think I see how he came to die. He was coming home, and he felt all the danger was over, and he could bring his treasure out again. When he came to the bridge he suddenly thought he might as well take the treasure out of the hiding place, then and there, and bring it

home with him. Only something happened when he was trying
to reach the hiding place, and he slipped or fell or something, and
was drowned in the river before ever he got the treasure."

"Look at that decoration stuff," said David. "They're very
worn away, but I believe they're meant to be roses."

"Tudor roses," said Adam.

"Adam," said David, "we could have moved that comma
farther back than we ever thought." He quoted softly:

> *"When Philip came, to the single rose*
> *Over the water*
> *The treasure was taken . . .*

Do you see, Adam? The treasure was taken to the single rose on
the bridge over the water."

"But I don't think any of the roses are put singly."

They burst through the bushes to make sure of the roses. There
were several groups of three, symmetrically placed; there was
also a date carved over the middle pier of the bridge. A.D. 1585, it
said. There were, however, no single roses.

"Let's look on the other side."

The best way would have been to have walked through under
one of the two arches, but the way was blocked under each arch
by high coils of rusty barbed wire. They were not deterred by
this, however, but started walking along by the highway, hearing
the occasional cyclist or car passing on the other side of the thick
hedge. At last, they found what they were looking for: the
hedge thinned for a little, and they were able to force their way
through, climb down a bank, and find themselves on the road-
way. Nearly opposite them was a most convenient gate, leading
into the water meadows on the other side of the road. The gate
was padlocked, and garnished along the top with more barbed
wire, and bore a notice: "Trespassers Will Be Prosecuted by
Order of Saml. Truelove." Adam and David paid no attention to
any of these intended obstacles and were soon on the other side,
with no worse than a tuft out of the seat of David's trousers. They

made their way through the Truelove meadows, following the course of the highroad back to the bridge again.

The bridge seemed very much the same on this side as on the other: the same overgrown bushes and trees, the same stonework, the same devices of grouped Tudor roses. The only difference was that high over the middle pier, where the date had been on the other side, there was the carved design of one extra rose by itself.

"The single rose!"

In the early days of the bridge, before weathering had so smoothed its surface and carving, the stonework would have given enough foothold to any climber. Now, the only way to get within reach of the single rose was by climbing the elder tree whose upper branches brushed against it with such irritating intimacy. Adam, unquestionably, was the one to make the attempt.

The elder tree was neither easily climbable nor stout. Adam worked his way up it, but when he began to reach the top the slender branches there not only gave warning creaks, but bent beneath his weight and let him fall away from the very stonework he was trying to reach. Clinging with one hand to the tree, and with the other straining toward the rose, Adam could touch it with his fingertips—no more.

David, below, was entirely absorbed in watching Adam, clenching his teeth in an agony of desire and hope. Neither noticed that Adam's struggle in the tree was whirling and whipping about its topmost branches, which, being above the level of the road, could not fail to attract the curious attention of any passer-by. There were always passers-by on the Castleford road, and always children playing about the bus shelter near the Council houses. The present strange agitation of a wayside tree brought together, in only a few minutes, a small crowd—a butcher's boy with his bicycle, two little girls, and old Mr. Barncroft, hobbling along to visit his niece.

Adam had indeed become aware after some time of the excited whisperings going on above him. He did not care. The foliage was too thick for spectators on the bridge to see what he was about, and he hoped at any moment, with an extra effort, to get a firm enough hold on the rose to press it or wrench it or slide it —whichever was the secret of its moving.

Suddenly, however, the leafiness was parted by Mr. Barncroft's outstretched walking stick, and behind it appeared the face and craning neck—not of Mr. Barncroft, but of Constable Platt. Adam had a vision of a yellow mustache and blue eyes and a deeper blue helmet, and heard a threatening, "Now then! Now then!"

Common sense and prudence, even in the excitement of treasure seeking, showed only one course to Adam. He changed grips and footholds quickly, fell a little, slithered a great deal, and jumped the last few feet to where David crouched at the bottom of the unhelpful elder tree.

Adam crouched beside him and put his mouth up to David's ear. "Did they see what I was after?"

David shook his head.

"What do we do now?" breathed Adam. His job had been the single rose; David's was the strategy of escaping Constable Platt.

From above their heads, as if to remind them of their danger, came the repeated roar of "Now then! Now then!" and the sound of Constable Platt stirring the leaves round with the walking stick. Perhaps he hoped to frighten the boys into breaking cover and making across the meadows, where he could see them and recognize them. David certainly believed this, and thought it wisest to lie low. The constable could get no nearer to them unless he went along the road, climbed the gate, and came back on the inside of the hedge toward the bridge. Then would be time enough to make a run for it.

Constable Platt, however, was acting from a mixture of motives. He knew that he was stationed in the Barleys to enforce the rule of law, but he liked, through the law, to rule alone. He never passed Sam Truelove's "Trespassers Will Be Prosecuted" notice without feeling a jealous irritation at his claim. He was quite disinclined to do Sam Truelove's dirty work for him: Sam could prosecute his own trespassers. Constable Platt would shout and thresh about in the branches to frighten the disturbers of the peace, without doing anything more for their identification and punishment. He considered that he had done all his duty in putting to an end the unseemly agitation of branches by the Queen's highway.

In time, therefore, the constable mounted his bicycle and rode away. Mr. Barncroft, his stick restored to him, used it to shoo away the children who were disappointedly lingering on; Mr. Barncroft's hobbling step was the last to die into the silence.

"Now," said David, relaxing his cramped muscles, "I think we'd better get into safety and then think again."

Adam cast one more glance up at the single rose, measuring with his eye.

"Discuss it later," urged David.

They went back the way they had come, over the gate and through the thin place in the hedge on the other side. They had to bide their time at both places, and slip across the road behind the back of a baker's van going in one direction and a woman with a baby carriage going in the other. They did not consider themselves safe until they were actually sitting in the *Minnow* again.

"What on earth were all those people doing on the road, anyway," said Adam crossly. "All those children you could hear, and an old man and a policeman and a woman with a baby, not to speak of traffic."

"Well, it is a road," said David, feeling Adam to be unreasonable.

Adam fell into frowning thought. "I don't think I could have reached the single rose even without interference," he admitted at last. "It was just about impossible. A better way might be to try from above, over the bridge parapet—perhaps on the end of a rope."

"What about the passers-by, again? They would never give you a chance."

"Not in the daytime," said Adam. "But by night . . ."

Nighttime—late at night—when the road would be deserted was the only time for their venture. They agreed to make the attempt that very night. In that agreement, they paddled serenely home.

Miss Codling was on the lookout for them as they came from the river bank toward the house. "Come along!" she called. "I want you to help me move my mattress from my bedroom on to the landing. I've decided to sleep there for tonight at least." She went on to explain that she thought she would find it less trying to sleep where her father's getting up and moving about would rouse her anyway, than to continue in her own bedroom, where she had to keep awake and strain her ears to hear whether he were beginning his wanderings. What did she do when he woke her? She followed him to make sure that he did not fall and hurt himself, and when he was tired she made them both a cup of tea, and perhaps they would have a little chat, and then he would go back to bed again. Miss Codling did not say why her father wandered, nor where, but David guessed that he would be waiting by the house doors—waiting for his dead son.

David felt very sorry for Miss Codling, with her sleepless nights. Adam's eyes, however, still sparkled; it seemed to him that there were no ills that might not be cured by the recovery of the treasure.

The boys helped Miss Codling to carry her mattress into the passageway outside old Mr. Codling's bedroom door, by the stairs. Like most mattresses, this one was clumsy to move, rather than heavy. Then they fetched the blankets and sheets for it.

"There!" said Miss Codling cheerfully. "It's tactically very well placed at the head of the stairs. There's a way round for people to walk, but in the middle of the night if Grandfather goes by, however quietly, I'm sure to wake."

"Or if anyone else went by," said Adam, in a voice from which all the gaiety had vanished.

"Don't be silly, Adam!" said Miss Codling sharply. "There's certainly nothing in this house for a burglar to come for."

David, watching Adam's expression, knew that he was not thinking of burglars. Adam, as well as Mr. Codling, would have to pass the watchdog that Miss Codling had made of herself if he went on any nighttime expedition. And Miss Codling would not be a watchdog to be disregarded.

They left Miss Codling making up her uncomfortable bed, and went out into the garden, where they could talk privately.

"We could drug her," said Adam desperately, "but we haven't the money to buy any good drugs."

David had no suggestion at all to make; they thought long but in vain.

"It's just unfortunate," said Adam. "I simply shan't be able to get away tonight, after all."

"The single rose isn't a job I could tackle alone," said David. "I should think not."

"Your aunt will have to move back to her bedroom some time," said David. "Perhaps she'll want to go back tomorrow."

"We'd better be about to help move the mattress back the minute she makes up her mind, or she might change it again."

"I'll come over after breakfast," said David. "To be on the safe side."

14

Search by Moonlight

"I SHOULD HAVE thought it was very drafty, sleeping on a landing, Miss Codling," said David. Miss Codling did not answer, so he went on. "I had earache once, and my mother said it might have been a draft that started it. She said it might have turned to mastoid, which is very serious."

"Your mother would never let you sleep on a landing, just because of drafts," said Adam.

"But David can never have asked to be allowed to do such a thing," said Miss Codling.

"Because he knows it would be useless," Adam retorted triumphantly.

There was a silence, and Miss Codling went on rolling out her pastry. Then Adam said, "It must be very hard and uncomfortable, too."

Miss Codling stopped in her work and held up her hand imploringly. The boys' care for her health and comfort had, at first, touched her. By now, however, after three days, it had begun to worry her. It did not seem natural. Besides, they hung about her all the day—even in the mornings—as though they were waiting for her to do or say something. She felt herself as harassed by their presence in the daytime as she was by her father's wanderings at night.

"Adam and David," she said, when she had gained an expectant silence, "why don't you go in the canoe as you used to? Why don't you amuse yourselves outside?"

"We thought you might need us suddenly to help you with some job or other," muttered Adam.

"I have no such jobs," said Miss Codling. "The work I am doing at present I prefer to do alone. I would rather you left me in my kitchen, and gave me a little time to myself."

"To think?" said David, hopefully. "To think things over?"

"David," said Miss Codling, leaning an elbow on her upended rolling pin, "I only want to be able to roll out pastry, without talking and without thinking and alone—alone. Just to roll out pastry."

There was something that struck them as almost desperate in the way in which she leaned on the rolling pin and gazed at them. They went slowly out of the kitchen. At the door, Adam turned and said, "If you did want us for anything, we shall only be in the garden."

Miss Codling altered neither her attitude nor her gaze; and the boys closed the kitchen door behind them, and went out on to the steps of the garden porch. They dared not go farther, in case Miss Codling made up her mind suddenly to move her mattress, and called for their help.

"Three nights!" said Adam. "The treasure waiting to be taken out of the hiding place, and me bottled up in my bedroom by a woman's whim."

"I don't think her whim is going to change," said David. "The longer she sleeps on the landing, the more she gets used to it."

"The doctor's coming to see Grandfather tomorrow morning.

Do you think it would be a good thing to tell him about the drafts and the danger of mastoid? Then he might order her back to her room."

"Yes, you tell him—you're next of kin, not counting your grandfather."

Adam shook his head. "You nearly had mastoid: it would have more weight coming from you. It's your duty, really."

David braced himself. "All right. When is he coming, exactly?"

"First thing tomorrow morning, he promised."

David arranged to arrive even earlier, and with this in prospect, went soberly home. There, he could settle to nothing, and found Becky's sociability particularly irritating.

"Can't you leave me alone?" he said crossly, and finally took to his bicycle. He cycled along the Castleford road, over the Little Barley bridge, past Sam Truelove's gate, and came to a stop on the hump that he now knew was the old, forgotten bridge. Here, under his feet, had once flowed a river; here, one moonlight night, Jonathan Codling had dismounted from his horse for the last time; here, under the single rose, had been hidden the treasure. The treasure was the only thing that remained—within a few feet of him, too. Yet he could do nothing about it. Already a carter, passing, had turned to stare, wondering why a boy chose to make his halt in such a dull, unpromising place.

He turned and rode slowly home again. As he wheeled his bicycle into the shed Becky ran out of the house. "You're late for tea, David, and someone's been for you, and you weren't here."

"For me?"

"A boy with red hair—he came in a shiny brown boat to the dock, and he saw me in the garden and called to me. Oh! Do tell me, David—is it Adam?" Becky had heard much of Adam, but never seen him; she had been out on the few occasions when he had been to Jubilee Row.

"Yes, of course," said David, eagerly. "What message did he leave?"

"He didn't want to leave one, at first; he said it was a secret." One had only to look at Becky's sparkling eyes and parted lips— the lips of a happy babbler—to guess why Adam had hesitated to entrust her with his message.

"Did he say nothing, then?"

"In the end, he told me to tell you: At the dock."

"At the dock? He must have said something more."

"No, he didn't. David, would he let you take me in the canoe some day? It looks safe after all, now it's so shiny. Would he, David?"

"Perhaps. But listen, Becky——"

"Oh, good!" Becky clapped her hands and twirled on her feet.

"Listen, Becky!" implored David. "We'll never take you, unless you listen."

"I am listening," she said, quiet at once.

"Adam must have said something else. You must have forgotten part of the message."

"He didn't—I haven't. Oh! But I have forgotten something." Her hand went into the pocket of her pinafore. "It was a present to you from him—at least, they weren't his to give away, because he picked them from our garden." She brought from her pocket a crumpled leaf and some bits of grass.

David stared at them amazed. Then he saw that the leaf was of privet, and he suddenly remembered; a privet leaf for today, and a hawthorn leaf for tomorrow, and blades of grass for the hours of day.

"How many bits of grass are there, Becky? How many exactly?"

"These." She scrabbled in her pocket again while David picked up the ones that had already fallen to the ground, counting them. "Eight—nine—ten."

"And here's another," said Becky. She peered into her pocket. "And there's just a very short one—do you want that?"

"Yes," said David. "Half a blade of grass—that makes a lot of difference." The leaf and the grasses all lay in the palm of his hand now, and together with Adam's words, said, as clearly as possible: "Today—tonight, at half past eleven at the dock."

"What are you going to do with them?" asked Becky, watching his face with keenest curiosity.

"Nothing."

"Can I have them, then?"

"Yes, here you are."

"And what is the secret?"

"Ah!"

He turned abruptly from Becky, to hide the smile of excitement that he knew was on his face. He left her poring over the leaf and grass, trying to understand their magic. She carried them indoors at last, and for years they lay, withered but still mysterious, wrapped in a silk handkerchief in a doll's chest of drawers.

The hours between tea time and bedtime dragged for David; and yet the hours between bedtime and half past eleven would go even more slowly and dangerously. The risk lay in his falling asleep. If he did so, he knew, there would be no hope of waking again before the next morning.

As soon as his mother had tucked him up for the night and left him, he crept out of bed and dressed again completely, except for his shoes, and then put on his pajamas on top of everything else. They would hardly button across his other clothes and were uncomfortably tight as well as hot to wear under the bedclothes. But that was all to the good—the more uncomfortable he was, the more likely he was to stay awake.

From downstairs he could hear the sound of a wireless program, and the faint murmur of his parents' voices: it was lulling to listen to. He stuck his bare feet out of the bed until they felt quite chilled and he felt wakeful again.

Once there was a moment of acute danger. There was the sound of a door opening and then Mr. Moss's footstep on the stair, with his wife's voice behind him, asking him to fetch David's trousers so that she could mend a tear she had noticed in the seat. Mr. Moss did not put on the bedroom light for fear of waking David; he spent a long time fumbling at the foot of the bed for the trousers, and David was longing for him to find them and go, when he remembered with a shock that he was wearing them. Luckily, however, Mr. Moss was not as persistent as his wife would have been. After a while he gave up the search and went downstairs. David could not hear what was said, but from his mother's tone in reply, he judged that she was taking the incident as another interesting example of a man's inability to find what was under his nose. Mr. Moss did not return, nor did Mrs. Moss come; she had evidently decided to leave the trousers until the morning.

The wireless program went on for a while; then it stopped. There was a too-restful silence during which David thought it wiser to do some sharp exercises with his legs and arms. At last, from downstairs he heard the sound of a door opening again, and both his parents were on the move. They seemed to spend a long time fidgeting with chairs, aimlessly opening and shutting doors, talking. Then David heard the sound of front and back doors being bolted—that would be his father. Then there were footsteps coming upstairs.

Mrs. Moss stole into her son's room, again without putting on the light. She felt over the bedclothes to make sure that he was properly covered. Then she tiptoed out again. He heard her go into Becky's room. And then there were noises of bathroom and basin, and the click of the landing light going off, and the stronger click of his parents' bedroom door shutting.

David counted a thousand, and then got out of bed, took off his pajamas, and shoes in hand, crept out onto the little landing. There was no line of light from the bottom of the bedroom door that had recently shut, and no sound from behind it: the house slept.

He tiptoed downstairs. There was a clock in the hall, and by the moonbeams through the fanlight he could read the time:

half past ten—only half past ten! He put his ear up to the clock and listened, but it was still ticking, and as long as it went it always kept perfect time. By now, however, David could not wait for time.

He unbolted the garden door very quietly and let himself out. The moon was almost at the full, and silvered the little garden so that it had a strange new beauty. David stepped almost reverently down the gravel path to the dock. There, for the first time, he dared to put on his shoes again.

Besides David, the River Say seemed to be the only thing alive and awake this night. David stooped and dabbled his fingers in the water, and found that it still had the warmth of summer sunlight in it. He could, he reflected, pass the time by taking a moonlight swim. Yet, somehow, the stillness everywhere and the unfamiliar blackness of the water made him decide against it.

Then he was aware of a regular, watery sound coming from upstream—and coming closer. Before he had time to know that he was feeling afraid he saw the *Minnow*—a new *Minnow,* all in black and silver. It glided up to the dock.

"You're early," whispered Adam.

"So are you."

David took his place and his paddle, and they turned the canoe back again toward the opening of the old channel. Presently David had to relieve his mind of a question that had been troubling him.

"Did you have to drug her?"

"Well, no," said Adam. "The doctor came unexpectedly tonight, after you'd gone, and saw Grandfather, and said he must get sleep at nights, and gave Aunt Dinah sleeping tablets for him. And he helped Aunt and me to move the mattress back to the bedroom, because he said Grandfather would sleep all night and so could she, in comfort."

"You didn't bribe him or anything?"

"It wasn't necessary."

Silence came again and stayed with them as they turned the

Minnow into the old channel, drove her up it, and finally left her as before. Now moonlit meadows stretched before them, with a light white mist that cooled their ankles and made the old channel an even fainter line than they had found it by day. They followed it to the old bridge and the Castleford road. The road was lightless and soundless.

David, obeying Adam's instructions, made his way through the Truelove meadows to the bushes under the single rose. He was to wait there, ready to catch anything that Adam might let fall. Meanwhile, Adam had secured a length of rope to the parapet, and, with its help, had lowered himself over the side of the bridge. He knew he could not rely entirely on the rope, so he had taken his shoes off in order to find even the slightest foothold with his bare feet. One foot was now helpfully braced against the stonework; the other dangled right over the single rose itself. He felt its excrescence beneath his toes and poked them against it vigorously, but apparently not with enough force to produce any result. He gave up the attempt with his foot. He lowered himself to the end of his short rope and used both feet now to find some kind of additional support. Then he loosed one hand from the rope and, perilously spread-eagled across the face of the bridge, reached down with it to the rose.

At first, it seemed to David that this tactic was going to be no more successful than before. Then a particularly strong push of Adam's hand suddenly drove the stone sideways and back into a cavity that as suddenly appeared to engulf it. It was the kind of thing they had hoped for, but it was still startlingly wonderful.

The unexpectedness of the stone's giving under Adam's blow threw him forward and destroyed his delicate balance. There was a light rattling of shale on leaves as his feet lost their grip on the stonework. His only support was the rope now, and he hung from that only by one hand; the other hand was in the hole, feeling. The whole weight of his body was on the rope and the hand clutching it. It was not the rope that gave, but the hand; it slithered, and slithered again, and suddenly the rope's end was swinging free. Adam's body smashed through the light branches of elder and fell the whole height of the bridge to the ground beneath. He lay face downward, quite still, with his body across the marshy depression that had once been the River Say that Jonathan Codling had known.

David, for a moment, could not move. He could only think, confusedly: "I've seen Jonathan Codling falling to his death." Then, in a rush, he was by Adam's side. Adam was still breathing.

When David asked if he were hurt, Adam answered, "I'm all right," but he spoke strangely, and without lifting his head or moving his body.

"I'll help you," said David.

"Leave me alone," said the strange voice.

David waited in obedience for a few minutes. Then he could endure it no longer. He laid hands on Adam's shoulders and prised him up from the ground until he could see his face. He was startled at its pallor and expression: this was not death, but it was the death of hope.

Adam sat up. "I'm all right," he repeated. He stood up. Except for the dirtying of his clothes, he seemed quite unharmed. "There was nothing in the hole. Nothing," he said, and turned, and began to lurch away over the moon-silvered grass.

15

Old Mr. Codling Laughs

THERE WAS no doubt about it. The hole behind the single rose was the hiding place Jonathan Codling had had built into the bridge in the anxious years before the Armada. There was no doubt that he had hidden the treasure there; if there was nothing in the hole now—well, then, Jonathan Codling's treasure was truly lost. In this knowledge, David followed behind Adam's defeated figure, attempting neither to walk with him nor to speak with him.

Adam crossed the main road and set off over the meadows again. He was still barefoot and seemed to have no thought for his shoes. After a hesitation, David ran back along the road to the bridge to fetch them for him. There were the shoes, and there was the rope. Remembering the minor disaster of the lost gardening twine, David was about to untie the rope when the idea occurred to him that he himself might look in the hole—to make sure that Adam, in his hurry, had not made any omission in his search.

David quickly took off his own shoes and swung himself over the bridge. He held the rope firmly with both hands, and felt round until one bare foot found its way into the hole. It was a square hole and quite bare. His toes dragged themselves over every wall and poked into every corner, finding nothing. There was something—a thin scrap of something—that they felt on the floor of the cavity, and that they secured, with some difficulty, between big toe and second toe. David hauled himself back on to the parapet and examined this find, without much hope. It was a strip of paper, with a roughly torn upper edge, and four lines of writing upon it. By the light of the moon he could read what was written—it was quite useless:

> *When Philip came to the single rose*
> *Over the water*
> *The treasure was taken where no one knows*
> *None but my daughter.*

David stuffed the paper into his pocket, gathered up the two pairs of shoes and the rope, and ran back after Adam.

Adam was just stepping into the *Minnow* when David rejoined him. There was still no conversation between them. As they paddled out into the main river the Great Barley church clock struck a quarter to midnight. It startled David to realize how short a time they had been out. His parents and Miss Codling would still be in their first sleep, unaware of doings by night and hopes proved as insubstantial as moonshine.

They parted at the Mosses' dock, having spoken no word more than what had been said under the single rose.

The next day, instead of sleeping late, David was awake especially early, and at once with the thought of Adam in his mind. As soon as he was free he went round to Codlings'.

"He doesn't seem to be feeling well this morning," said Miss Codling, when he asked for Adam. "He's in bed. Go up and see him."

David went upstairs and knocked on Adam's door.

"Who is it?"

"Me—David."

"No!" violently. There was no further sound, so David opened the door and looked in. He was at once transfixed by the glare of Adam's eyes over the top of the bedclothes. "I'm too ill to see you!"

"Were you hurt last night, after all?"

"Don't keep asking me that—no, I wasn't."

There was a silence. Then David began timidly, "About the treasure——"

"What's the use of talking about it? It's gone—stolen! We showed the way to the hiding place when we first went there. In the next three days somebody went and got it. Mr. Smith probably—yes, he's gloating over it now."

David had to contradict. "Someone found the hiding place and stole the treasure, but we couldn't have shown them the way. Look at this."

He held out the strip of paper that he had not dared to show to Adam the night before. Adam took it unwillingly even now, and went red with anger as he saw the familiar rhyme. He choked. "It was left there for us to find—as a sneer! To make sure we knew someone had got there before us! Mr. Smith— I'm sure it was Mr. Smith—he followed us after all. He——"

"But, Adam, it can't be that. This must mean that whoever found the hiding place did it by working on the clue of the rhyme—else why was it there at all? We didn't give the hiding place away."

Adam began to be more puzzled than angry. "Yes, I suppose that's true. But then, how could Mr. Smith—or anyone—know that rhyme? It's always been more or less of a secret."

"When the Smiths called on your aunt, she may have told them."

"She wouldn't."

"Or perhaps, while she was out of the room, they looked in her bureau."

"It's kept locked."

"Perhaps it was unlocked that day."

Adam threw back the bedclothes and began getting into his pajamas, with an air of resolution. "It won't be pleasant, and I don't expect it'll get us the treasure back, but we'll have to talk to Aunt Dinah."

They went downstairs together and found Miss Codling.

"You shouldn't go about with bare feet on these stone floors. Adam," she said anxiously, "even if you are feeling better."

"Aunt Dinah, please sit down."

Miss Codling sat down as though mesmerized.

"We want to tell you something," said Adam, "and it'll take some time, and you may feel like interrupting before we've finished. But I want you to promise not to say anything till we have quite finished."

Miss Codling looked at them wonderingly. "It's not a trick?"

"No, it's just so that we can have our say."

"Very well. It seems strange, but—very well."

Then Adam told his aunt the whole story of their treasure seeking, undertaken secretly and against her wishes—and yet, Adam insisted, for her good. Several times Miss Codling's mouth opened as if to speak. Then David, who stood by Adam throughout, put up a warning hand, like a policeman's; and Miss Codling remembered her promise and was silent.

Adam brought the story right up to David's finding of the strip of paper in the hole in the bridge. "This is the paper, Aunt Dinah," he said. "And what we want to know is do you know how anyone could have known of this rhyme—do you perhaps even recognize the handwriting?"

Miss Codling took the paper, and, strangely, she smiled. "Yes, I recognize the handwriting very well." She rose and went to the bureau. She unlocked it and took out the old cigar box and from that lifted the two papers. She unfolded the one that was old Mr. Codling's copy of Judith Codling's Narrative. She laid David's slip of paper along the bottom of the copy; the rough upper edge of David's paper exactly fitted the rough bottom edge of Mr. Codling's copy. One had been torn off the other.

"Somebody tore it off!" gasped Adam. "You must have left the bureau unlocked some time—when the Smiths were here, it would be."

Miss Codling did not understand what Adam meant about the Smiths, but she was clear about one thing. "This bureau has never been left unlocked. Your grandfather carried the key until your father died, and he fell ill; then I had it."

"But, Aunt Dinah . . ." Adam's voice trailed away as he realized that his aunt was looking at him with a kind of compassion.

"I said, at the very beginning, that you and David would be on a wild-goose chase if you began looking for the treasure. I didn't want you to begin. You see, I knew that even if you found the hiding place, wherever that was—I didn't know—the treasure wouldn't be there."

"You knew that someone had stolen the treasure?"

"Not stolen," Miss Codling corrected him. "You can't steal your own property. You see, Grandfather had already found the treasure, long ago."

"Grandfather—Grandfather——"

"Yes. He looked, as you looked, and I suppose he was as clever as you were, for he found the hiding place, as you did, and he found the treasure there. I only knew because I happened to walk into his study, unexpectedly, when he had it turned out on the table in front of him."

"You saw the treasure?"

"Yes. It was very beautiful." She paused, half to remember, half to give the boys time to ask any questions; but they were too amazed to speak. She went on, "He told me then that he was going to keep it until John—my brother—your father, Adam —it was the time when we were expecting him—came home. Then he would bring it out as part of the celebrations. I wanted him to put such a valuable collection into safety in the bank in Castleford, but he wouldn't hear of it. He said that John might come home unexpectedly, any day, any time, and then the treasure wouldn't be there for him to see at once, and there'd be all the trouble and delay of fetching it from a bank." She smiled to herself. "He liked to have his own ideas and carry them out on his own. Well, he said he'd at least hide it, somewhere handy but very safe. He promised."

"Where did he hide it, then?"

"I'm sorry, Adam, but he would never tell me, then or since. And I think it must be as thoroughly hidden by your grandfather as it ever was by Jonathan Codling—more thoroughly, for there's no clue."

"But, Aunt Dinah, he must tell us now—we need the treasure so badly."

Miss Codling sighed. "I often used to ask him. He always said he would get it out when John came home—not before. I've given up asking him, now."

"You must explain to him, Aunt Dinah, and ask him again. You must."

"No, Adam. It does no good. It only upsets him."

"Aunt, please—" Adam swallowed something in his throat. "I don't want to have to go to Birmingham at the end of this summer."

There was a long silence in which David felt that Adam and Miss Codling had forgotten his presence. Then Miss Codling picked up Adam's hand and held it in hers. "I'll try asking him once more."

Miss Codling insisted that Mr. Codling was not to be worried until he was up and dressed and had had his mid-morning cup of tea. Then she went in to him, where he sat in his study by the window. She purposely left the door ajar, and Adam and David peered through the crack and listened.

"Father," she said, and knelt beside his chair, the strip of paper between her fingers. He answered her only absently, but presently looked down at her, and then she held the paper up toward him.

He looked at it, and then took it. "Why, Dinah!" he said, and laughed to himself—it was like the grinding of rusty keys in locks. "Why, Dinah! You've been cleverer than I thought! So you've found the single rose and the hiding place!"

It had been agreed between Miss Codling and the boys that it might be better not to mention their exploits to Mr. Codling. So she simply said, "Yes, the hiding place is found." There was such a long pause that David wondered if Miss Codling had lost courage altogether; but at last she went on. "Father, dear, don't you think that anyone who could find the hiding place really deserves to know where the treasure is, too?"

"You will know—you'll see it for yourself—when John comes —any day now."

"Couldn't you tell me now, Father?"

Adam and David could see Mr. Codling's head over the back of his armchair, shaking from side to side, again and again. "No need, no need," he said. "When John comes."

"But, Father—"

Miss Codling never pressed her father as much as this, and he was showing signs of impatience. "No, no, Dinah. I say, no." Then he seemed to relent a little. "You've been clever enough to find the hiding place by the rhyme; well, now you can find the treasure by the rhyme, too."

"But, Father——"

"Why do you think I went back and put this in the hiding place? For someone as clever as you. But wait!" The boys heard his fingers among the writing materials on the table. There was a pause; then he pressed the paper into Miss Codling's hand again. "There! There's your chance! Yes, I suppose you might even find the treasure before John gets home. I shouldn't mind. You haven't much time, though—he'll be home so soon—so soon. Now, not another word!" His hand waved imperiously in the air. The interview was over.

Miss Codling came out to the boys, shutting the door behind her. "It was no use. He said——"

"We heard everything," said Adam. "But didn't he write something?"

With a gesture of despair, she held out to them the paper she had taken into the room with her. At first, it did not seem to them to be written on in any new way. Then, they noticed that one word had been crossed out and another written over it, in faint straggling capitals, very unlike Mr. Codling's first, firm script. The second line of the rhyme now read: *UNDER the water.*

16

John Codling Comes Home

NOT ONLY Miss Codling felt despair. Adam and David had found difficulty enough in wringing the secret meaning from the rhyme that Jonathan Codling had left as clue. Now, they felt the impossibility of finding yet another meaning buried in it—Mr. Codling's meaning.

Adam, it is true, fastened savagely on the altered phrase: "Under the water." His grandfather had sunk the treasure in the River Say, he maintained, and they must have the whole river dragged to recover it. It was useless for David to point out that sinking the treasure was as good as throwing it away, and for Miss Codling to point out that only a millionaire could afford to drag the river. Their reasoning with Adam only tinged his obsession with black despair. He spent his time now prowling up and down the river bank, staring hungrily into the water. At first, David went with him, more to keep him company than for any other reason. But Adam did not want company—he wanted nothing but the impossible treasure. In the end, David took to staying away from Codlings'.

The very air at Codlings' seemed uneasy nowadays. Old Mr. Codling was sleeping soundly, thanks to the doctor's prescriptions, but he was no better in himself: he seemed more expectantly on edge than ever. Miss Codling suffered from the double worry of her father's nervous excitement and Adam's moodiness —for Adam's mingled thoughts of lost treasure and of Birmingham made him ill-tempered and obstinate. His aunt had never known him like this, and she was at a loss. She found that she could make him neither eat properly nor go to bed at any reasonable time—not by reasoning, nor by persuasion, nor by downright command. He haunted the river bank until daylight had gone and the waters seemed more black and secret than ever.

He came back by moonlight one evening. The moon was at the full, but there were the clouds of a summer storm gathering in the sky, and her light was not always clear and free. Adam did not mind. He picked his way with accustomed sureness through the riverside woodland to the lawn at the back of Codlings'. There he halted. The garden door had been left open in the thundery heat, and he could see against the light in the hall that his grandfather was standing there, looking out into the garden —looking and listening.

Adam was sure that he had not been seen, and—apart from his own feeling for solitude, nowadays—he did not want to be seen. The appearance of anyone so unexpectedly would be sure to upset his grandfather. But Adam had forgotten the moon. At first, he was standing hidden in clouded darkness: then, suddenly, the moon swept out from behind the clouds and lit brightly the trees, the lawn, and the boy. Before Mr. Codling's eyes it brought the vision of a moonshine-ghostly boy: Adam was no longer a stranger with dark-red hair, but a familiar-seeming boy with a head silver fair—a boy as fair as John Codling had been. Old Mr. Codling saw his son's hair, and it made him see too for the first time what Miss Codling had always seen in Adam's face—

the features of his dead father. Mr. Codling took a step toward the moonshine boy. "John!" he called, softly and warmly. "John!"

For a moment, Adam was too frightened to speak or move. Then, the necessity of undeceiving his grandfather gripped him, and he moved forward. "Grandfather—" he began.

Mr. Codling never heard. With a violent suddenness he had turned back to the house, one foot on the upper step. "Dinah!" he called, and "Dinah!" again. Joy made his voice ring out, loud and strong, as it had not sounded for many years. "John's come home!" he shouted. "John's here!" he shouted. "John——" His voice ended abruptly, and he fell forward up the steps.

Adam ran to him across the lawn at the same time as Miss Codling came running from the house. Miss Codling reached him first. She knelt by him, and put her arms under his breast; her face and her whole body bowed over him.

"Quick, Adam!" she said. "Run and fetch the doctor!"

He started off down the drive, running, and then heard her calling him back again. He halted, and she called him again, and he went back and stood by her. She still knelt by Mr. Codling, her face looking down at him. "Adam," she said, "I don't want you to run, and alarm yourself, and alarm the doctor. There is no need for hurry and alarm. Grandfather has died, you know." She looked up at him for the first time and smiled, to reassure him; but all that Adam could watch upon her face were the tears that moved, and, as they moved, glittered in the moonlight.

17

The Board at the Gate

THE STORM CLOUDS gathered slowly that week and then broke. Old Mr. Codling's funeral took place in a downpour of summer rain.

Mr. Moss arranged for time off to attend the funeral as did many of the older inhabitants of Great and Little Barley.

"Everyone was there," said Mr. Moss. "Mark Tey came, to represent the Parish Council, and someone came from the cricket club, and the bowls—although some of the younger ones can't have known him at all, even by sight. Old Alice Hellin was there, and Roger Ramsden and Gertrude from the *Codling Arms*, and Arnold Alexander—Ernest Alexander's son. Frankie Ellum was there, from the paper shop. Edward Nunn was there. Even Squeak Wilson was there. He crept in late and sat in the back pew and looked like a mouse the cat has caught; I saw Miss

Codling spare a word for him afterward, and shake hands with him, too."

"She must be in a sad way," said Mrs. Moss.

"A sad way," agreed Mr. Moss, "but she has spirit. Like her father—although the Barleys won't see his like again."

He shook his head and sighed; and David wished intensely that he had known Mr. Codling in the old days, when he had made his century at cricket and played bowls and ruled the Parish Council with Mark Tey. Now Mr. Codling had withdrawn into a remote and golden past that he would share forever with Robin Hood and Bonnie Prince Charlie and Nelson at Trafalgar.

When the talk of the funeral was over, and Mr. Moss had gone to his work, and Mrs. Moss back to her housekeeping, David felt at a loss. Going to Codlings' to see Adam was out of the question, he knew, and he had nowhere else he wanted to go—nothing else he wanted to do. Becky wanted him to play with her, and that he did for a time, swinging her to and fro on the front gate. He tired of the occupation long before she did, and wandered away in the direction quite opposite to Codlings'. He went on foot, being too dispirited even to get out his bicycle.

While David was away, Miss Codling paid her visit. Becky was still swinging herself on the gate when she came into view. Becky watched her unfamiliar black figure coming along the Row, stopping to look at the number on each house until she reached the Mosses'. By then, Becky was hanging over the gate, plainly staring. Miss Codling nodded gently at the number on the gate, and at Becky.

"Is your mother in?"

Becky moved her head up and down slowly, still staring.

"Can I come in and see her?"

For answer, Becky held the gate open, and Miss Codling walked through, and up the path to the front door. Becky let the gate swing back behind her, and followed slowly after, like a dog in the tracks of a suspicious stranger. Miss Codling pressed the bell, and while she waited, turned and smiled at Becky.

"You look like David's sister, Becky."

Becky was frightened by this magic penetration; she began to back slowly away down the path again, still staring. Meanwhile, the front door was opened by Mrs. Moss, drying her hands on her apron.

"Yes?" she said to Miss Codling, certainly not recognizing her —taking her perhaps for a hawker.

"Are you Mrs. Moss?"

"Yes," said Mrs. Moss, again hardly less forbiddingly.

"I'm Miss Codling, Adam's aunt," Miss Codling said, and faltered a little. "I wondered—"

Mrs. Moss's steamy red hand had already gone out to Miss Codling's that fidgeted in its unfamiliar black cotton glove. "Come inside," she said, and the front door closed behind them.

When David wandered home some time later, Miss Codling was still there. He was just going into the house when he was arrested by an amateurish whistle from the pear tree. He went over to it, and to his surprise saw Becky, who had scrambled somehow into its branches—a most unusual feat for her.

"Davy!" she called down to him softly. "Miss Codling has come, and she's been a long time with Mother, and they've had tea out of the best tea cups, and they're still talking, and you can see everything from up here."

David climbed up beside Becky, and with her had a fine view of the tea party. Mrs. Moss's apron had disappeared and her sleeves were rolled down. She and her visitor were sitting in the best room and using the best china, but they were both very much at their ease. Miss Codling had taken off her rusty black hat— it was the first time David had ever seen her with a hat—and put it on the arm of her chair. Her gray head nodded as she talked, and when she stopped talking, Mrs. Moss would begin. The conversation as David saw at once was what his mother called "a quiet chat," and any interruption would be unwelcome. He stayed up in the pear tree until Miss Codling took her leave. Then he and Becky went indoors to their mother. She was standing at the window, looking after Miss Codling, and then when Miss Codling had disappeared, still looking out at nothing.

"What did she come for?" asked David.

"Miss Codling? Oh, we had a quiet chat. David, you shouldn't make Becky climb trees without a pinafore—she has tree green all over her dress."

"I didn't, Mother. What exactly did Miss Codling say?"

"This and that."

"What?"

"Well, for one thing, she asked if Adam could come and stay here for a few days, and, of course, I said yes."

"Here!" cried David, joyously dumfounded.

"Here!" echoed Becky.

"It's because Miss Codling has to go to Birmingham to see some relations and make some arrangements."

"I know—about Adam's going to live there with his cousins. It's that, isn't it?"

Mrs. Moss did not answer at once, so David repeated, "Isn't it?"

"Partly," said his mother, "but Miss Codling's business doesn't concern us anyway. What concerns us is that Adam's coming here. I shall put him to sleep in Dick's room."

"Next door to mine," said David.

"When does he come?" asked Becky.

"Tomorrow."

The next day Adam paddled down in the *Minnow*, with his pajamas and toothbrush in a brown-paper parcel in the bow. His was a welcome arrival. Mrs. Moss kissed him as though she had done so since he was a baby; and Mr. Moss told him, just as he would have told David, to wipe his shoes on the mat and not bring all the mud of the river into the house. David, with Becky just behind him, took him up to his bedroom, and pointed out to him the photograph of Dick's ship, H.M.S. *Harbinger*, hanging over the washstand, and showed him Dick's collection of birds' eggs.

They neither of them spoke of old Mr. Codling's death—there was nothing to be said on either side. When they were alone together, however, Adam reopened, very soberly, the subject of the treasure.

"I still want to find it," he said. "I still hope to."

"I'll still help you then," said David.

Adam nodded in acknowledgment. "Now that my grandfather's dead, of course, the only way—the one and only way—of finding the treasure is through his clue. This time, I think, we want to go at it calmly—calmly." He frowned at David as though David had been trying to rush him.

" 'Under the water,' " said David thoughtfully, and very slowly, to fit Adam's new mood.

"I've been thinking we can work on more of a clue than that. If Grandfather had wanted that to be the only clue, he would have crossed out the rest of the rhyme. It would have been such an easy, sensible thing to do."

"You mean, the whole of the rhyme ought to be taken as the clue?"

"Yes, every bit of it, I believe. Now, we can split it up and have a go at each bit separately—I mean, ask questions, as detectives do in books."

Adam ticked off his questions methodically on his fingers: "Who is *Philip*? He can't be Philip, the Duke of Edinburgh, for instance, because Grandfather couldn't have been thinking of him all those years ago before I was born. Had Grandfather a friend, perhaps, called Philip?

"Then, what is the *single rose*? Is it really a rose—the rose in Jonathan Codling's picture, or a rose in the garden, or even a watering-can rose? Or did Grandfather know someone called Rose?

"*Under the water*—well, we've thought of that a bit. I don't expect, after all, that Grandfather just threw the treasure into the river. Perhaps he hid it in a secret tunnel going under the river —only I don't think there is one.

"And then, *None but my daughter*. Aunt Dinah was Grandfather's only daughter, so it must mean her. She knows where he took the treasure—she *knows*!" Adam flushed with a kind of anger. "And yet, of course, she doesn't know she knows."

"Like Sarah Codling," said David. "She knew the secret of the hiding place, because she knew the rhyme. But she never realized she knew."

"Yes. So the last question is what does Aunt Dinah know about—I mean, that has to do with a Philip and a rose. And that brings us back in a circle to the first question."

"It sounds rather difficult," said David. "Have you asked your aunt anything, yet?"

"Not yet. There's plenty of time yet."

David hesitated. Then he said, "What about Birmingham, though?"

"I know. I go to Birmingham at the end of these holidays; but, after all, there are other holidays, and then I can come down here and stay with Aunt Dinah, and we can work on the clues then. It'll be a long job, anyway. All right, I'm patient; I can wait. We'll work away steadily, and sift through all the possibilities, and in the end we'll solve all the clues, and find the treasure, and then Aunt Dinah will be well enough off to have me back here for good." There was a quiet triumph in Adam's voice.

The starting point of their inquiries clearly ought to be Miss Codling, and they had to wait for her return. Adam had a letter from her on the third day of his visit to say that she would have to be away a few days longer than she had expected.

"She wants to see the headmaster of the school I'm to go to," said Adam as they sat round the tea table.

"I said that was the kind of thing she was going to Birmingham for," said David. "The only reason, really."

"Of course."

"Have some cake, Adam?" said Mr. Moss suddenly. "You'll be sorry to leave the Barleys."

"Yes, please," said Adam. "Well, I shan't really leave here, because I can always come and stay with Aunt Dinah, you know. I shall do that—often. David and I have been making plans."

"You might like to come and stay with us again—with David," said Mrs. Moss.

"Thank you very much," said Adam, surprised. "Only I think I'd feel strange if I didn't stay with Aunt Dinah at Codlings'. That's my home. I was born there."

"Still—" said Mrs. Moss, but she did not go on.

Mr. Moss, who had been listening intently, with the cake knife held over the cake, now cut an enormous slice, and laid it on Adam's plate. "There!" he said, loudly. "And you can have jam with it, too, if you like." He got up abruptly and went out into the garden. David heard him muttering angrily as he went, "It's a shame—a downright shame!" The remark seemed very mysterious.

While they waited for Miss Codling's postponed return, the boys tried to put the thought of the treasure out of their mind. As Adam had said, there was no need for rush under their new, long-term system. Instead, they played with Becky and took her on several short trips in the *Minnow*—never, by order, out of the sight of Mrs. Moss, who sat on a chair on the dock and knitted and watched. So they passed the time quietly until the day fixed for Miss Codling's return. Then, Adam packed up his things and thanked Mrs. Moss, and he and David prepared to paddle the *Minnow* back to Codlings'.

"But, David," said Mrs. Moss, "I think perhaps Miss Codling would rather see Adam alone. She'll have some important things to tell him."

"Only about my cousins and the new school," said Adam. "He might like to hear that."

"I still think it would be better if David didn't go with you," said Mrs. Moss.

"But why?" asked Adam, puzzled.

Mrs. Moss moved her hands helplessly as if she could not explain further; and, Adam insisting, David and he went together after all.

They tied up the *Minnow* at the usual place, and went through the Codlings' woodland to the house. It was the first time that David had seen Codlings' without old Mr. Codling: the place seemed strangely the same.

Then they both noticed someone digging in one of the flower borders. "Why, it's Squeaker Wilson!" cried Adam. "He's digging up some of Aunt Dinah's clove pinks!"

The sound of Adam's voice made Squeak Wilson look up, and the sight of Adam's indignant face made him bundle up his plants and scuttle round the corner of the house. Adam was just going after him when Miss Codling, who must have seen them from the window, came out.

"Aunt!" cried Adam, forgetting all about Birmingham. "Did you see Squeaker Wilson? He was stealing some of your best plants!"

"I told him to take some," said Miss Codling. "He does a little as a jobbing gardener sometimes, and that kind of thing helps him."

"But they're your best clove pinks!" said Adam, dumfounded. In all his experience he had not known his aunt to be a selfless gardener; gardeners were not like that.

Miss Codling was positively impatient of the idea of her pinks. "Never mind them!" she said, and drew the boys indoors. She was still wearing black, but it could not be that alone that made her look so pale. She talked in a worried way, and yet at random, as it seemed.

"I've only just got back," she said. "I had such a busy time at Birmingham. And I was writing letters to Castleford, too, to start getting arrangements made there. I thought there would be such delays, and lo and behold! Oseley and Webb have got farther ahead than I really meant them to."

"What firm are Oseley and Webb?" asked Adam. "Are they the lawyers that have Grandfather's will?"

"No," said Miss Codling, darting him a strangely alarmed glance. "No, not lawyers. As a matter of fact, your grandfather's will was so very simple that there isn't much work lawyers need do. And there was very, very little to leave, beyond this house."

David felt now that perhaps his mother had been right. Miss Codling would not want to talk about her private affairs with anyone but Adam. He got up. "I think I'd better go—it'll take some time to walk home."

"I'll just come with you to the top of the drive," said Adam.

"Oh, no!" cried Miss Codling. "Don't do that! I mean, why doesn't David go home by river?"

"It's really better if the canoe stops here with Adam, because I've always got my bicycle at home," said David. "No, I'll walk."

Miss Codling seemed distressed. "Don't go yet, then," she said. "I've important things to say about the arrangements I've been making." Yet she seemed unable to tell them whatever was on her mind, and David felt even more strongly and uncomfortably that whatever it was concerned Adam and should be told to him alone.

Again David tried to take his leave. Again Miss Codling tried to detain him. In the end it was arranged that, as Adam insisted on going with David to the gate, Miss Codling would go too.

She talked as they went. "Grandfather didn't leave much. What we lived on, almost entirely, was a pension he had; that stopped when he died. You do understand that, don't you, Adam?"

"Yes, Aunt Dinah."

"There's the house, of course. That's really the only thing of any value that Grandfather could leave, and you can't eat a house."

"Of course not."

"I mean," said Miss Codling, "it's unrealized capital—and all we have. We haven't any income any more."

"What is unrealized capital?" asked David, not because he really wanted to know, but because he felt that Miss Codling might like to be asked, and Adam was showing no interest.

"I mean," said Miss Codling, "that the only money that Adam and I have in the world is tied up in the house, and that's very awkward."

Miss Codling had been holding them all back by the unusual slowness of her pace, but now they were almost at the top of the drive. Suddenly Adam said, "What on earth is that?"

He pointed to a brand-new notice board that had been planted just inside the gateway. The board faced outward, toward the road. The boys left Miss Codling, who had come to a dead stop, and ran round to the front of the board to see what it was. It had written on it:

TO BE SOLD
Oseley and Webb
House and Estate Agents
Castleford

The boys stared. Then David said, "It's a mistake, Adam."

"No," said Miss Codling, coming to them. "It's not a mistake. The only mistake was in their putting up the board so early, before I had time to tell Adam. It's as I was trying to explain to you, Adam. We have to sell this house altogether, in order to have even a little money to live on. I shall have to leave Codlings' and Great Barley when you do, and go to Birmingham to the cousins. They've been very kind."

Adam did not appear to be listening to his aunt. "Adam!" she said, trying to attract his attention. He turned away and began to walk back to the house. "Adam!" she called after him. "Come back and listen!" But he began to run.

Miss Codling put her hand out to David's shoulder as if to steady herself.

"Shall you like living in Birmingham?" asked David for something to say.

"No," said Miss Codling, and leaned upon him heavily as if she were very tired. Presently she took her hand from his shoulder and drew herself up. "Well," she said, "you'd better get home, David, or your mother will be wondering where you are."

"Yes," said David. "Shall I go now?"

"Certainly, you must go now."

David set off, but turned round several times to look back. Miss Codling stood in the gateway for some time, watching him, or perhaps just thinking; she did not wave. He met and passed Mr. Smith, who was also on foot. When David next turned to look back, Miss Codling had gone, and Mr. Smith had drawn level with the gateway. There, Mr. Smith stopped to read the new notice board. He studied it for some minutes; then he turned into the Codlings' drive.

18

Pip-squeak

THE STORY of the treasure as Adam and David had planned it, with themselves as heroes, was to have had a leisurely and happy ending; now, it was rushing to a very different conclusion. The questions about Philip, and a rose or Rose, and any tunnel "under the water" had to be put to Miss Codling in frantic haste, and she knew none of the answers. Next should have come the slow "sifting of all possibilities," upon which Adam had been relying. But there would be no time for that in the short time left before the end of the summer holidays, and there would be no more holidays at Codlings' for Adam. By the end of the summer, Adam and his aunt would be in Birmingham for good, and Codlings' would be sold—sold to Mr. Smith. That was the end of the story.

"Mr. Smith is the villain," said Adam.

"Nonsense!" said Miss Codling. "On the contrary, we're very lucky to have an offer for the house so promptly."

"Why should he want Codlings' in such a hurry?"

"He's not in a hurry. He told Oseley and Webb that he's always thought he should like to have it."

"Why?"

"Well," said Miss Codling, angrily, but almost crying at the same time, "we wanted to live here, didn't we?"

"That's different."

Miss Codling did not answer, but David felt the force of Adam's questioning. Codlings' was neither beautiful nor convenient, nor in good repair, and its garden was mostly in an even worse state. Those familiar with it—born in it—might love it and be sad to leave it, but why should a stranger want it? Was not Mr. Smith's offer sinister?

"It does seem queer about Mr. Smith," said David.

"He's a villain," insisted Adam.

"Nonsense!" repeated Miss Codling, and to forestall further contradiction, began to move away at once. "There's Squeak! I want a word with him."

The frequency of Squeak Wilson's visits, and Miss Codling's kindness to him, were irritations to Adam in the present situation. The house was not yet sold to Mr. Smith, but in the meantime Miss Codling was giving away to Squeak all kinds of things —not valuable things, but things that seemed to go with the house and the garden—as though she felt that she was already giving up possession. She gave him her clove pinks, and old Mr. Codling's worn blue dressing gown to be cut up into dusters, and as many potatoes as he liked to dig and carry away, and other things.

She defended her kindness by saying that Squeak Wilson was so poor, and that old Mr. Codling had been harsh in dismissing him years ago. Miss Codling said Squeak had never had a strong head, and he had got drunk one day in the kitchen at Codlings', and Mr. Codling had discovered it, and in a terrible fury had sacked him. The story was uninteresting except that it explained Squeak Wilson's extraordinary terror when they first met him at Folly Mill. He had seen in Adam the family resemblance to formidable old Mr. Codling, and Mark Tey had pushed his nervousness to panic by his gibe about drinking unwisely.

Squeak Wilson was as fearful of Adam now as he had been at their first meeting; if there was any danger of their meeting face to face in the garden, he would gather his tools and slip away. His furtiveness only increased Adam's distrust and dislike.

One day Miss Codling let fall that she had given Squeak a message to leave with the Smiths on his way home. There was an outburst of anger from Adam. "Why do you trust him?" he stormed.

"Someone had to take the message," said Miss Codling. "Would you have taken it, Adam?"

"No! You know I wouldn't!"

"Or David?"

David was hesitating unhappily when Adam answered for him, "Nor David!"

"There you are then. I could have stopped what I was doing and walked round. But, on the other hand, Squeak Wilson goes right past the gate on his way home, so I asked him, and he was quite willing."

"Willing! Of course, he's willing! He's probably in league with the Smiths."

"Don't be silly, Adam."

"His name's Squeak, and he is a squeaker, and nobody ought to trust him. He's a telltale—you've only to look at him. He's a traitor——"

"Adam! I will not have it! Squeak Wilson is a poor, harmless old man you've managed to scare half out of his life. What's all this rubbish about his being a traitor?"

"He's called Squeak because he's a squeaker," said Adam stubbornly.

David saw that Miss Codling did not understand, and was growing angrier and angrier, so he explained: "A person who squeaks gives away his friends—betrays them."

"So that's it!" said Miss Codling scornfully. "But he's not called Squeak for that reason at all. Squeak is just a shortening of Pip-squeak—Pip-squeak was his nickname—Pip-squeak Wilson."

The boys' conception of Squeak Wilson dissolved: not a squeaker after all, but only a little pip-squeak of a man. He was certainly that.

Adam recovered his self-possession quickly, and his ill temper. He shifted his attack. "Anyway, why do you have to send messages to the Smiths, at all? Why do you have to be friendly with them, and kind?"

"This wasn't a particularly kind message. Mr. Smith asked if he might buy the portrait of Jonathan Codling with the house. I had to tell him that the picture was not for sale because I wanted it, if possible, to belong to my nephew when he grew up."

At any other time, Adam might have been softened by this; now, he could only think and feel in one way. "They wanted the picture!" he cried. "They want Jonathan Codling's picture, because they want Jonathan Codling's treasure! It's all a plot—a plot! And you'll do nothing against it! You know where the treasure is—the rhyme says so—you know who Philip is—and about the rose—and 'under the water'—and yet you can't tell us, and you spend your time sending polite messages to the Smiths instead!"

This seemed to David to be going too far, and he glanced fearfully at Miss Codling. To his surprise, he saw that she had changed color. There was more of apology than reproof when she spoke. "You're right, Adam—at least partly right."

"That it's a plot?"

"No—about the rhyme. I don't know where the treasure is, or the meaning of the rose, or 'under the water'; but now I realize that I've always known a Philip that your grandfather knew too."

"Oh!" breathed Adam and David together. "Who?"

"The Philip we were just talking about—Philip Wilson. When I was a little girl, people called him Pip Wilson, and then they made a joke of it—because he was so small—and called him Pip-squeak Wilson, and then Squeak Wilson. I'd forgotten where his nickname came from until you began talking about it just now."

"Squeak Wilson," said David, and there was a long pause.

Then Adam asked if Squeak's wife had been called Rose—or had he grown roses?

"Grandfather would never let him touch the roses here. And his wife's name was Ellen, and so is his daughter's—Ellen Perfect."

"Then what does the rhyme mean about Philip?"

Miss Codling shook her head.

"The rest of the rhyme must mean something—something to do with Squeak Wilson."

Miss Codling sighed and said, "After all, Squeak may not be the Philip of your rhyme." With that unhelpful suggestion, she left them.

The next time that Squeak Wilson came to Codlings', Adam and David were lying in wait for him. Before he was off his tricycle, David was holding it by the back of the saddle, and Adam by the handle bars and basket, and with his face within a few inches of Squeak's own.

As they questioned him, Squeak trembled with fear. Of roses and underwater places and hiding holes he knew nothing; the idea of hidden treasure only bewildered him.

"But, at least, your name is Philip," said Adam.

Even his own name seemed to take Squeak by surprise. "Why, yes, but there's none's ever called me that this many a year. Except," he faltered, "except your grandpa. 'Philip' your grandpa used to call me, when he was put out."

The memory of old Mr. Codling "put out," and the nearness of his alarming grandson, became too much for Squeak. He slid sideways from his tricycle to escape to the refuge of the kitchen and Miss Codling's protection.

Adam and David were left gazing at each other across the tricycle. They were dissatisfied, but not entirely disappointed.

"He's Grandfather's Philip, all right," said Adam, and David nodded.

19

A Dead End

ADAM AND DAVID had found a Philip. Was that really the beginning of a solution of all the clues that would lead them
to the treasure? And would it lead them there quickly
enough? There were other events, whose sequence was sure,
rapid, and threatening. Twice already Miss Codling had paid
visits to Oseley and Webb, in Castleford, and it was understood
that the business of selling Codlings' to Mr. Smith was going
forward.

The sale was no longer talked of between Miss Codling and the
boys. Adam did not even discuss it with David now. Yet David
felt that Adam was painfully sensitive to the signs of what was
going on, and sometimes gave himself up to despair. He began
to insist, for example, that the *Minnow* should be kept moored
to the Mosses' dock instead of to the Codlings' bank.

"She's yours," he announced.

"Oh, no!" said David, startled. "You haven't even gone yet."

"As good as. We might as well begin now: she's yours, and she stays at your dock."

"But we both join at her—I don't want to have your share in her as well as my own. You'll come from Birmingham in the holidays and stay with us, as Mother said, and we'll go out in the canoe every day, and it'll all be the same as before."

"No, it won't," said Adam. "And I shan't come back, ever." There was a resolute sadness in the way he rejected David's invitation.

David said, after a silence, "Anyway, she might as well stay tied to your bank until you go. You don't know that something may not turn up, after all, to stop your going."

"No! I won't have you pretending everything's going to come all right in the end! It's not going to—I can see it isn't!"

"All right, then," David said pacifically. "I'll keep the *Minnow* at our dock, but I'll paddle up here in her every day."

"Just as you like."

Adam's grimness quite spoiled any pleasure David might have taken in paddling to and fro in the *Minnow*, tying her up at the dock every evening, and finding her waiting there for him every morning. As for being the *Minnow's* sole owner, David had never dreamed of such a thing since he first met Adam, nor did he wish it now. It was Adam who was intent on thrusting proprietorship upon him.

Adam swung occasionally from this black mood of gloom into one of irrational, almost frantic hope. David was paddling up to Codlings' one morning when he saw him making his way, on hands and knees, over the tree bridge from the Nunn side. He was pushing a garden fork in front of him. He reached the bank at the same time that David stepped from the *Minnow*.

"Have you been digging for the treasure over there?" asked David, in surprise.

Adam nodded. "I was thinking about the clue, 'under the water.' Part of that land is often under water."

"But I thought you'd forked it all over, long ago. You said you had."

"All except the boggy bit and the dogs' graves."

David remembered headstones, low and half covered with ivy, that yet had glimmered from the shadows of that neglected woodland. "Did you dig them up?" he asked, awestruck.

Adam nodded.

"And did you——?"

"Nothing. Nothing but bones—skeletons." He slowly rubbed earth from his right hand, with a tuft of grass plucked with his left. "Mr. Nunn once told Aunt Dinah that he thought the ghosts of those dogs go rabbiting in his fields on moonlight nights. It must be fun, even if you are a ghost. Better than Birmingham, anyway." He threw away the grass, and turned from David and the river, trailing the fork after him.

David followed him at a little distance until they came out on the lawn. Here, Adam waited for him to catch up.

"Do you see that rose tree?" he said, pointing. "It's called the Empress of China. It has big single roses—a bit like dog roses, only much bigger and a streaky pinky-yellow, as though they're fading, even when they're only just out. My grandfather was very proud of it. He planted it."

Adam handed the garden fork to David. "Hold that," he said. He passed quickly indoors; he was back again in a minute. "She's busy in the kitchen," he said. "It's all clear."

He took the fork from David, and, with speed and force, drove the prongs in at the foot of the rose tree.

"Here!" cried David, bewildered and horrified. "Adam!"

"I told you," Adam gasped as he dug away. "It's a single rose —the only single rose in the garden."

David watched in a state of dazed apprehension: he seemed to be in a waking nightmare. It was almost a relief when the inevitable spectator appeared. Squeak Wilson came, trundling a wheelbarrow and whistling. He stopped both, when he saw Adam and what he was doing. For once, Squeak was too appalled to be frightened for himself.

"That's the Empress of Chiny you're at there!" he shrilled.

Adam worked on, paying no attention.

"That's your grandpa's Empress of Chiny rose! He'd be that upset!"

Adam turned his head. "Go away and be quiet!"

Squeak left his wheelbarrow and went away, but he could not have obeyed the rest of Adam's order. In a few minutes, Miss Codling appeared at the garden door, with Squeak peering out from behind her.

"Adam!" she shouted—no, she screamed it, rather.

Adam had only a little more digging to do, and he did not stop now. David could see the sweat rolling off his cheeks like tears; his muscles flowed and knotted and flowed again; the fork thrust and heaved and whirled up and away, like a gleaming, deadly instrument of war.

Miss Codling screamed again, and set off across the lawn toward Adam. She reached him at the exact moment that the fork completed its work: it had made a deep, raw hole, empty now of any rose-tree roots, and empty, too, of anything else. There was no treasure. Lifting his eyes from the pit, Adam looked across the corpse of the Empress of China to his aunt. She was trembling with a rage that at first prevented speech.

Adam began heavily to explain that he had dug up the single rose in the hope that the treasure might have been buried under it. "It was just a chance for us," he said.

"A chance!" cried Miss Codling. "For a chance, you dig up and kill—yes, kill!—the Empress of China rose! The most beautiful rose, the rarest rose in the garden! I tell you, Adam, you've done a murder for the lowest motive of all—gain—money—treasure!" She almost spat, in her contempt. "If we go from here, we go. Others have lost more than we are losing, and have gone out with decency and with dignity. But you—you'd drain dry the

River Say, and pull this house down, and root up everything that has ever been planted and tended here! For money—money!"

"But, Aunt——"

"Is there nothing you would not do?" she stormed. "Kill the living—dig up the dead, no doubt—"

This last thrust was more bitter than Miss Codling knew. Adam turned from her and began to run clumsily for the shelter of the trees, holding one arm across his eyes—David was almost sure he was crying. David followed to give what comfort he could. He looked back once, and saw that Squeak Wilson had picked up the fork—gardening tools seemed almost to grow to his hands. Miss Codling was bending over the rose tree, like a mourner.

Later in the day, Miss Codling met Adam and David again, face to face. She was calm, but very cold. "I think you should know," she said, "that I have to go to Oseley and Webb's on Saturday to sign the papers for the sale of Codlings'. I tell you so that you may be spared further exertions."

Meanwhile, however, the boys had already determined on "further exertions" of a reasonable, unobjectionable kind. The new idea was David's, and he offered it as some kind of consolation to Adam.

"You see, Adam, I think it's no use trying to work on odd clues, like 'the single rose,' that we haven't really solved yet. I think we ought to work from what we *do* know—from 'Philip' being Squeak Wilson."

"How?"

"Well, find out all about Squeak—and not just by asking *him*, either. I've been asking my father, but he doesn't know much—nothing interesting, anyway. But I'd been thinking——"

"Go on."

"Well, the only person I could think of who knows everything that's happened in Barley for a long way back, and likes to talk about it, is Mr. Tey, of Folly Mill. Should we go to see him?"

"All right."

So they paddled up to Folly Mill—it was the first time Adam had been in the *Minnow* since the day they had learned that Codlings' was for sale, and the voyage was certainly the dreariest they had ever made.

This time they arrived at the mill while it was still working. There was no one to be seen, until a man in white dusty overalls leaned out of an upper window and asked what they wanted. He told them that Mr. Tey would probably be in his office, and pointed the way. They found what was the office by catching sight of Mr. Tey inside, at a desk; he beckoned them in.

They found themselves in a shadowy little room, facing Mr. Tey over what was rather like a counter in a shop—only this counter was piled with a confusion of things that no single shop, in its senses, would have sold. There was an old-fashioned weighing machine, with a handful of cobnuts kept in its scoop; a dumpy leather bag whose handle was worn shiny by the grip of more than one generation of millers on their way to Castleford corn market; a pile of old ledgers; a large fragment of mirror, carefully propped up, so that Mr. Tey could examine the length of his beard and trim it; there was a basket with some eggs in it; and a very antiquated kind of mousetrap that needed repair, and would be repaired some day—a white kitten sat on it now, licking its fur. A gentle dust lay over everything except the kitten.

"Come in," said Mr. Tey gravely, composing his features into an expression of gloom. He began to talk of the funeral of old Mr. Codling, and—going farther back—of his memories of him years before; some reminiscences the boys had heard from him on their last visit.

At last, he drew to a conclusion. "And I hear you and your aunt will be leaving Barley now," he said to Adam.

Adam nodded.

"And who is the house going to?" (David felt the delicacy of his avoiding any word of sale.)

"To the Smiths."

"Which Smiths would they be?"

Adam told him.

Mr. Tey shook his head. "They're a poor lot—hardly belong to the village at all, with their trips to London. London indeed!" Mr. Tey here spared time faithfully to give his opinion of London. "And then they say Mrs. Smith's so haughty, she'll walk down the street with not a how-d'ye-do to people she knows as well as I do you. And their daughter a wretched thing they won't have seen about the place—they're downright cruel to her in that, I've heard."

"You do know a lot about everybody, Mr. Tey," said David, hoping to take over the direction of the conversation a little.

"I heard a bit about the Smiths from Squeak Wilson," said Mr. Tey.

"Oh!" exclaimed Adam and David together, astounded that Mr. Tey had so played into their hands. Before he could say more, they had swept him away on to the subject of Philip Wilson.

Mr. Tey talked willingly, as ever. He had known Squeak since he was a boy—they were both much the same age. He remembered, in detail, Squeak's marriage, his daughter, his widowerhood; the jobs he had done; his eccentricities. For the boys' benefit, he remembered particularly Squeak's relations with old Mr. Codling, right up to the episode of his drunkenness—"drunk as a lord on your grandpa's own wine"—and the final break. But, in all he remembered, even prompted by the boys' most cunning questions, he told them nothing that could possibly help in the solution of the mystery of the rhyme.

They slipped off their stools to go.

"Well," said Mr. Tey to David, "I expect you really came for him." He nodded to the kitten, who was now playing with a cobnut on the counter. "Have you remembered a basket for him?"

"No," said David. "We didn't really come for that—I mean, we haven't brought a basket."

"He'll need to go in a basket with a lid if you take him back by canoe. Cats get near frantic sometimes when they're on water. You'd best come again with a basket with a lid."

"Yes," said David. The kitten was a pretty thing, but the fetching of it had no urgency, compared with the urgency of Adam's problems.

They left Folly Mill and paddled downstream again. At Codlings', David put Adam ashore and went on homeward alone. It was the end of the day—the end of Thursday. Then would come Friday; and then—nothing on earth could stop it—Saturday.

20

Mrs. Perfect Can't Quite Remember

SATURDAY MORNING, and David was paddling up to Codlings',
saying to himself, "Well, it's too late now." This was Saturday, and Miss Codling would be on her way to Castleford
to sign the papers of the sale. It would all be over; and he was
almost glad—except that he was so miserable. Not being able to
do anything, and yet having the whole day to do it in—yes, he
was glad that yesterday was over. Except that he was so miserable
today.

Yesterday he and Adam had done nothing but think. Their
thoughts had twined round the clues of the rhyme. They had
thought carefully, then desperately, then wildly, then wearily,
then almost boredly. If the solution of the clues had not meant
so much to them, they would certainly have been bored to tears.

David left the canoe at Codlings' and walked slowly through
the trees to the house, still thinking, "It's over—all over." He
was, therefore, very surprised to catch a glimpse of Miss Codling
through the windows. Adam came outside to him with a per-

fectly ordinary explanation. They had taken for granted that
Miss Codling would catch an early bus to Castleford. In fact, she
was not going until the half-past-twelve bus, and Mr. Smith,
who was catching an early train back from London, would meet
her with a taxi at the bus station in Castleford. Then they
would go on to Oseley and Webb's together.

There stretched before David an hour or so of the same inaction
as they had endured yesterday. He must do something.

"I shall talk to Squeak," he said.

"He's not here this morning. He told Aunt Dinah he'd a
grave to dig this afternoon, so he was going to take this morning
off at home."

"Well, then, I'll go and see him at home."

"What about?"

David was going to say, about Philip—about the single rose—
about anything that might lead to the treasure. But Adam would
only point out that they had already asked about these things very
thoroughly.

"I shall ask him about the Smiths," said David, with an air of
inspiration.

"Why?"

"Well, if it's true that they're cruel to their daughter, I shouldn't
think they're the kind of people your aunt would want to sell to."

"They'd have to be Crippens before she'd give them up."

"Crippens?"

"Crippen was a murderer. I mean, the Smiths would have
to be really bad criminals, hiding from justice."

"Well, you believed once they were hiding from justice."

"I'm not so sure now. Anyway, I don't see how we could
ever prove anything against them, really and truly." Adam was
certainly in the deepest gloom. "I'll come with you to Squeak's,"
he added.

"No," said David, feeling that he could as well endure the
company of a death's head. "I mean, you only scare Squeak,
anyway."

So David went up the village alone. As he walked, his spirits, almost unbelievably, managed to sink below their previous level. Drearily he paused outside Mrs. Trudgett's sweet-shop window. Its sights did not cheer him as once they would have done. He did, however, buy three licorice bootlaces—it was all he could afford. He ate one length, although he did not like licorice: he felt it might brace him a little. The other two he kept as a kind of bribe for Squeak.

Mr. Tey, in his conversation of two days ago, had described fairly closely where Squeak Wilson lived—in a little whitewashed cottage at the back of the church. David found it easily.

There was no doorbell or knocker to the front door, so he knocked with his knuckles. A peaceful silence followed his knocking, and his repeated knocking. All he disturbed was a spider who had built an extensive web between the door and its lintel. The web seemed proof that the front door was seldom—if ever—used.

David left the front of the house and followed a flagged path that led round the side into a paved yard at the back. The yard was bright and hot with morning sunshine; in the shadow of the overhanging thatch stood a basket chair, in which Squeak Wilson was asleep.

The sound of David's steps on the stone woke him. He eyed his visitor uncertainly: he had seen him often with Adam, but he did not know whether to fear him on his own account.

"Good morning, Mr. Squeak," David said politely. "I've brought you some licorice."

He held the bag toward Squeak, open; Squeak looked in, and his eyes brightened. "Lickerish!" he said. "Now, lickerish has flavor!"

He took the bag, and at once, to David's surprise, leaned far back in the basket chair, tilting it up and back. Without needing to look, Squeak threw the bag of licorice into the hollow space revealed under the chair. David saw fleetingly that the bag joined company with other objects—a clay pipe, a seed catalogue, an

Old Moore's Almanack. Then the solid wickerwork sides of the chair were allowed to sink to the ground again, and the treasures and the hiding hole were again hidden from view.

Squeak winked at David, as if to say, mum's the word about *that*. "My daughter fancies sweets give me the indigestion," he explained. "But they don't." David could see that he was put into a very good humor by the gift. If there was questioning to be done, now was the time to do it.

"You must have done odd jobs for a lot of people in the Barleys," David began.

"That's the bare truth."

David would have liked to lead Squeak into unprompted reminiscence, but Squeak was by no means as communicative as Mr. Tey. When at last they reached the subject of the Smiths, he said, surprisingly, "No, I never worked for them."

"Never!" said David. "But Mr. Tey once told us you knew a lot about them."

"Maybe," said Squeak.

This mystery, David found, after some talk around the point, was easily explained: Squeak's widowed daughter, Mrs. Perfect, had done cleaning work for the Smiths. From her he had had the story he had passed on to Mr. Tey.

By now the influence of the gift of licorice was lessening: Squeak's eyes were becoming wary; his replies briefer and more enigmatic.

"It was Ellen worked for them," he said.

"Does she still?"

"Cleans the church."

"Where is she now?"

"Cleaning the church."

"Could I go and talk to her?"

"Dessay."

"I mean, would she mind?"

"Dunno."

David felt that defeat was in the sleepy, sunny little yard. He left it and made his way to the front of the cottage and so, by a side gate, into the churchyard. The clock on the church tower, he noticed, said ten minutes to twelve.

As he went up the path between the tombstones, he reflected that here—somewhere—old Mr. Codling was buried. If only it had been night, and moonlight, instead of the sunny middle of the day, and if only he had dared, David could have wished that the ghost of Mr. Codling might walk and tell its secret. But old Mr. Codling lay at rest at last, side by side with his son, for whom he had looked so long. He cared nothing for clues or treasure now; that was left for his grandson.

David passed inside the church. The first thing he saw was a broom leaning against the font, and a bucket near it. Mrs. Perfect herself was farther up the church, working with a duster. David decided to wait for her to finish: the conversation he planned to have with her was going to start with a barefaced lie. He would prefer not to be in the church to deliver it.

Mrs. Perfect took some time. She dusted and polished the brass lectern, and then flicked round some pew ends as though in a hurry. But then she took a great deal of time dusting the oblong-winged butterflies in the carved woodwork of the pulpit. David grew impatient. While she was still at work, there was a whirring sound from overhead, and then a clanging, and the church clock struck the hour—noon. In half an hour from now, Miss Codling would be boarding the bus for Castleford.

At last the work was finished, and Mrs. Perfect gathered up her bucket and broom, and prepared to leave. David slipped forward and held the door open for her.

"Thank'ee," she said, surprised at his presence, and perhaps, too, at his politeness. She passed out into the sunshine, with David just behind her.

"Mrs. Perfect," said David, gravely, "Miss Codling sent me."

At the name, Mrs. Perfect stopped and turned as David had hoped—and expected—that she might. David had more than once been present when Miss Codling had given Squeak this or that oddment, and had noticed that Squeak would end his thanks by saying, "And my daughter'll think kindly of you, ma'am, as she always does."

"Miss Codling wants your advice," said David, and again saw that his words had their effect: Mrs. Perfect was pleased.

"You see," said David, "she's thinking of selling her house— you may have heard—to the Smiths that live by the river, and she wants to make sure that they'd be good people to own it. She heard you'd worked for them, and wondered what you thought of them."

"I worked for them," Mrs. Perfect agreed. She was pleasant in her manner, but her style of conversation at first reminded David of Squeak's.

"Wasn't there—isn't there—a daughter?"

"So I've heard."

"And weren't they cruel to her at one time?"

"Not that I know of. But they were very queer about her."

"Yes?"

"They wouldn't have her down here at all—at least, Mr. Smith wouldn't—not at any price."

"Well, I'd call that cruel," said David, but only halfheartedly, thinking to himself that Miss Codling might not call it cruel— not criminally cruel. "Anyway, they can't have been fond of her."

"But they were," said Mrs. Perfect. "That was what was so queer." She leaned on her broom, and, after a leisurely pause, went on. "Mr. Smith spoke of her nicely, when he *did* speak of her, and Mrs. Smith was always fidgeting for them to be off on one of their London jaunts to see her. She lived in London with her granny—Mrs. Smith was quite open about that; but why the child wasn't allowed to be with her own mother—" Mrs. Perfect shook her head. "That was Mr. Smith's willfulness, and, for all her ways, Mrs. Smith didn't know how to manage him. 'Twas right-down pitiful. I wouldn't have liked poor Perfect that's passed on to have seen it. Nor even Father, though he's quiet enough—though can be sly."

If Mr. Smith wasn't cruel to his daughter, perhaps he was cruel to someone else, David thought. He asked if Mr. Smith had ever beaten his wife.

"No, but it's not only beating that shows the master," said Mrs. Perfect knowledgeably. "Now, I'll tell you something I saw with my own eyes. One day, Mr. Smith was poorly—he's queer insides, and the slightest thing upsets him. Well, this time he was right-down ill, and Mrs. Smith was fair off her head with worry. She says to me, 'I'll get Betsy to come down'—Betsy is the daughter's name. I said to her, 'You do it; it'll be a comfort to you.'

"Well, she was on the telephone to London—I was polishing the floor at the time—when there was a funny noise and there was Mr. Smith coming down the stairs to stop her, and almost having a fit because of it. Between us we got him back to bed, but he made her promise first that she'd never try telephoning that way again without his permission. And she promised, for he looked that ill she couldn't have done otherwise. He swore then he wouldn't have his daughter seen in the village—and when I say 'swore,' I mean 'swore,' I hadn't been used to such language— I've always kept Father's speech clean—and I gave my notice that very day."

"Was that all?" said David, disappointed.

"All? You never heard such language: it haunts me." She shook her head. "After that, I was glad to get the church cleaning. It's a steady job, and I will say the Rector's not foul-mouthed."

"I meant, was that all Mr. Smith did wrong?"

"I don't know that it was *wrong*," said Mrs. Perfect, "apart from the swearing."

"And there's nothing else queer about them?" He remembered Adam's idea. "Their name isn't a false one? It really is just plain Smith?"

"Now, there was something . . ." said Mrs. Perfect. She knit her brows, evidently trying to recollect.

"Were they—were they called Crippen?"

"No, the name was Smith, but not plain Smith: it was Something-Smith."

"Crippen-Smith?"

"No. Now what was it? They were called just Smith in the village, but sometimes letters came addressed to Mr. Something-Smith. Mr.—now, what was the name?"

Mrs. Perfect leaned on her broom handle and gazed up into the sky for inspiration.

"It was something about a tree," she said at last.

"A tree?"

"A kind of tree."

"You mean, they had a name like Sycamore-Smith?"

"No. Now, it's coming back to me: 'twas Somethingworthy-Smith, but there was a tree in it, too."

David looked round the churchyard. "Yewworthy?" he suggested.

"No, but it was short, like that." Now Mrs. Perfect looked down the path to the churchyard gate, which was shaded by an enormous elm tree. "Now, was it Elmworthy?" she questioned herself. "It doesn't sound just right, and yet it might have been Elmworthy. It was a tree, and a short tree, and it might very well have been Elmworthy."

"Elmworthy." Now that he had the name, David saw how useless to him it was. "And is that all—I mean, all I can tell Miss Codling?"

"Isn't that all she wants to be sure of? That I know no real harm of Mr. Smith and his lady?"

"Yes, of course," said David. "I'll tell her that." He turned dejectedly away, and so left Mrs. Perfect and the churchyard, the church and the church clock. As he turned into the village street the clock struck a quarter past twelve behind him. Miss Codling would be going for her bus. Going through the village, David saw Miss Codling on the other side of the road; she was hurrying although she was in good time. He was glad in a way that

she did not notice him, since he had found out nothing that
would even delay her going to Oseley and Webb.

David arrived back at Codlings' and began to look for Adam.
He was not in the house. His name, called aloud indoors, echoed
mournfully as if the place were already abandoned. After a while,
however, he was found at the bottom of the garden, staring at the
fowls.

"Well?" he asked, looking sharply at David.

"Nothing. A lot of stuff about the daughter, but nothing bad
enough. And their name really is Smith, too—Something-Smith."

"What do you mean—Something-Smith? Something isn't a
name."

The name, so unimportant, had slipped from the grasp of
David's mind. What had it been?

"Well?" said Adam, with an impatience bordering on real
anger.

It had been Somethingworthy, she had said—yes, a Treeworthy
—some kind of tree. Which?

"Well?" said Adam. In a moment, he would be in a rage.

David cast his eyes desperately about for inspiration as Mrs.
Perfect had done—about and up—up to the heights of the great
ash tree that shaded the Codlings' henhouse.

"Ashworthy-Smith?" he said, only tentatively and half to himself.

Adam's mounting irritation seemed to explode into something
frantic that was not anger. "Ashworthy!" he roared. He sprang
upon David, and held his arm in a grip that hurt. "Ashworthy!
Are you sure?"

"Yes," said David. "I mean, no—I mean, Mrs. Perfect wasn't
at all sure, except that it was a tree, and short, and I can't remember——"

"It must have been Ashworthy, because the other name was
Ashworthy, don't you remember? I'm sure it was!"

"The other name?" said David, bewildered, thinking, wasn't it something else Mrs. Perfect had said—then, "Oh!" he said. "I've remembered. It wasn't Ashworthy; it was Elmworthy. Mrs. Perfect looked at an elm tree—I remember now—and said, 'Elmworthy.' "

"But you said yourself, David, that she wasn't sure except that it was the name of a tree and something short: ash is as short as elm."

"Ashworthy?" said David. "Well, perhaps, I suppose. Only I don't see——"

"I'll swear the Smiths' name is Ashworthy, and I'll swear the other name is Ashworthy too."

Before David could ask again what Adam meant by "the other name," he was being taken at a run across the garden and into the house. Adam planted him in the hall in front of Jonathan Codling's portrait. "Wait there!" David stared, in great confusion of mind, at Jonathan; Jonathan gazed back, with his usual knowing look.

In a moment, Adam was back with a chair, had mounted it and twisted the picture round, so that they were now looking at the family tree pasted on its back.

"There!" Adam's finger wavered only a second; then it stabbed directly at an entry near the beginning.

"Sarah Codling b. 1577; d. 1630; m. A. Ashworthy Esq."

"There!" cried Adam. "She married an Ashworthy; I knew I was right!"

"She married an Ashworthy, and the Smiths' full name is Ashworthy-Smith," said David. But he felt hardly clearer in his mind about what it all might mean.

Adam, however, was quite clear. "There were only two sets of people that would be sure to hear the rhyme of the treasure from Sarah Codling. One would be her own family, the Codlings; the other would be the family she married into, the Ashworthys. The Codlings handed the story of the rhyme down and hoped for the treasure some day; why shouldn't the Ashworthys have done the same? There may be Ashworthys now, at this very minute, who think they'd like to have a look for that treasure. And it seems to me more than suspicious that the name Ashworthy's cropped up just now. Somebody, for no reason at all, wants to buy the house, and all the time he's hiding his full name, and his full name is Ashworthy-Smith! Isn't that true?"

"Well, perhaps."

"Perhaps? And if it's true that the Ashworthy-Smiths are planning to deceive and rob us, do you think Aunt would sell to them?"

"Well——" began David; he was grasping at a hope.

"No, she wouldn't!" Then Adam's excitement seemed suddenly to cool. He put the portrait back, the right way round; he adjusted it exactly. Then he began to take the chair away. "And it's all too late. She'll be at the bus stop now. We can't possibly catch her and tell her and stop her."

"On my bicycle," David began and then remembered that his bicycle was at home in the shed; he had come by canoe. Then, "By canoe!" he cried. "Adam! We might just do it yet, by canoe—by canoe to the bridge!"

"How? How?"

"The bus from Great Barley takes the winding road, and it stops a lot, too, before it crosses the bridge at Little Barley on the way to Castleford. If we could get to the bridge——"

"By canoe!"

"Before the bus did—there's a bus stop near the bridge—we could get on the bus there—we could talk to your aunt—we could explain—we could stop her—"

As he spoke, David was already running toward where the *Minnow* lay peacefully moored; Adam was behind him.

There was just a chance for them if they were quick. The *Minnow* had never gone so quickly before—probably had never in all her reveries at the end of her mooring rope dreamed of being able to go as quickly as this. The two boys, working like pieces of exact, whirling machinery, flashed her past familiar landmarks that seemed like shapes in a dream—the Smiths' house, the old channel, the dock. At last, ahead, lay the bridge.

On the air was borne a low humming—the Castleford bus was coming. There was no time to slow up and draw neatly into the bank. Adam, who sat in the stern, steered the *Minnow* full tilt into the sloping bank of mud by the bridge. And even before her bow had come to rest in it, David was up, and from the canoe had taken something between a stride and a leap ashore. One foot went into deep mud and, for a second, seemed to be stuck there forever. Then something gave, and David's naked foot came out. He bothered no more about the loss than to shout "Shoe!" to Adam as he stormed up the bank. He burst through the hedge onto the highroad as the Castleford bus came into sight. There would certainly not be time, he realized at once, to reach the proper bus stop, which was more than a hundred yards down the road; he must just hope that the bus would stop for him without his being at the proper stop. He stood at the side of the road on one leg—the leg that was shod—and raised his hand, with an appearance of firmness and confidence that he was far from feeling.

21

The Bus to Castleford

WHILE DAVID stands with his hand up and the bus is coming nearer, there is time to explain something of importance in the running of the Castleford and County Omnibus Service.

The buses in this Service are, of course, country buses. For instance, the bus that is coming—and it is a little nearer David by now—is a single-decker. You never see a red bus in London that is a single-decker. The rules for buses in the country, too, have always been less hard and fast than in the towns. In the old days you only had to mention where you lived to the conductor of a country bus, in order to be set down at your very door if the bus went near it. There were several informal ways of making the bus stop to pick you up: you could wave from a window to it, and it would stop and wait for you; you could send someone ahead with the message that you were just coming, and it would wait for you. The most important thing was that it would stop anywhere—anywhere—along its route, to pick up and put down passengers.

Then, after many years, and to everyone's interest, notices labeled "Bus Stop" began to appear along the Castleford and County bus routes. People argued a good deal about the matter. Some used the bus stops; others paid no attention to them. The buses had to stop at all the new bus stops as well as at all the other places where people wanted to get on and off. The buses, in fact, seemed to have to stop even oftener than before the notices had been put up.

This state of affairs was not at all what the Management of the Service had intended. A meeting of all the bus drivers and conductors was called, and the Management pointed out that the bus-stop notices had been put up so that the buses should not have to stop anywhere but at the notices. People must learn, said the Management, that even in the country, you must get on and off only at bus stops. People must be taught a sharp lesson; bus drivers absolutely must ignore signals from people not at bus stops.

Mr. Moss was one of those who had to teach would-be passengers this unwelcome lesson; it was a thankless duty. Old Mr. Barncroft, of Jubilee Row, had given Mr. Moss a piece of his mind because Mr. Moss's bus had not stopped for him when he waved his stick. He was in the doorway of Mr. Ellum's shop—exactly halfway between two convenient bus stops. "And me lame!" said Mr. Barncroft indignantly. Mr. Moss, however, had pointed out that Mr. Barncroft knew the time of the bus, had had nothing else to do that afternoon but catch the bus, and could easily have gone straight to the nearest stop instead of expecting to be able to gossip with Frankie Ellum until the very minute he boarded the bus. The new rules, said Mr. Moss, if they were observed, could save his bus so much stopping time that it would be in Castleford quite ten minutes earlier. Moreover, Mr. Barncroft wasn't as lame as all that.

Mr. Barncroft was very angry with Mr. Moss, and for a time

took to walking to Tidfield railway halt and catching a slow train from there to Castleford. Then he slipped back into using the bus. He was never, apparently, convinced of the justice of the new rules, but he was waiting exactly at the bus stop when he next wanted to be driven into Castleford.

The bus is much nearer to David now. Mr. Moss himself happens to be driving it—and if you think that *that* is at all in David's favor, you mistake the working of Mr. Moss's mind.

Mr. Moss was humming contentedly to himself as he drove round the bend of the road and came within view of the Little Barley bridge. Then he caught sight of the figure at the side of the road, and the outstretched hand. He assumed, at once, the special, unseeing, cold expression that was necessary in the passing of these would-be boarders of buses. They were no better than pirates; and the drivers of the Castleford and County buses had thought that this kind of piracy was stamped out. No one now attempted it. Yet, here, standing by the Little Barley bridge and far from any bus stop, was another impudent one, due for a lesson.

The bus drew a little nearer, and Mr. Moss suddenly realized from what he saw out of the corner of his eye that the person at the side of the road was his own son. That he should dare! Mr. Moss almost choked with indignation.

When David saw his father's face behind the windshield, he knew he had no hope. The last accusation to which Mr. Moss would lay himself open would be that of favoritism.

The bus was almost level with David now, and it had not slackened speed at all. Mr. Moss looked at David, with the most deliberate hostility, from head to foot—and then was struck by the strange fact that he seemed to have only one leg and one foot. He was level with David before he saw the other leg and the other foot—naked. He was already past David, when the thought occurred to him that his wife would certainly not like it at all: there was no sign of David's other shoe, and he was a long way from home.

Mr. Moss put his brakes on rather suddenly, jarring the bus to a standstill, so that many of the passengers looked to see why it had stopped so abruptly. David, as he came up with it, saw their heads turned toward him—there were several faces he knew— Mrs. Tey's, for one. There was one head, under a rusty black hat, that did not turn: Miss Codling was on the bus, but quite unaware that David was about to board it.

The conductress slid the bus door back, and David climbed in. At the same time, up at the front of the bus, Mr. Moss twisted himself in the driver's seat, to call back through his little window, "Florrie, keep him safe—I'll have a word with him in Castleford!" The passengers who had not already seen David turned to have a good look now. Only Miss Codling's head never moved.

The conductress, Florrie, knew David. She usually did duty on Mr. Moss's bus, and she had been to Sunday tea with the Mosses, bringing her young man with her. She forced David into the seat at the very back of the bus and in the corner, and sat down next to him, with her knitting. The bus set off.

As Adam, free at last of the *Minnow* and the mud bank, came out onto the highroad he saw the bus rolling away toward Castleford, and he saw the back of David's head through the rear window. "He's done it!" he sighed with relief.

David was not happy, however. He could see Miss Codling, some way up the bus; there was even an empty seat beside her. But between him and the bus gangway sat Florrie, like a wardress. He could so plainly see Miss Codling's hat, nodding evenly with the motion of the bus; but she never turned her head. David dared not call out to attract her attention. Florrie looked grim enough to gag him at once with her knitting. He would have to wait until the bus terminus in Castleford when Miss Codling would be passing quite close by his seat as she got out.

At the terminus, everybody stood up and began filing off the bus. Florrie stood up too, but still keeping the position that prevented David's escape. Upright, her body was an even more formidable barrier: he could catch only glimpses of the people passing her. He was almost frantic lest he should miss his chance. Then, at a little distance, he saw Miss Codling, fullface. She actually looked at him, and, to his horror, looked through him: her eyes were unseeing, and her face wore such an expression of misery as she had never allowed herself in his and Adam's presence. She did not recognize him, and in another second David had lost sight of her. He called to her, but no one the other side of Florrie's body could have heard him. Then, through the crook of Florrie's arm, he saw a familiar black cotton glove —Miss Codling's. It was already level with him. In another moment, it would have passed. Boldly, he darted out his hand to catch hold of it. He could no longer see, and his fingers fumbled in vain among coats and shopping baskets. His fingers glided, without his knowing it, over the strap of Miss Codling's handbag. Then the handbag, the gloved hand, and Miss Codling herself had passed. Surely his chance had gone forever.

"Bag snatching!" cried a thin, unpleasant voice. "I saw him attempting it!"

From behind Miss Codling, Mrs. Tey had pounced upon David's unsuccessful hand, and now held it tightly by the wrist. The suddenness and excitement of the arrest made an uproar that could not be contained in the narrow gangway of the bus. Besides, Mrs. Tey was still being carried along in the stream of passengers getting out. She still held tightly to David, and Florrie still tried to keep in front of him. All three were swept out of the bus and onto the pavement behind Miss Codling, whom Mrs. Tey immediately tried to secure as a witness.

"Bag snatching?" said Miss Codling, bewildered. And then, catching sight of the accused, "David!" in a tone of the greatest astonishment.

"I must speak to you, Miss Codling," David said.

"The person you speak to is a policeman," said Mrs. Tey.

"The person you speak to is your father," said Florrie, breathless through being hustled, and much annoyed.

"Now!" Mr. Moss had left the driver's seat and come round to the back of the bus to claim David for sternest questioning. He found David in the middle of an excited little group, and with Mrs. Tey's fingers clamped round his wrist, like a handcuff. Mr. Moss must have heard her accusation.

Mr. Moss was taller than any of the three women—even than Florrie. He lowered one large hand into the midst of them and picked Mrs. Tey's fingers off David as though they had been green fly on roses. "I'll trouble you!" he said, in a way that made Mrs. Tey shrink and seem to lose all interest in the case. She sidled away, pursued by Mr. Moss's glare.

The group was breaking up. Mr. Smith was waiting and had already stepped up to Miss Codling. Now he touched her on the arm and raised his hat. "Miss Codling, if the brawl does not concern you—I have the taxi waiting."

"You can't go—you mustn't!" cried David.

Mr. Smith's eyebrows rose, and Miss Codling said uncertainly, "Why not, David?"

"You mustn't."

"But why?"

"Adam and I—" began David desperately, not in the least knowing how he should go on.

"Oh!" said Miss Codling, with sudden coldness. "So this is one of Adam's ideas. I'm afraid, David, that I have important business. I cannot keep Mr. Smith waiting."

"Please, Miss Codling! Please!" David was almost crying, but it did not seem as if that were likely to move Miss Codling. She was just turning away, when Mr. Moss gently detained her.

"Miss Codling," he said gravely, "I don't know the rights of this matter, but David's usually a reliable boy." His face clouded over a moment after, with the memory of David's recent behavior, but he added nothing to what he had already said.

THE BUS TO CASTLEFORD

"That's true," said Miss Codling. "David, say what you have to say, quickly."

How could he? How could he tell Miss Codling, in front of these other people—in front of Mr. Smith himself—the long story of Mrs. Perfect, the elm tree, the ash tree, the family tree? Besides, he realized for the first time that Adam's theory was far-fetched—silly. David was silent. Miss Codling made a gesture of impatience, and began to turn away—this time, not even Mr. Moss would be able to stop her.

"Miss Codling," said David at last, with desperate significance, "you'll be sorry if you sell to Mr. Ashworthy-Smith."

He saw from her blank face that his shot had misfired: Miss Codling did not understand. Over her shoulder, however, Mr. Smith's face went a dark red. David thought it was the sign of a terrible anger, and instinctively cowered back. The face became a deeper and deeper red, and when it seemed as if it could go no darker without becoming quite black, color began to ebb from it, leaving it a dreadful gray. At the same time there was a choking sound from Mr. Smith's open mouth, and he swayed and stumbled. Miss Codling and Mr. Moss caught at him, and the taxi driver ran from behind and held him up. There was a moment of confused alarm in which David thought that he had murdered Mr. Smith in the presence of witnesses.

Then Mr. Smith, still gray-faced, still supported by the driver's arm, was speaking—although only in whispers and gasps, "I'm not well. It's nothing, but—Miss Codling, my apologies—I—home!" He waved his hand, unable to speak more, and closed his eyes, exhausted. Miss Codling gave the taxi driver his address, and Mr. Moss and he between them helped Mr. Smith into the taxi. Miss Codling would have got in with him— "He should have someone with him," she said anxiously—but Mr. Smith showed such painful distress at the idea that she thought it better not to insist.

The taxi drove off toward Barley, leaving Miss Codling, Mr. Moss, Florrie, and David staring.

"Well!" said Mr. Moss, at last. He looked at David as if he were now going to have with him the "word" he had promised. Florrie folded her arms to enjoy it at ease. But Mr. Moss only said, "You'll go home by the next bus, David."

"And I'll go with him," said Miss Codling. "We can have a talk together on the bus."

In the time before the next bus, Mr. Moss treated them all to cups of tea and sausage rolls at the busmen's coffee stall. The party was a silent one. Mr. Moss asked no questions about the strange happenings of the last hour, and sternly crushed in Florrie any signs of curiosity. Miss Codling was quite silent, thinking, and waiting to be alone with David. David was too thankful to want to talk.

In the bus back to Barley, David told Miss Codling the whole story.

"Well," she said at the end, "it's very striking."

"And Adam's idea's right—it must be right, or Mr. Smith wouldn't have had a fit, or whatever it was, just because I said his name."

Miss Codling nodded, as though she were really impressed. "Davy," she said, "you have been most kind and resourceful." Yet she seemed, strangely, not to share in his soaring spirits.

At the bus stop in the middle of Great Barley, Adam was waiting. His brow cleared when he saw his aunt and David get off the bus together, and saw David's brilliant smile. He handed David his shoe—cleaned of mud, and with only the shoe-lace broken—without a word. He kissed his aunt as though they had met again after long separation and estrangement.

It was a glorious end to the day, for both the boys. David went home, half dancing, in spite of the clipclopping of his loose shoe. He had Miss Codling's permission to tell his parents everything. He told the story to his mother first. Mrs. Moss stared, and wrung her hands—when David went barefoot into Castleford; and shook her fist—at Mrs. Tey; and seemed much more moved by the thought of what might have happened to David than by the thought of what might have happened to Codlings' and its treasure. Mr. Moss, when he came home in the evening, made a better listener. He listened to the account of Adam's and David's deductions and actions; he sympathized with their triumph; he even accepted the importance of David's mission as an excuse for his hailing the bus so incorrectly.

David went blithely to bed that night. Yet if he had heard his father's remark just after he had closed the door behind him, he might have felt differently.

"All very well," said Mr. Moss, "but if they don't sell to this Andrew Ashworthy-Smith, they'll still have to sell to someone."

22

The Smiths at Home

MISS CODLING sat at her father's writing desk, an envelope between her fingers.

"I wonder if you would deliver this for me, David?" She twisted the envelope slightly, so that David could read the direction on it: *Urgent*. To Mrs. Andrew Ashworthy-Smith.

"I just want it delivered, and a simple answer brought back— Yes or No. I don't want anything discussed—that's why I would rather you went than Adam or me. They won't question you. You would be just a messenger. You'd just wait on the doorstep until you got your answer, Yes or No, and then bring it back to me."

David was silent. He would have liked to know what Adam thought, but Adam stood behind his aunt's chair, his eyes on the ground.

"I could send it by Squeak, but the letter is important, and Squeak—well, he isn't always reliable. I could post it, but it

might be days before I had my answer, and I must—I *must*—
have an answer quickly. Will you deliver the letter for me,
David?"

"What does it say?" David blurted out, at last.

"You have done so much, you have some right to know. I
am writing to Mrs. Smith, instead of to Mr. Smith, because if he is
ill, he ought not to be bothered with business. On the other
hand, I must know as soon as possible whether he is likely to want
me to go on with the sale of Codlings' to him. That is what I
have said in the letter."

"Still to sell Codlings'!"

"David, don't you understand? Whoever Mr. Smith is, the
house must still be sold; and so far he has been the only person to
show any willingness to buy it."

"Sell Codlings'!"

"Unless we sell, Adam and I have no money—nothing to
live on."

Miss Codling advanced the letter, for the third time, toward
David. He drew his hands back, as though from an instrument of
murder. Adam lifted his head and said heavily, "Aunt Dinah's
quite right. There's no other way."

"Will you, David?"

David took the letter.

A little later, when he stood on the Smiths' doorstep, he felt
some nervousness for himself, as well as gloom about his mission.
He had rung the bell, but after the sound of the bell had stopped,
there was so long a silence that he began to hope that the house
was empty, or that the inmates were all asleep. Perhaps, even,
Mr. Smith had died—how would that affect Miss Codling's course
of action?

Then there were footsteps, and the door was opened by Mrs.
Smith herself. David offered her the letter. "And, please, I'm
to wait for an answer."

Mrs. Smith took the letter, but as though she did not fully
understand that it was for her. Her whole manner was somehow

distracted; her eyes, behind the thick lenses of her glasses, looked red, as if with crying. Perhaps Mr. Smith was dead.

Mrs. Smith turned the letter over in her hand twice, and then opened it and read it, at first with the same absent-minded air, and then with close attention. Her first remark brought Mr. Smith unmistakably to life. "He's been waiting for this—for some word from Miss Codling. He seems to have nothing but that business of buying the house fixed in his head." She began to cry quietly as she spoke. "And he won't take care of his health, and he came home from Castleford so dreadfully ill in that taxi." She wiped away her tears and controlled herself. "Anyway, I can't give any answer myself. I must ask him. Wait here."

She left David on the doorstep. Miss Codling seemed really to have foreseen exactly how the mission would go, and David felt more confident. He looked through the open door into the Smiths' house: it did not seem alarming—the colors were cheerful; there was sunlight; there were bowls of flowers. But the answer that Mrs. Smith finally brought was by no means a simple Yes or No, but: "He wants to see you."

"Oh, no!" cried David. "It wouldn't be any good. I mean, I'm just a messenger. I can't—"

Yet he was inside, and the front door shut behind him, and Mrs. Smith was pushing him upstairs in front of her. She only let him pause on the landing, because she had something to say in a lowered voice. "You're a sensible boy?"

"Sensible?"

"I mean, he's been so ill—he mustn't be excited or worried. He oughtn't to be thinking about business at all—but he's always headstrong, and he won't let me do anything for him. He insists on speaking to you alone. Promise you won't upset him—you'll be sensible?"

"Yes," said David, without being quite sure what he had promised.

Mrs. Smith nodded at him as though to seal the agreement.

Then she softly opened a door, pushed him inside, and as softly closed the door behind him.

David felt himself almost sightless: the windows of the room let in hardly any light—heavy curtains were draped over one, and a thick blind was drawn down over the other. There was less light from outside than from the fire, that in spite of the summer day, flickered in the hearth. The room seemed too still to be anything but empty, but David peered nervously round. He could distinguish vaguely the shapes of empty armchairs, and a table, and a tall cupboard with glass doors, from behind which came glints of gold and deep, rich colors, where the firelight gleamed on the contents. Over the fireplace hung a mirror, round whose frame gilded mermaids and dolphins sported; mermaids leaned forward, combing their hair and gazing at themselves in the glass. David was marveling at them when his eye was caught by a faint movement in the shadowy depths of the reflection. He turned quickly to face whatever it was.

"Who's there?" he asked.

There was no answer, but David saw the shape of a couch in the far corner of the room, and someone lying on it.

"Who's there?" he repeated.

There was a further silence; then a whispering voice said, "Andrew Ashworthy-Smith. Come here. I can't shout."

David went over to the couch, and looked down on Mr. Smith's face: it was very pale, and the eyes were shut. Suddenly the eyes opened widely at him. "You're the boy that called me by that name in Castleford, aren't you?"

"Yes."

"Why?"

"Well," said David, "we knew—Adam and I knew—Adam's Miss Codling's nephew, you see—we knew that your name was partly the same as the name of someone Sarah Codling married— Sarah Codling, you see——"

"I see; I know." With a gesture of the hand, Mr. Smith silenced him. He let his eyelids droop, wearily. "Miss Codling wants an answer to her letter. The answer—" he paused, breathing slowly. "My daughter will give her the answer." Again his eyes flew open to stare at David. "Does that surprise you?"

"Your daughter? I don't know. I mean, I don't understand. Your daughter?"

Mr. Smith laughed to himself—a whispering laugh that seemed to exhaust him for a little. "So you don't know everything!" he said presently. He reached his hand to a bell rope that hung by his side, and pulled it feebly. David heard the bell ringing downstairs. While it was still ringing, the door opened—Mrs. Smith must have been waiting outside.

"You're not feeling worse, Andrew?" she said hurriedly.

"No, but Elizabeth is to be sent for at once."

"You are feeling worse!"

"No! Rubbish! You misunderstand! This is a matter of business: Elizabeth is to act for me, with Miss Codling."

"But, Andrew, Betsy's hardly more than a child! And her grandmother may not want——"

"I said, telephone to Elizabeth." The man on the couch strained upward painfully, until he had half raised himself on his elbows. "Telephone!" David could feel the strength of a single-aimed, passionate will—"willfulness," Mrs. Perfect had called it. Perhaps this was Mr. Smith's debt to a Codling ancestry, but Mr. Smith's temper was unsoftened by any of the gentleness that even queer old Mr. Codling had shown. The Codlings living by the Say seemed to have some of the character of their river: the Say might have times of impetuous flood, but its habitual flow was gentle, steady. The stream of Mr. Smith's desires was smoothly racing until it met some obstacle; then it boiled into appalling whirlpools and torrents. To all this Mr. Smith added a characteristic by which men, not rivers, are sometimes distinguished—unscrupulousness.

"I care nothing about Elizabeth's age, or her grandmother. It is essential to my plans that she should be here. Telephone her."

"Yes, Andrew, I will—oh, I will!"

Mr. Smith subsided. He rested a while, and then spoke calmly, almost genially. "And this boy—he has his answer for the time being; he can go."

Mrs. Smith laid a hand on David's shoulder, and began taking him with her out of the room. As they reached the door Mr. Smith called, "Boy!"

"Yes?"

"I never asked your name."

"David—David Moss."

"I shan't remember that. But I shall remember you as the boy who knows everything, except that he doesn't know quite everything. You will, when you see my daughter!" Mr. Smith's speech ended in a kind of wheezing, which David could just recognize, fearfully, as a paroxysm of laughter. Meanwhile, Mrs. Smith was fairly hauling him out of the room, and then downstairs.

"There!" she said. "You've got your answer. Go."

"But Miss Codling wants a real answer, Yes or No."

"When Betsy has seen her father, she'll give you that."

"But it's urgent. When will the answer be?"

"I'm going to put a trunk call through to London now. She'll be down tomorrow morning, at least."

"And when can she tell Miss Codling?"

"Oh, soon after that—very soon, I'm sure. Go now—go!" Mrs. Smith pushed David out of the front door and shut it. As he stepped off the doorstep he heard her, inside, lifting the telephone receiver and asking for Trunks.

He walked back to Codlings' in confusion of mind. When he had told Miss Codling and Adam his experiences, he felt that he had done no more than share his bewilderment with them.

"Never mind, David," said Miss Codling. "I don't see what else you could have done. It's all very odd. Anyway, we shall know more when this Elizabeth Smith comes."

"She's the girl they wouldn't have seen in the village at any price," said Adam.

David shivered. "I wonder . . ."

"People who are so unfortunate as to be deformed or ugly in some way are to be pitied, not feared," said Miss Codling. "Anyway, whenever the bell rings tomorrow, I shall go and answer it myself. You both understand? No one is to answer the bell but me."

The front doorbell did not often ring at Codlings': there were few visitors. Yet it rang that afternoon, some hours later. Miss Codling was at work in old Mr. Codling's study, with both the boys. They were sorting books: the few books that Adam and Miss Codling would have room for in Birmingham; the more valuable books that they hoped to be able to sell in the auction; others that would go to some village jumble sale. As Miss Codling said, they must sell the house and leave it, and before that, they must clear it of all its contents. The job would be a long one, and the sooner it was begun, the better.

"Bother!" said Miss Codling at the interruption of the bell's ringing. "Answer it, Adam!"

Adam left his aunt and David still at work and went down the hall to the front door. He could see obscurely through the frosted glass; the caller was no one he knew from the village. Yet somehow, strangely, there was familiarity. He paused for a moment, with his hand on the doorknob, almost as if afraid. Then he opened the door, and the caller half turned to face him; she parted her lips to speak, but remained silent, her mouth still absurdly in an oh! of stupefaction.

They looked at each other, as a face looks at its reflection in the mirror—only, here, which was face and which was reflection? Two living faces and yet the same dark-red hair, the same eyes, the same pallor of skin, the same line of feature.

The girl gazed as if permanently robbed of the power of speech; Adam was the first to recover himself a little, because he could at least make some guess at an explanation. He bowed in a stiff, old-fashioned way to the image of himself—a bow that fitted the oddity of the situation, and yet seemed all the stranger since the girl could only be a year or two older than himself. "Please come in."

She followed him down the hall, still without speaking. She stopped when he stopped at the portrait of Jonathan Codling. He made a turn to look at it, and silently invited her to do the same. Side by side, they seemed to lose themselves in the study of it.

Meanwhile, in the midst of her work among the books, Miss Codling had paused to listen, wondering who the visitor might be. The delay in Adam's appearance and the odd silence suddenly alarmed her. With David at her heels, she went to the study door, opened it, and looked out.

The creak of the door made Adam and his companion turn together. Miss Codling and David saw them both fullface, and between and behind them the face of Jonathan Codling. The centuries shrank to nothing; the three faces looked like an artist's study of one close family group; the resemblance was overwhelming.

Miss Codling, like Adam, quickly recovered herself, and swept forward. "Elizabeth Ashworthy-Smith," she said, "we did not expect you so soon." She did not offer her hand, and her voice was severe in tone. She led the way into the study, and the door was shut upon Adam and David.

They waited in the hall, and then in the kitchen; they waited longer and longer. They grew hungry. It was time that David —who had not meant to stay to tea—went home, but there was no question of his going until they knew the purpose of this visit and its outcome.

At last the study door opened and Miss Codling came out, with her visitor. They moved slowly down the hall to the front door, where they halted. Elizabeth Smith said something—it was the first time that the boys had heard her voice: it was hesitant and soft—so soft that the words were indistinguishable at a distance. Miss Codling answered, "Yes, tomorrow, please," and bade good-by, taking the girl's hand in her own as she did so. Then she turned back into the house.

Adam and David rushed forward into the hall to meet her. "Well?"

Miss Codling looked musingly at them—especially at Adam. She put her finger under his chin and tilted his face upward. "Elizabeth Ashworthy-Smith and Adam Codling: a common ancestor four centuries back, and this freak of resemblance—this face." With her other hand, she moved a lock of Adam's red hair. "She might be your sister—your elder sister—and a sister to be proud of."

"Proud of?"

"She is—yes, she is going to be beautiful."

Adam snorted.

"And if—as I have no reason to doubt—she grows up as good as she will be beautiful——"

"Good!" burst out Adam. "What about her father? What's he been up to?"

"His business."

"What is his business?"

"He's a dealer in antiques and art treasures."

"So that's it!" The boys began to understand.

"He is the kind of businessman—" Miss Codling hesitated, and David felt sure that the memory of her interview with Elizabeth was influencing—softening—the choice of words she made. "Well, he runs an important business with branches in New York and Paris, and no doubt—no doubt at all—he is very astute; but he is not—well, he is not perhaps the nicest kind of businessman." Miss Codling allowed herself to go on with greater firmness. "And as a man—and especially as a family man—he is certainly one of the most selfish and stupid. Perhaps, indeed, he can't feel real fondness for any mere human being, but to keep that child apart from her mother all these years—" Miss

Codling positively stamped her foot. "All the treasures in the world cannot justify it!"

"It's the treasure he's been after all the time?"

"Yes, so he told Elizabeth before he sent her here. His grandmother was an Ashworthy from Cumberland. The story of the treasure has been steadily handed down by the Ashworthys, and then by the Ashworthy-Smiths. But Mr. Smith was the first one of the family to start looking for it. In the course of his business, more wonderful and valuable things must have passed through his hands, but he set his heart on this. As far as I can understand such a man, I think the treasure must have become an obsession—almost a madness—that has in secret devoured all his thought and feeling. He told his wife and daughter nothing of what he intended, but he found out where the remains of the Codling family still lived, and he settled as near to them as he could. What exactly he meant to do next, I don't expect he knew himself. To begin with, I suppose, he wanted to get on intimate terms with us—you remember, he brought his wife to pay a visit here. On that one and only visit he saw the portrait of Jonathan Codling in the hall—perhaps he saw Adam too."

"He did," said Adam.

"Anyway, the queer family resemblance to his daughter must have struck him at once. He would realize that if he ever allowed her to be seen in Barley, the secret might be guessed."

"Well, then," said Adam, who wanted to dislike all the Smiths, "Mrs. Smith must have known too, because she came with him on the visit when he saw the picture."

Miss Codling was amused, but not at Adam. "It seems that Mrs. Smith must join to her over-docility a kind of obstinate little vanity. She is very short-sighted, and yet won't be seen wearing glasses in public."

"That's true," said David. He remembered meeting her blind, blank stare in the village street.

"So Mr. Smith could rely on his wife's not noticing any

resemblance; he could also forbid his daughter ever to visit her parents here—and enforce his order." Miss Codling wagged her head in a way that reminded David of Mrs. Perfect in the church-yard. "Some men are indeed masters of their households!"

"Mrs. Perfect thinks Mrs. Smith gives in to him too much," said David.

"Far too much. A mother to allow herself to be separated from her daughter! Your mother, David, would never stand for such a piece of nonsense for Becky."

"But I don't think my father——"

"Of course not. Nor is giving way to husbands by any means good for them. Poor gentle, silly Mrs. Smith has not only allowed her daughter to be made lonely and often unhappy, but en-couraged her husband to become a selfish rogue. Yes, a selfish rogue!"

"That's it!" cried Adam, with enthusiasm.

Miss Codling at once calmed herself, probably regretting the lengths to which she had been carried. She returned to the story. "Anyway, Mr. Smith was so clever that by the time Codlings' came up for sale his secret was still safe. He could pose as just an ordinary person thinking of buying just an ordinary house. He was convinced the old hiding place was somewhere on the property, and so he would in the end get his hands on the treasure if only he kept quiet about it."

"Whereas now——"

"Now, he is known as a kinsman—a kinsman, although a very remote one—who is bent on laying his hands upon a family treasure. Well, he's been forced into the open about it. When the grandmother in London had Mrs. Smith's message, Elizabeth was sent rushing down by the very first train, and took her instructions from her father at once. He told her everything—everything, that is, except about her resemblance to Adam and the portrait. I think he must have held that back as one little joke he could still enjoy against people he is sure are really so much less clever than he. That was the last piece of trickery. Now, everything is known. Elizabeth came round here with orders to lay all his cards on the table—not a very pleasant job for her!"

"What's going to happen next? Does he still want to buy the house?"

"Certainly he does."

"Then nothing is changed, really."

"Indeed it is. If Mr. Smith has a head for business, so have I. Selling a house and garden is a very different thing from selling a house and a garden and—somewhere—a treasure."

"What's very different?"

Miss Codling's eyes glinted. Her voice had an edge to it as she said: "The price!"

23

From Cellar to Roof

D AVID WAS NOT foolishly romantic, but he could not help feeling some shock at the enthusiasm with which Miss Codling now threw herself into bargaining with Mr. Smith. Before, she had seemed to act only from a sense of necessity; now, the thought that she had nearly been cheated roused her fully. Again and again during the week she sent Elizabeth Smith back to her father with a rejection of the terms newly, and newly again, proposed. She wanted a better bargain.

What Miss Codling and Mr. Smith were arguing about now was not the price of the house and garden as much as the price of exclusive information about the treasure. Miss Codling had already admitted that her father had found Jonathan Codling's hiding place, removed the treasure, and hidden it again on his own account. She said, quite frankly, that the clue *he* had left behind was even more obscure in meaning than Jonathan Codling's. So far, they—that is, Adam and David—had been able to solve only one small part of it, and thereafter they had stuck. Miss Codling had no reason, as she said, to think that Mr. Smith would be any more successful than two quick-witted boys.

Elizabeth Smith carried Miss Codling's explanations to her father. He sent back to say that whatever the clue to the present whereabouts of the treasure—however little information it yielded —he was prepared to buy it when he bought the house. He would pay handsomely, he said, at this price; at that price, retorted Miss Codling. So, through Elizabeth, they haggled, Mr. Smith's offer slowly rising, and Miss Codling's even more slowly sinking. One day the two offers must meet in agreement.

Meanwhile, looking ahead to the time of that agreement, Miss Codling was pushing on with the sorting of the contents of the house. After the books in old Mr. Codling's study, there was the collection of stuffed birds in glass cases, which he had chosen to range against his bedroom walls. Most of the specimens would have to go to a jumble sale; some might be welcome in the natural-history section of the museum in Castleford.

Apart from old Mr. Codling's study and bedroom, the in-habited rooms of the house were sparsely and poorly furnished, and the other rooms were quite bare. When David mentioned this at home, Mr. Moss looked at his wife. "I hope we never fall so short that we sell our sticks of furniture to live on." And, as if in answer to this, Mrs. Moss at once started making another great cake for David to take with him on his next visit to Codlings'.

Besides all the rooms of the house to be gone through, there were the outlying buildings. In the potting shed, for instance, Adam and David brought to light a regiment of flowerpots, which Squeak took off Miss Codling's hands. The garden tools there were all in good condition—Miss Codling was too careful a gardener ever to have neglected them. One or two that Squeak coveted were given to him; the rest were listed and stacked, to go into the auction sale.

Adam and David even crept into the half-ruined summer-house and handed out to Miss Codling the junk they found there

—the old canoe cushions that went straight on to Squeak's bon-
fire, wormy skeletons of deck chairs, and rusty croquet hoops.
The set of bowls, in their case, were the only things of value, and
Miss Codling decided to present them to the Barley Bowling
Club.

Elizabeth Smith would often arrive, as she had done on her
first visit, to find Miss Codling and the boys busy at their dusty
work. After delivering the latest message and offer from her
father, she would start helping them, or if they seemed very
weary, she would slip away to brew tea in the kitchen where she
now seemed quite at home. Miss Codling said she made an
excellent cup of tea, but then she liked everything about Elizabeth—except her father. Miss Codling already spoke of her as
Betsy, and David followed this example, but nervously, for he
knew that Adam did not approve of the familiarity. You might
have thought that no one could help liking Elizabeth Smith, but
Adam achieved that seeming impossibility quite easily. He spoke
to her only when he had to, and then with a stiff politeness
that was really far from polite; he called her Elizabeth, always.
Miss Codling and David nodded and applauded when Betsy,
beaming, poured out the tea and talked—she loved talking, perhaps because she had so little opportunity in her grandmother's
quiet household—but Adam would only scowl down at his plate.
It was amazing that, with such a difference of expression, the two
faces could still be so alike.

In these circumstances, Betsy became David's friend, but not
Adam's. To David, she was garrulously confiding in a way
that reminded him of Becky—he saw what it might be like to
have an elder sister as well as a younger one. This talk, however,
was much more exciting than Becky's. He heard, for example,
of things that Betsy's father had done on business trips abroad:
he had climbed to the top of the Eiffel Tower in Paris, and seen
police cars chasing gangsters in New York, and—rather surprisingly—been taken in a Red Indian canoe to shoot rapids.

"I say!" said David, at the last. (It seemed a pity that Mr.

Smith was not a nicer person, with all that experience.) "Have you shot rapids?"

"Not yet. I haven't actually been in a canoe at all yet. I rather wondered . . ."

She hesitated, and David, who suddenly saw what she was wondering, tried to bring the conversation back to safety. "Go on telling me about rapids and Red Indians."

"I wondered," said Betsy pleadingly, "whether you'd take me in your canoe. You've told me all about the voyages for treasure, and I do want to see the places you went to—Folly Mill, and the bridge Darius Codling built, and oh"—she clasped her hands together, and her eyes sparkled—"especially the secret river!"

"The secret river?"

"I mean, the old channel that no one knew about until you found it."

"I could take you by road and show you Folly Mill and Darius' bridge, any time."

"And the secret river? I could go with you in the *Minnow* to see that?"

David went red. "There's nothing worth seeing—really there isn't, Betsy."

"But couldn't we? I'd paddle and do just what you told me."

"Well, you see—you see, the canoe isn't really mine. I mean, I share it." Betsy waited for him to go on. "With Adam."

Betsy still did not see what David was trying to tell her. Indeed, she said, "Well, he wouldn't mind my going in it with you, would he?"

David wanted to say, No, he wouldn't. But he knew that would be useless. "I'll ask him," he said miserably. "In private."

The private conversation was even unpleasanter than David had expected. It gave Adam his opportunity for an outburst against the Smiths, and against Betsy in particular.

"I don't trust her," he said.

"Well, I do," said David. "And your aunt does. You heard

her say she thinks Elizabeth's going to be as good as she'll be beautiful."

"Beautiful!" said Adam scornfully. And then, "They say she's like me."

"So she is."

"Ah!" Adam pounced. "You're not going to say I shall grow up to be beautiful." He pushed a threatening face toward David.

"No, of course not."

"Very well. Either she's not going to be beautiful or she's not like me. Choose. You can't have it both ways."

"But it's something quite different——"

"Choose."

"All right!" cried David, driven beyond all patience. "She jolly well is going to be beautiful, so she's not a bit like you."

Adam had hoped for an answer the other way round—that Betsy was not going to be beautiful, and—if one thing followed another—was not going to be good, and probably wasn't good now. He gave David a glance of deep reproach, and turned on his heel. Then he remembered that he had never dealt with the question that had opened the conversation. He came back.

"I said the canoe was yours now, and so it is, and you can do what you like with it. But—well, if I still had a share, I'd rather the canoe were rotting at the bottom of the Say than with *her* in it!"

He left David appalled, as if by blasphemy.

Adam had expressed only a wish, but such a passionate one that David knew he must respect it as much more. He told Betsy that Adam did not want them to use the canoe, and that was that. She did not argue, but her eyes rounded as though she were going to cry—whether at the thought of now never being able to see "the secret river," or at the sting of Adam's unkindness, David could not tell. He noticed that after this she never tried to tease Adam into an answer or a smile any more.

Adam could not accept Betsy, because he still could not accept the idea of losing the house. He must certainly have despaired by now of solving his grandfather's clues, but perhaps he still hoped, even by chance, to come across the hiding place of the treasure. David had noticed that as they took the books off the built-in shelves in old Mr. Codling's study, Adam had softly rapped and pressed and pushed at the back of each shelf. In his grandfather's bedroom he had done the same to the walls against which the specimen cases had been standing. In the potting shed he had examined every inch of the hard-beaten earth floor. He had done the same in the summerhouse. Finally, he raised with his aunt the question of looking through the cellars—"for anything you might be able to sell."

"But there'll be nothing there, Adam. The cellars haven't been used for as long as I can remember. The steps down to them crumbled and were never repaired; your grandfather said they weren't safe, and always kept the door locked."

"Still," said Adam, "I could be very careful going down the stairs, now you've warned me, and I might find some bottles of very old wine that had been forgotten, and they could go into the auction."

"I don't for a moment think you will find anything," said Miss Codling, "but you can go if you promise to be careful. The cellar-door key hangs on the key ring with the others. It's labeled. Take the torch with you. You'll be able to slither down the stairs all right, but if you can't get back easily, you must shout for David or me."

"I think I'd like to go too," said David. Adam said nothing to this, but as he did not repel the suggestion, they went together. As they were clambering down the broken stairway Adam said, "It's not really bottles of wine I'm after, at all."

"I thought not."

"We might come across Grandfather's hiding place here. There might even be a secret tunnel leading from here under the river. And just where it passes under the water, we might find the treasure. One of the clues is 'under the water.'"

"But what about the other clues—Philip, and the single rose, and your aunt knowing where the place is?" To which Adam gave no answer.

The cellar was dank and dark. In spite of their chilling feeling of being buried alive, the boys conscientiously examined the walls and floors: everywhere there was nothing but the most solid of masonry. The racks for wine were, as Miss Codling had foreseen, quite empty: there was not a bottle in the place. All they found, in one corner, was an old horn lantern, made almost unrecognizable by its winding sheet of cobwebs—black, sticky cobwebs that only a cellar spider would have had the heart to make.

They did not, after all, need Miss Codling's help to get up the stairway again, although it was more like scaling a treacherous mountain slope than walking up ordinary steps.

Miss Codling was shocked at the dust they had rubbed into themselves in the cellar. "Why ever did I let you go down there!"

"But look what we've found," said David, holding up the lantern. "Is it valuable?"

Adam was scraping the cobwebs off it. "It's old, anyway," he said. "Perhaps the museum would like it with the stuffed birds."

"There was no wine at all," said David. "Not a drop."

"Well, you see," said Miss Codling apologetically, "although this house may have the biggest cellar in Barley, it's a very long time since any of us had enough money to keep anything in it. And, although it may be the biggest cellar, I can see from you two that it must be in a dreadful state."

"Oh, well," said David, "it doesn't matter about a cellar if you haven't any wine anyway."

"But of course we have!" cried Miss Codling suddenly. "All those years ago! I'd quite forgotten! We have some wine—at least, wine of a sort—homemade stuff."

"Oh?" said David. "Not in the cellar?" He could only show polite interest. His eyes were on Adam, cleaning the lantern.

"It was made from an old recipe that Adam's grandfather found," said Miss Codling, addressing David, who was the only one who seemed to be listening. "We made it—how clearly I remember now!—to cheer up Adam's mother. Only she wasn't his mother yet; she was expecting him to be born in the spring. The summer before, I was making the wine—it was a great bother: you had to add all the different ingredients of fruit and flowers as they came into season. All the time, my father kept telling Adam's mother that the wine would be in its jars by the time the baby was born, and we could try a first taste of it to celebrate John's homecoming." Miss Codling sighed and shook her head. "Poor Father! He was so pleased with his idea—so excited! He wanted the wine to be kept in a specially safe place —we'd lost a jar of it, quite early on—so that it should be ready for the celebrations. Then, John was killed, and Adam's mother died, and there was no question of any celebration, and the wine is still where my father stowed it so hopefully—in the roof."

"In the roof!" said Adam, waking from his inattention. "Why on earth did he choose to put anything there?"

"I've no idea," said Miss Codling, "except that it was a safe place because no one ever went up there. It was an odd place to choose, but your grandfather would never be dissuaded. Up he went into the roof with his wine."

"He went up into the roof to store wine?"

"Adam, I've just said so."

"I mean, only for that?"

"Well, I believe he went several times afterward. He said he wanted to make sure the wine was safe."

"But you said he chose that place just because it would be so safe there? And it was only wine after all."

"Oh, Adam! What does it matter anyway?"

Adam, in spite of his aunt's irritation, was not going to let the subject drop. David had seen hope spring into his face again. Old Mr. Codling's excuse for going up into the roof, again and again, seemed very thin. Homemade wine, indeed! Perhaps there was a hiding place in the roof into which Mr. Codling had put something far more precious—the treasure.

"Don't you think, Aunt Dinah," said Adam, "that David and I ought to go into the roof and get that wine down before you forget it again?"

Miss Codling did not want to abandon the wine, but she was loath to let them go. "It'll make you even dirtier."

"But, Aunt, we're already so dirty, it's just the time to choose to go."

"You'll be filthy again when Betsy arrives—she's sure to come."

Adam frowned. David said quickly, "Betsy doesn't mind dirt; it's just chance that she's so clean to look at."

"Oh, very well, then!" Miss Codling gave in for the second time that day. "There's a trap door in the ceiling of your grandfather's room, Adam. You'll need the stepladder to reach it, and the torch again, when you're up."

Miss Codling held the quaking old stepladder, while first Adam, then David, mounted toward the trap door. Adam pushed at the door. "Harder!" cried Miss Codling, from below. He got his shoulders underneath it and heaved, and suddenly the trap door rose and clattered back out of sight, leaving a square of blackness, into which the boys climbed one after the other.

Are the tops and bottoms of houses always equally black? wondered David, while he waited for Adam to switch on the torch.

Miss Codling's voice came from below. "The wine jars are under the tank, I think you'll find."

At the same time Adam's torch went on, and the beam swept round. It lit up joists and other timbering, the slates of the roof sloping above their heads, and a great zinc tank from which pipes passed downward through the floor.

"Under the tank—can you see them?" called Miss Codling.

"Not yet," Adam called back. His light beam had never paused at the tank, but swept on. Free of his aunt's supervision,

Adam had given up all pretense of merely fetching the wine. He was already at his work of searching, rapping, pressing, pushing. He quickly worked his way round to the far side of the tank leaving David in darkness—in complete darkness, he thought at first, until as his eyes became used to it he saw where it was broken: a thin thread of light outlined a rectangle the width of a man's body and half his height. David stared at it wonderingly, and then called Adam—softly, so as not to be overheard by Miss Codling.

"I say, there's a door or something that leads outside."

Miss Codling did not hear what was said, but she heard the hasty sound of Adam's rejoining David, and then their footsteps moving away together.

"Where are you going?" Her voice floated up with anxiety in it. "Haven't you found the wine? What are you doing?"

They did not answer. They found, when they reached David's rectangle, that it really was a door. They unlatched it and pushed at it. Very many years had passed since those hinges had been made to move; they resisted as if they had some long-standing secret to keep. The boys pressed together, with all their strength, and yet with caution, fearing some murderous drop from the roof top might lie immediately on the other side.

The door opened onto something quite different: a kind of minute courtyard, floored with lead and with the slopes of the slate roofing for its four walls. It was a well in the middle of the roof of the kind that is quite often found in old houses. From below roof level, one would never have suspected its existence. It made a charming secret retreat, airy and sunny; it was a perfect hiding place. And alas! it appeared to be bare of anything but a little dust and a few dead leaves.

A gutter came down from the roof ridge in an angle of the roofing. Where a gutter comes down, a boy can always go up. David could not resist the invitation, and Adam, after gazing about him in incredulous disappointment, followed him up.

Together they peered over the ridge, looking outward and

downward—far—far. Codlings' was an exceptionally high-built house—probably the highest building in Great Barley, not counting the church. It gave a view over roof tops and tree tops, and far out over the countryside. The boys could see the River Say winding away toward the bridge at Little Barley; they could see the railway line, and the place where it crossed the little iron bridge over the old channel of the Say—they watched a train pass over on its way to London; they watched its smoke drift with the wind over the water meadows—drift and dissolve.

"I say!" said David, awed. "You're lucky to have a roof like this, Adam!"

"Yes," said Adam. "And I feel somehow that somewhere about in this secret part—somewhere—Grandfather must have put the treasure. It's the kind of place where I'd hide a treasure, especially if the only way to its hiding place lay through my own bedroom."

Adam was about to slide down from the roof ridge to resume his search when David stopped him. "Look!" His eye had been caught by a movement below in the drive leading to Codlings'. It was Betsy, but who was with her? The sunlight glinted on a bald head. "It's Mr. Ashworthy-Smith!" cried David. "He's coming here!"

Adam and David dropped back into the well at once, to return the way they had come—there was no thought of finishing the search for hiding places now. As they came near the trap door again they could hear Miss Codling's voice, in a continuous wail of anxiety that had probably begun some time ago. "Adam! David! What are you doing? Haven't you found the jars? Why don't you answer? If you don't answer, I shall come up myself! Adam! David!"

"Coming, Aunt Dinah—just coming!"

"Don't forget the wine," whispered David, "or she'll know we were up to something."

Adam fumbled under the tank where they were supposed to have gone in the first place.

"How many jars did she say?"

"Three, I think."

"Well, there are four." Adam brought them out—four jars rather like Chinese ginger jars, only larger. Each one was sealed across the top and dated nearly fifteen years before; one was actually labeled, "To be the first opened, on the return of my son, John."

They carried the jars over to the open trap door and handed them down to Miss Codling. Before she could ask why they had been so long, Adam and David told her of the two visitors that they had "happened to see." The news was quite enough to distract Miss Codling from any further questioning. She only waited to hold the stepladder firm while they came down it; then, she hurried downstairs. The boys were left to bring the wine jars. They put them with a pile of other odds and ends in the kitchen, and then went outside to brush themselves down, and wash under the pump. While they were outside they heard the ringing of the front doorbell, and Miss Codling going to answer it; when they came back to the kitchen they found Betsy there.

"Your aunt and my father are having a private interview," she explained timidly to Adam, as to the master of the house. "They didn't want me, so I came in here. I—hope you don't mind."

In acknowledgment of this, Adam grunted. He went over to the door that led into the hall and propped it slightly open; then he sat by it, his eyes fixed steadfastly on the floor.

David made some quiet conversation with Betsy—was glad her father was well enough to walk out again, and so on—but she had not her usual spirit for talking. To amuse her and to while away the time, he got out a set of checkers from the kitchen drawer. Adam must have recognized the rattle of the wooden pieces for, without turning, he said: "My checkers!" No more; but David and Betsy did not play. They all fell into silence, waiting—listening for the click of the opening of the study door.

When it came, Betsy went out into the hall, and the two boys, without following her, posted themselves for observation. Adam took the view through the crack of the door; David took the keyhole.

Mr. Smith came out of the study with Miss Codling: they both seemed pleased—he jovially triumphant, Miss Codling as if there were some innocent joke she was looking forward to enjoying later and at length. Mr. Smith waved a slip of paper at Betsy —a slip of paper with writing upon it, and with one of its four edges rough from being torn. Even at a distance the boys recognized it as the paper they had found in Jonathan Codling's hiding place on the bridge.

"Well," said Mr. Smith, "the bargain's struck at last, Elizabeth! And I believe both sides are satisfied. You have a very good price, Miss Codling, and I—well, I have got what I wanted." He tucked the slip of paper into his wallet, put it into an inner breast pocket, and slapped himself there joyfully.

"I hope it really is what you want." Miss Codling looked guilty when she had spoken: it was just possible that she hoped it, but she clearly did not expect it.

"I have no doubt that I shall find the treasure."

"Yet the clues in the rhymes seem difficult to understand."

Mr. Smith was amused, and almost teasing in his manner. "My dear Miss Codling, I am grateful that you are selling me this rhyme, but I shall not worry deeply if its clues do not lead me directly to the treasure. There are other methods, more laborious, but at least sure."

"Other methods?"

"You said, did you not, that your father declared he had re-hidden the treasure 'in a handy place'?"

"Yes."

"Would that place, therefore, not have to be somewhere in the house or grounds?"

"Yes, but they are large, Mr. Smith."

"But not limitless. For the garden, I shall have every inch of it dug deeply over—every path dug up, every bush and tree uprooted, every plant disinterred." Miss Codling's hand moved up to her mouth, almost as though to prevent herself crying out: her face became slowly colorless. Mr. Smith went on, cheerfully: "If the treasure is not to be found in the garden, it must be in the house. I shall have wallpaper and woodwork stripped away; I shall have brick taken from brick, if necessary, until the whole house is pulled down; I shall have the foundations dug up. In the end, I shall find the treasure."

Miss Codling stretched out a hand and rested it on the wall; her fingers crept over it, as if touching something more than its surface. Still she said nothing.

Mr. Smith was full of the kind of high spirits that blind even observant people, and Mr. Smith had never been observant of human beings. He noticed nothing unusual in Miss Codling. He bade her a brisk good-by, and taking his daughter's arm, moved down the hall and out of the front door. Still Miss Codling stood, half leaning against the wall, half caressing it, with a look of dreary horror upon her face. Adam was about to open the kitchen door wide and go to her, when Betsy came swiftly back into the house.

"I said I'd forgotten something." She came close to Miss Codling as if to speak of private and important matters, but whatever it was could not be said after all. Instead, she took the hand that was resting on the wall and held it between both of hers. "Dear Miss Codling."

"I am quite all right," said Miss Codling, but her lips moved stiffly, as though the muscles of her face were chilled by winter cold. "One should foresee—one should foresee the worst—one should be ready. I was not ready." Miss Codling began to cry. Betsy brought out her handkerchief, but Miss Codling's was not a grief whose tide handkerchiefs could dry. Suddenly, but gently, she pushed Betsy from her and slipped back into the study. The door shut and there was the sound of the key turning in the lock.

Staring at the closed door, Betsy called distressfully, "Oh, David! Adam!"

Adam did not answer the call, but David came out to her. "Don't cry, Betsy! It's not your fault! It really isn't!"

"It's my father's!" she wept. "He doesn't know about the way people feel."

This was true, and yet so small a part of the whole unpleasant truth that David said nothing.

"Do you think, David, I should make Miss Codling some tea? She always says it revives her."

"I don't think she wants any now," said David. "But I'll make her some later. I know how."

Betsy wiped her eyes. "Will you? Because I shall have to go."

"You'll be coming again?"

"You—you think Miss Codling will want to see me again?"

"Yes," said David firmly, and meant it.

"Then I'll come. But you know, I shan't be able to come much more, anyway. I've done the business my father wanted. The house is sold, all but the signing of the paper. My father doesn't want me here any more, and my grandmother is expecting me back in London. Besides—"

She did not finish her sentence, but David knew that she meant that soon Adam and his aunt would not be living at Codlings' any more; soon Codlings' would not be a house any more. The unspoken thought was too much for Betsy. She turned and ran from the house.

In the time before tea would be—in David's judgment— acceptable to Miss Codling, he and Adam went up into the roof well again, to finish their search for a hiding place. They searched more thoroughly, perhaps, than they had done elsewhere, because they knew that this was the last place left for them to look. Once more, they found nothing.

When in due course David, bearing a cup of tea, knocked on the study door, Miss Codling opened it at once. She seemed her usual self, except that her face was pale and her eyes red rimmed. She took the tea gratefully, and then looked at David and at Adam beyond him, and shook her head. "You two have been poking about again and getting dirty, I can see. What do you still expect to find? Silly, silly boys!"

Two days later, while he was on his paper-delivery route, David opened the wooden box at the Codlings' gate as usual. He was about to push the paper in, when his eye was caught by something small and green in the bottom—a privet leaf. There was a closefitting lid to the box, and it was quite impossible for the leaf to have got inside without having been put there. There was nothing in the box, however, besides the leaf—no blades of grass. The leaf lay there alone, having somehow a desperate air.

David picked it up and cycled down to the house. He wanted to see Adam, without Miss Codling, and he was lucky enough to attract his attention through the kitchen window. Adam came outside to him.

David opened his hand to disclose the leaf. "Didn't you put this into the box?"

"Yes."

"A privet leaf meaning 'today'?"

"Yes."

"But no special time of day? There was no grass with it."

"No."

"Well," said David, baffled, "I don't see."

"It wasn't exactly a message for you. There was nothing you could do. I put the leaf there to mark the day—the day Oseley and Webb's man came with the paper for Aunt Dinah to sign—the paper that makes the sale to Mr. Smith."

"Today!" cried David desperately. "Perhaps something will happen to stop her signing it, even at the very last minute. Perhaps——"

"I put that leaf there yesterday," said Adam. "The man came yesterday after you'd gone, and the paper was signed."

The house was sold. Suddenly but undramatically what they had been fighting against had happened; it was already something in the past.

David was still gazing at the privet leaf: he could see now that it was browning and curling at the edges; it would soon be no more than another dead leaf. Adam stretched out his hand and took the leaf from him, dropped it to the ground, and set his heel on it.

24

Heigh-ho!

DAVID THOUGHT he had never felt such misery in all his life. At Codlings' everyone, every day, seemed sad—with the exception of Squeak Wilson. David shared in their feeling, and carried some of it home with him.

At home he met sympathetic interest in the Codlings' plight. His family did not remain for long subdued by distress, however. One breakfast time, when David sat in his usual dejection, Becky was beaming and beating her spoon on her plate in an ecstasy, Mrs. Moss was smiling, and Mr. Moss was distinctly looking pleased.

"There!" said Mrs. Moss, and laid down the letter with the foreign stamp that she had been reading aloud. Dicky Moss had written some time ago that his ship was coming through the Panama Canal, bound for home. Now he had written to say that he would be home even sooner than he had expected. Indeed, they were to expect him only when they saw him; he wouldn't waste time telegraphing or telephoning; he would come straight down to Barley as soon as the *Harbinger* had docked and he was free.

"There!" said Mr. Moss. "Aren't you glad, David, to be having Dick home again?"

"Yes," said David, and indeed he was; but his gladness could not blot out his misery. In some ways it made it worse. He had so often told Adam about Dick and about the things they could do together some day, all three of them. He had promised that he would get Dick to show the tattoo marks on his forearm and tell how they had been made far off in Hong Kong. Dick would imitate a seal's cry for Adam and teach him jujitsu and tell about his voyages in the *Harbinger*. Now after all, Dick and Adam might never meet.

"It's a pity your Adam will be gone before Dick comes," said Mrs. Moss. But she went on immediately to wonder whether hot pot or potato pie would be better for Dick's first meal at home. Or would he prefer bacon and eggs—only it must be ham and eggs for such a homecoming? Puddings were easier: Dick's favorites were jam-at-the-bottom and syrup pie. David loved syrup pie too, but he could not feel any pleasure at the prospect of it now. He slipped away from the bustle of his mother's preparations for Dick's return.

There was bustle at Codlings' too, but a joyless one: the clearing out of the house went on, and plans for departure were being made. The house, of course, was already sold, but Mr. Smith had said that Miss Codling and Adam could move out as late as they liked.

It was strange to David to think that of the five people bustling about Codlings' he would very soon be the only one left in Barley. Miss Codling and Adam would have settled in Birmingham; Betsy, even before that, would be back in London; and Squeak Wilson—poor, queer old Squeak, everyone was saying, was going the longest, saddest journey of them all. He was certainly an old man, but he had seemed still snugly set in life. Now, mysteri-

ously, he sickened—nobody could say precisely of what. He was
as much an oddity in sickness as in health: he declared he felt
no pain, that he was not ill; he would not go to bed, but huddled all day in his basket chair in his back yard, staring at nothing
and muttering to himself. He ate hardly anything, his daughter
said, and seemed hardly to sleep. He stayed in his chair until after
the sun had gone and she had given up arguing with him to
come indoors. When she got up in the morning and looked out
of the window there he was in his chair again as though he had
never moved, exactly as the day before, except that he looked a
little smaller, a little weaker.

Whatever Squeak's sickness, it had come very suddenly. On
the day after the signing of the deed of sale, he had been at Codlings' as usual, working on the wooden frame in which Jonathan Codling's portrait was to travel to Birmingham. He seemed
quite well, and cheerful too. He was not at all affected by the
gloom of the other four—he seemed not to realize it. Miss Codling stood in the kitchen, making her sorrowful arrangements,
while Squeak hammered and whistled away behind her.

"Perhaps, David, you'd take the bowls up the village to Frankie
Ellum today. He's not actually President of the Bowling Club,
but he'll pass them on to Edward Nunn, who is."

"Yes, Miss Codling."

"And we must get on with the list of the stuffed birds, so that
Adam can take it in to the Castleford Museum for the curator to
choose from. The ones they don't want and the auctioneer can't
sell—I don't think your father would mind if we just left them
here as rubbish, do you, Betsy?"

"Oh, no. He couldn't mind."

"Then there are the jars of homemade wine from the roof."
Miss Codling unearthed one of the jars from the heap of stuff
that had further accumulated. She hesitated, then said, sadly,
"I think I'll leave them, too, for your father to do what he likes
with. I had meant to sell them, or at least that we should drink
them. But then I remembered how my father had intended the

wine to be opened to celebrate a happy homecoming." Miss
Codling sighed. "There was no homecoming, and now there
seems nothing to celebrate."

Miss Codling fell silent, and Betsy and the two boys had
nothing to say. It seemed to David that the whole kitchen was
filled with a heavy sadness; yet, even now, thin and merry,
Squeak's whistling went on.

"Well," said Miss Codling, with an effort, "we shall never get
anything done at this rate. David, will you take the box of bowls
up now? And if you go on with the listing of the specimen
cases stacked in the hall, Adam, Betsy can help me as I go through
the papers in the bureau. It's almost the last job of that kind."

They went their ways, leaving Squeak still in the kitchen, still
whistling.

That was Squeak's last day at Codlings' before he fell ill—
David was the last to see him there. David had been up the village on his errand to Mr. Ellum, and was coming back down the
Codlings' drive. It was the sleepy end of a hot afternoon. The
foliage of the trees seemed to shimmer in the heat; the flowers—
wild flowers and cultivated tangling together in the neglected
borders—breathed their scents heavily. There was something
dreamlike about the garden that, with the house, was so soon to
disappear at Mr. Smith's command.

A voice somewhere down the drive began singing in queer,
thin tones that might have come from another world. David
felt almost frightened until he saw that the singer was Squeak
Wilson going home, the capacious basket of his tricycle piled
high, as usual. He paid no attention to David even when he drew
level with him. Now, David could hear the words of his little
song:

> *"Heigh-ho!*
> *Heigh-ho!*
> *Heigh-ho! Sweet summer!"*

All the sweet summers that David had ever known came drifting into his mind, and last came this one—the best of them all, that he had shared with Adam. He heard the swish of the *Minnow* as they paddled her along the Say; he saw again the moonlight silvering the water meadows by Jonathan Codling's bridge; he smelled—yes, he really smelled—the delicious scents that follow in their order the summer through—only these were mixed together all at once—hawthorn and cowslips in the meadows; in the garden, apple mint and clary, honeysuckle and roses. A wave of summer sweetness moved over David as Squeak passed, singing.

They did not greet each other—Squeak did not seem even to see David. He appeared, as David reported later to Miss Codling, to be, if anything, more cheerful than usual. The only sign of what was to come was, perhaps, in the wavering course he steered up the drive on his tricycle. He did not seem quite in control of it; on the other hand, he certainly did not seem to care.

The next day, Squeak did not turn up at Codlings', and they heard from Mrs. Perfect that he was not well. Miss Codling, in spite of all she had yet to do, was going to see him at once, but Mrs. Perfect dissuaded her. "He's gone queer about visitors, and won't see anyone. Besides, he will have it he's not ill."

Not long after Squeak had ceased to come to Codlings', Betsy came to say good-by. They had all known that this would be her last visit, yet Adam was nowhere to be found for the occasion. Miss Codling was sure he would be sorry to miss Betsy, and made her promise to call the next morning on her way to Castleford station.

The next day Betsy called, in a taxi. She stepped out, clasping a hatbox and bearing a sheaf of flowers and looking altogether almost grown-up.

"What flowers!" sighed Miss Codling. "Surely they're from a hothouse?"

"Yes. The gardener grows them in Father's greenhouse, and Father gets him to make a bouquet for Grandmother."

"Their stalks are done up properly in silver paper," said David.

"A greenhouse!" Miss Codling murmured. There was something she envied Mr. Smith, after all.

Betsy broke into her rapture by saying uneasily that she would have to go soon to catch her train.

"Of course! Now, where's Adam? Adam!" cried Miss Codling, and again, "Adam!"

Once more, amazingly, Adam had vanished. Miss Codling and David left Betsy in the kitchen while they went about in the house and garden, calling him.

David came back to the kitchen first. He was fairly certain, although he did not like to say so, that Adam had deliberately hidden himself so as not to be drawn into any leave-taking. Betsy's thought must have followed David's. Together they waited in the kitchen, listening to Miss Codling's voice calling in the distance: both felt the uselessness of it. Presently the voice ceased; Miss Codling had given up and was coming in again.

Betsy began to take her leave of David—rather formally, to suit her present appearance. "I have had a nice time here. Thank you for taking me to see Darius Codling's bridge and Folly Mill."

"It was a pity you couldn't see the old channel too."

"Yes, it was rather a pity."

At that instant an idea came to David. "I say! Of course, you're going by the London express from Castleford, aren't you?"

"Yes."

"Well, then, you'll cross the channel—you'll see it! Look out for a choked-up stream that goes under a girder bridge—your train goes over that bridge!"

"Oh, David—David!"

"You'll see it best on the Little Barley side, I should think—and you must be pretty careful not to miss it. I mean, there are plenty of other meadow ditches and things, and there isn't much left of the channel."

"And the train goes so fast! But I'll stand in the corridor and look. Oh, if I could be certain of not missing it!"

"Well . . ." began David as his second brilliant idea of the morning began to take hold of his mind. Further speech was cut short, however, by Miss Codling's worried, bustling return. They must give Adam up, she said. Betsy, if she were to catch her train, must not wait a moment longer.

As she stepped into the taxi, Betsy said to David, "And I'll look out for the old channel."

"You won't miss it."

"Well, I *might*."

"No," David contradicted her. "If you keep a lookout on the Little Barley side, you won't miss it."

"But, David——"

"*You won't miss it.*"

There was no time to stay and probe mysteries. Miss Codling was already fussing for Betsy to be off, and telling the taxi man to drive fast but not dangerously. Betsy said her last good-bys, and the taxi drove away.

As soon as the taxi had left and Miss Codling had gone indoors again, Adam sauntered into sight. He looked as if he expected David to have something to say to him, but David had urgent business of his own. He made a detour round the house, to throw Adam off the scent, and then hurried to the river bank and set off downstream in the *Minnow*. He thought he was in time, but he had an appointment for which he could not afford to be even a few seconds late. He did not stop paddling until he reached the girder bridge over the old channel.

After all, he was in plenty of time. He waited under the bridge as he and Adam had done on their first voyage, until his hand on the metalwork felt the vibrations of the approaching train. Then he pushed out again to the Little Barley side of the bridge, in full view of the line.

The train was going very fast, but from some distance away David could see Betsy standing in the corridor. The window was down, and, in spite of still being encumbered with her hatbox and flowers, she was almost leaning out. David, to catch her attention as soon as possible, raised his paddle in salute.

Betsy saw him. Understanding leaped into her eyes at the sight of the boy, the canoe, and the reedy little waterway. Her lips parted in a smile of breathless joy—joy that seemed to light a flame in her.

"Oh!" said David, startled into speaking aloud. He saw at last what Miss Codling had meant when she said Betsy would be beautiful.

Betsy had been taken by surprise, and the train was already whirling her past, but there was an instant in which she had time for a gesture of gratitude. Her arm shot out and the bouquet flew from the car window and through the air, falling in a shower of separate flowers.

She had gone. The rest of the train roared by until the conductor's car itself passed, with the conductor leaning from his little window to watch a boy in a canoe—a boy fantastically surrounded and bedecked with orchids, camellias, and maidenhair fern.

Some of the flowers in the stream were still held together by their wrapping, and kept it afloat on the water. With the end of his paddle, David rescued the silver paper for his collection; he began smoothing it out on the side of the canoe, thinking. He had managed to show Betsy the old channel she so much wanted to see, and without betraying Adam. Yet he was not happy. His mind was haunted by an idea Adam had put there when he had spoken against Betsy's going in the *Minnow*. As he remembered Adam's words, David crushed the smooth silver paper into a pellet in his pocket—pressed fiercely with his fingers and thumb until his nails ached. At last, without shaking the spectral idea from his mind, he started back along the river. He did not go back to Codlings'. Instead, he went home, and tied the *Minnow* up to the dock. Then he lingered, staring at her—certainly he had not stared longer on the first morning that he had found her there.

His feelings were painful, his thoughts confused; behind everything was the sense of people going away, of things coming to an end. He realized that he did not enjoy going in the *Minnow* any-

more. She was not a boat for one boy to go in alone. He had
paddled up to Codlings' every day without noticing it, but now
he knew. Would it perhaps be different when Dick came? He
thought not. The *Minnow* was used to Adam and David, and to
no one else: they were her masters.

David began to gather stones together into a heap. Presently
Becky came down to the dock to watch him.

"What are you doing, Davy?"

"Never you mind."

"Shall I help you?"

"If you like. I want the heaviest stones."

"What for?"

"Never you mind."

Between them, they gathered quite a pile of stones, and then
David found an excuse to send Becky indoors. To sink a boat,
you would need to waterlog her, having put enough weight into
her to make sure she really went to the bottom. There, as Adam
had said, she would rot.

From the house Becky called, "Aren't you coming, David?
What are you doing?"

"Nothing." No, daylight was not the time to do this deed.
He must wait for the night. Then, he could steal down to the
dock and, with only the moon for witness, send the *Minnow* to
the bottom of the river. She would settle into the mud and be invisible before morning. She would have disappeared as inexplica-
bly as she had come.

A scruple attacked David. He could hardly do this to the *Minnow* while Adam, her part-master, was still in Barley. The time
was coming soon enough when he would be gone.

That night, then, the *Minnow* rode the water as buoyantly as
ever. But, the next morning, David went to Codlings' on his
bicycle, instead of by canoe: he was never going anywhere by
canoe again. The *Minnow*, surprised but unsuspecting, waited in
vain at the dock.

25

Treasure for Tea

BROWN-COATED MEN from the auctioneer's went about the Codlings' house, chalking numbers on things to be sold. Miss Codling supervised them, and at the same time dusted and polished suitcases and trunks for the move to Birmingham. Meanwhile, she had given Adam the mission of taking to the Castleford Museum the completed list of stuffed birds, together with several objects easily portable that the curator would be glad to have anyway.

Side by side on the bench by the Great Barley bus stop, therefore, sat Adam and David, and much else besides. David had come so far with Adam to help carry the things—there was the horn lantern from the cellar as well as several curiosities from Miss Codling's bureau, including, for instance, an old map of the county, and a housekeeping book, in manuscript, which had been compiled by Miss Codling's great-great-great-grandmother.

Adam and David were early enough to have to wait for the bus. They had nothing to do, but there was plenty of coming and going along the village main street—plenty of passers-by to stop and talk with them. A station wagon drew up, and Mr. Nunn poked his head out.

"Will you thank your auntie for the bowls?" he asked Adam. "A sweeter set I've never seen on the green."

He went on to ask when exactly the auction sale would take place, when Miss Codling and Adam would be leaving Barley, and so on. At Adam's every answer, he shook his head as though he deplored what was happening—and as though he blamed it at least partly on Adam.

"So your auntie won't be coming over the river any more to look for the orchis in my bit of woodland." He shook his head. "And what about those dogs' graves—your grandfather's dogs, weren't they?"

"And my father's—yes."

Mr. Nunn shook his head. "Your grandfather would never have stood for this, nor your father. They would not. Ah, well! Perhaps it's a mercy they're not here to see it!"

Mr. Nunn shook his head once more before he drove away.

Next came Mr. Tey. He got off his bicycle to give the boys the latest news of Squeak Wilson. Squeak was worse, he said; he was very queer—queer in mind, as well as in body. "Not long for this world," was Mr. Tey's opinion.

Then, as if one thought led by natural association to the other —"And how long are you in Barley?" he asked Adam.

Adam told him grimly.

Mr. Tey sighed and fell to stroking his beard. No one had anything to say. At last Mr. Tey turned to David. "Well, what about this kitten?"

"Kitten?" repeated David, blankly.

"You were coming up by canoe one day, with a basket, to fetch it. You hadn't forgotten?"

"No," said David, because that seemed the answer expected. Had he really taken pleasure in the thought of a kitten, once? And had he been planning an expedition by canoe to fetch it—by the *Minnow*, who had already made her last expedition on the River Say?

"Pity you won't be coming up together," said Mr. Tey to Adam. "You and your aunt will be gone for good by then, no doubt." He offered Adam his hand in farewell. David saw that Adam's hand, as it slipped into Mr. Tey's, was trembling slightly. Then Mr. Tey remounted his bicycle and rode away.

Still the bus was not due. Down the street Frankie Ellum came out of his shop and looked long in the boys' direction, shading his eyes against the sun. That very morning David had told him that Codlings' would not be wanting any newspapers after this week; and Mr. Ellum had expressed his regret that such an old family should be leaving the village. He looked now as if he were in half a mind to stroll down the street for a word with Adam on the same subject.

"I hope *he's* not coming to ask when we're leaving, and to say good-by," said Adam, in a voice that shook with something between irritation and tears. But Mr. Ellum went inside his shop again.

"I wish the bus would come." But it did not come. Instead, from up the road appeared the figure of Mr. Ashworthy-Smith.

"Pretend to be busy," said Adam, and at once unrolled the map he was carrying, and began poring over it. David took up the book of housekeeping, opened it at random, and began to read. He listened for approaching footsteps, while in order to appear to be reading he really read—he found himself in the middle of a remedy for whooping cough.

Mr. Smith's slow steps became clearly audible as David read that a cooked mouse was sovereign against the cough. Against this prescription, someone had written in the margin (there was much marginal annotation) "Cured my sister's son, James." A later hand had written a further comment: "Arrant nonsense!"

Mr. Smith's footsteps were very near now. Ahead of him ran an obsequious little breeze; it was already fluttering the pages of David's book, so that now, as he listened to Mr. Smith's approach, he was at the same time reading "How to Get Rid of the Cock Roach."

Mr. Smith's footsteps stopped at the bench. The little breeze, before going on again, gave a last turn to the pages of David's book. Now, he was reading a list of ingredients for some recipe— one among them, being underlined in red, caught his eye. To Mr. Smith's gaze he, at least, must have presented the appearance of a genuinely and deeply preoccupied boy. Mr. Smith spoke. "I shall, I think, join you in sitting for a moment."

Both boys looked up—although David still kept a finger on the spot in the book in which, it had seemed, he had felt so lively an interest. They moved up in order to make room for a third on the bench. Mr. Smith sat down with a thump. "A most convenient place to rest! I make it the turning point of the constitutional that the doctor encourages me to take."

Adam kept silence, so David said that he hoped Mr. Smith felt better. Yes, he did indeed.

In spite of all that had been happening recently, Mr. Smith— with an amazing kind of innocence—seemed to assume friendliness in all around him. He rejoiced, too, in a bounding cheerfulness, which David, at least, found difficult to snub. Mr. Smith simply could not realize that he was nothing more than a grasping, plotting, unscrupulous, heartless, destructive villain. Perhaps, David thought, people never see themselves as others see them.

"Well," said Mr. Smith to Adam, "and is your aunt well?"

"Yes."

"Finding things tiring just now, I expect?"

"No."

Mr. Smith, puzzled, gave Adam up, and looked past him to David. David's attention had been about to slip back to his book; now it was recalled. "How's the boy that knows almost everything?"

"Very well, thank you."

"Knowing as much as I do now, eh? Knowing really everything, except for one little thing? Just a little mystery of a hidden treasure still left to be solved, eh?" And Mr. Smith laughed at his own joke, as no one else seemed prepared to.

There was another silence. And then, to David's surprise, Adam spoke in a kind of mutter. "Do you think you will solve it—I mean, just by the clues—before you need to—that is, before you start—" Adam's mutter became quite unintelligible as his mind quailed before the vision of Codlings' and its garden under search by Mr. Smith.

Mr. Smith took his meaning, without at all perceiving the feeling behind it. "I wonder . . ." he said, very seriously. "I wonder . . . The clues in the rhyme should be enough by themselves, with the alteration of one word—that was what your grandfather expected, evidently; yet they seem not to be. I have the feeling that there's some piece of knowledge that's missing, and without which the other clues can't fully be solved. Yes, a piece of knowledge that would draw the other pieces together, like a magnet, so that all, coming together, mean one thing—the exact whereabouts of the treasure. But whether that last piece of knowledge will ever turn up . . ." Mr. Smith shook his head, but not despondently. He had, as they knew, another way of seeking out the treasure.

"Ah!" said Mr. Smith. "I think I hear your bus coming—I expect it is the bus that you're here for?"

"Yes," said Adam, and began to gather up from the bench the things he was taking with him. As he stretched out a hand for the book still on David's knee, David caught his wrist lightly, both to prevent him and silently to attract his attention. Nothing was said, for both boys were conscious of Mr. Smith at the other end of the bench. David pointed at something he had been reading; Adam, leaning sideways, read the words: *a single Rose.* The phrase was not only underlined in red; as if to make the emphasis certain, someone had written by it, in the margin: *N. B. B.*

Nothing that came before or after the phrase seemed to explain its underlining and the note. It was only one of a number of ingredients: there were cowslip heads, a sprig of mint, a cupful of clover honey, a single rose . . .

"Yes, it's the bus," said Mr. Smith.

Adam turned back the page of David's book to see the beginning of whatever recipe it was. The recipe was headed FLOWER WINE, and it started: *To make one jar of Flower Wine, take* . . . The boys read no farther in the recipe; in the margin they had seen writing in the same red ink as on the later page. They read:

> *4 jars made by D. of wh. P. W. opened & drank—w' out permission—1. This privately refilled by me & labeled as 1st to be opened when J. comes home. To prevent further loss, hid all 4 UNDER the water tank in the roof, as my d. knows.*

The note was signed with the initials B. A. C. and dated nearly fifteen years ago.

"Well, here's your bus," said Mr. Smith, "so I think I'll leave you." He rose, and started back the way he had come. The boys paid no attention to him or to the approaching bus. They were reading a story that they seemed already to know—that they did already know, piecemeal. Things that they had heard at different times from Miss Codling, Mr. Tey, and from Squeak Wilson came together with this new information, as if drawn by magnetism.

The initials were no obstacle to their understanding. D. must stand for Dinah; P. W. for Philip Wilson; J. for John—Adam's father; and B. A. C. for Bertram Arthur Codling—Adam's grandfather. The underlinings in the marginal note, together with the underlining over the page, gave them almost the wording of old Mr. Codling's rhyme-clue: "Philip—single rose— UNDER the water—my daughter knows."

Philip had come to the single rose when Philip Wilson had come upon the jars of Flower Wine, one of whose ingredients was a single rose. He had been tempted; he had opened a jar, tasted it, drunk deeply of it—that was what Mr. Tey had meant by "drunk as a lord on your grandpa's own wine"; that was what Miss Codling had meant by her tactful "we lost a jar." When old Mr. Codling had recovered from his natural rage at the loss— and sacked Squeak for it—he had observed the coincidence of this "Philip" and this "single rose." What was easier, to his ingenious mind, than to profit from the coincidence—to take it further? He privately refilled the emptied jar with Something—even yet Adam and David hardly dared name it to themselves—Something that would make that jar the best of all. He had accordingly labeled it as the first to be opened in celebration of his son's return—the boys had seen and read that label. Then Mr. Codling had had to think of a hiding place "over the water." He had hit upon the water tank in the roof. His daughter was well aware of the place chosen, although she could not know that a fourth jar —the most precious of all—went there with the other three.

"Only he should have hidden it *over* the water tank, not under it," said David—the first remark either had made since Mr. Smith had moved out of earshot. "Why didn't he?"

"Because there's no top to speak of on the water tank," said Adam triumphantly. "Didn't you notice when you were up there? I did. But Grandfather must have made all his plans—even to leaving the rhyme paper in the bridge—before he realized that. It was easier, then, to alter the clue by one word, and put the jars *under* the water tank, than to start thinking of an entirely new place."

So all the pieces had come together—every one: the story was complete. David closed the book, and he and Adam swiftly collected the papers and other things from the bench. The bus— unhailed, unnoticed—had already passed them as they set off hurriedly toward home. By the time they overtook Mr. Smith they were running. "Hey! Hey!" he called after them, in surprise. But they paid no attention, for they never heard him. They sped on.

The kitchen at Codlings' was empty. Adam and David made at once for the corner where stood the pile of things that Miss

Codling was intending to leave behind to be dealt with as the new owner thought fit. Adam and David burrowed into the pile like two terriers.

"Here!" cried David. "But it's not the jar with the label." The jar was set aside; the search continued. Adam found the next jar, but again it was unlabeled. They went on looking. They sifted through and through the heap, until all its objects lay scattered over the floor. Everything had been examined—looked into, looked under, moved, or shaken. The realization came over the boys simultaneously. They sat back on their heels, staring at two jars where there should have been—where there were not—four.

Into this scene of disarray walked Miss Codling. She would have allowed herself amazement and anger if she had not seen from the faces before her that here was a crisis of the extremest kind.

"What is it?"

They told her that once more they had located the hiding place of the treasure, and once more they had found the treasure gone. Miss Codling listened carefully to the details of their story; she examined the recipe book; she examined the two remaining jars; she looked where Adam and David had already looked for the missing jars. Not for a moment did she question the correctness of the boys' deductions and their importance. She was baffled now, like them.

She stood in the middle of the kitchen floor. "Where can those jars be?"

"They've been stolen," said Adam. "The treasure's been stolen."

Miss Codling only half assented. "There's so much I don't understand. Why were two jars taken?"

To Adam and David this question seemed less interesting than the question, Who?

"Could one of the auction men have taken them?" David asked—very hesitantly, for the suspicion was monstrous.

"No," said Miss Codling. "I'm positive they've never even set foot in the kitchen. Besides, why should they want to steal a wine jar? They know nothing about any clues to hidden treasure. For that matter, who did?"

David paled; his hand went into his pocket and felt for a hard, heavy, rounded little lump—a pellet of silver paper. He clutched it as a talisman to ward off evil.

But Adam's hand slammed on to the table. "I know who stole it!"

"No, you don't!" cried David. "It wasn't her!"

"She knew about the treasure; she knew about the clues. She went through the papers in the bureau with Aunt Dinah, and could have looked into the recipe book and seen what we saw. And on the last day she called she could easily have taken the jar."

"You don't know—you weren't even there!"

"I was up the tree by the front door, and I saw her arrive with that hatbox thing over her arm—it would easily have held the wine jar. And I heard you and Aunt Dinah calling me over the house and garden for nearly ten minutes, and she must have been alone in the kitchen all that time—plenty of time."

"It's not true!"

"It is. The treasure went in that hatbox. It's probably halfway to New York or Paris, by now."

"No—no—no!" shouted David.

Miss Codling laid a hand on David's shoulder. "Of course Betsy didn't do it. Not Betsy." She faced Adam almost defiantly. "Why should anyone steal the treasure jar, *and another*? And, remember, there would only be room for one jar even in that hatbox. Where did the other one go?"

That question at least was answered in the next ten minutes. While Miss Codling sat wrapped in the deepest speculation, Adam and David roved aimlessly to and fro, searching where they knew there was no point in searching. They preferred to avoid each other's company. David kept to the house, Adam to the garden. There, among the bushes by the back door, Adam came across a wine jar, lidless, empty. He searched for and found

the lid: it was—and always had been—without any label. With
bitter triumph he brought jar and lid into the kitchen to show to
his aunt and David. "There you are! There's the other jar—the
other one that she hadn't room for in her hatbox!"

David felt the grounds of his faith in Betsy slipping from under
him; he looked desperately to Miss Codling for help. She gazed
with interest at the jar. "Opened—emptied of wine—left!" she
said, with a kind of satisfaction. She rose, composedly shook out
her skirts, and made the amazing statement: "I feel sure, as I
think things over, that the treasure has not been stolen at all.
There has just been a mistake."

"A mistake?"

"The treasure has not really been stolen at all." More she
blandly refused to say, even in the face of the boys' plainest dis-
belief and despair. "With the money from the treasure, Adam
and I shall live happily ever after, and at Codlings', too. And
you shall visit us, David." She smiled like some goddess conscious of her power for good. "Now, of course, we must get busy
setting things here to rights again. The trunk and suitcases can
go back into the attic, and Jonathan can come out of his packing
and go up on the wall again—I'm sure he wouldn't have enjoyed
Birmingham any more than we should. Yes, you can both start
on that, while I tell the auctioneer's men that the sale is canceled."

Miss Codling's assurance was amazing, but, to her companions,
never convincing, and in her short absence from the kitchen, the
boys' blackest and bitterest feelings rose irresistibly. She returned
to find them grappling and fighting as if to the death. Between
grunts Adam repeated again and again: "She—was—a—thief!"

David, almost speechless, fighting back, yet spared breath to
gasp, "Not!"

Miss Codling prised them apart. "I wish you'd trust me," she
said reproachfully. David was dabbing with the back of his hand
at an injured eye, and trying to wrench himself free to attack
Adam again; Adam doubled his fists eagerly.

"In the circumstances," said Miss Codling, "I think you're

better quite apart. Adam, you can get on with the jobs alone, and David will come with me."

She selected from the baggage that Adam was to remove an old-fashioned Gladstone bag, and opened it. "We need something to take our minds off this whole business. This worrying is too ridiculous."

Miss Codling took one of the two remaining jars of wine, put it into the bag, and then snapped it shut. "There! That's just the thing to put Squeak Wilson onto his feet again."

"Are you going to see him?"

"Yes, and you're coming with me, David."

"He won't see visitors."

"He'll see me," said Miss Codling.

Miss Codling gave David the bag to carry, and marched him away; they left Adam scowling among the suitcases.

The jar of wine made the Gladstone bag heavy, and David was thankful when they reached Squeak's cottage. There was a note pinned to the gate to say that Mrs. Perfect had gone out shopping. "All the better," said Miss Codling, as though nothing could go wrong for her on this lucky day. She left David at the front of the house, while she went round to the back. David heard her shoes on the flagstones, and then her voice, loudly and yet gently. "Squeak! Wake up!" There was a cry from the dozing Squeak —even from where he was, David realized that he sounded weak and ill. Then Miss Codling's voice sank into a reassuring, confidential murmur, and the rest of the interchange became inaudible.

The church clock had chimed the half and the three quarters before Miss Codling reappeared. She seemed well satisfied with her visit.

"Is he going to die?" asked David subduedly.

"Of course, he is," said Miss Codling, "some day. So shall we all. But not yet. No, indeed!" And she looked as though she was glad to be able to say she had put a stop to that nonsense.

They met Mrs. Perfect coming back from her shopping. She was already wearing a funereal air. She was bewildered by Miss Codling's assurance that there was really nothing wrong with Squeak at all.

"He's going," Mrs. Perfect repeated several times with reproachful emphasis, as though she had expected more sympathy from Miss Codling.

"He'll be as right as rain," Miss Codling contradicted. "And I've left him with a jar of homemade wine—a thimbleful a day would not come amiss for a convalescent."

"Thank you," said Mrs. Perfect gloomily.

"And I told him that I should tell you about the wine because— well, frankly, he might keep it quite to himself and overindulge. Moderation leads to health, Mrs. Perfect."

"Health!" said Mrs. Perfect. "Health!" David said nothing, but he felt himself on Mrs. Perfect's side, against Miss Codling's mad optimism.

After leaving Mrs. Perfect, Miss Codling made a point of calling at Mr. Ellum's paper shop to say that she would be wanting the papers to be delivered as before. "We are not moving from Barley, after all, Mr. Ellum," she said gaily.

By the time they reached Codlings' drive, Miss Codling was singing to herself; David would hardly have been surprised to see her swinging the Gladstone bag in time with her song. Certainly, David had never seen her in higher spirits—and never with less cause for them. An unpleasant—a horrible idea began to steal into his mind.

Miss Codling led the way into the kitchen again. Adam stood exactly where they had left him, with exactly the same expression on his face.

"Adam!" cried Miss Codling. "Not a thing done that I asked for!" She kissed him, and almost startled him out of his set scowl. "Never mind! It's been a tiring day for you both—at one time it almost seemed disappointing!"

She laughed; neither boy said anything. "Well, we'll have tea. While I get it, you must clear some of these things back into the attic."

David, his eyes fixed apprehensively on Miss Codling, began to pick up the Gladstone bag she had just put down. "No, no, David, you can manage more than that. The big trunk first. One of you at each end. That's it!" Laughing still, she shooed them out of the kitchen.

As they climbed up to the attic, David whispered to Adam, "I think—I think it's all unhinged her mind."

They were too frightened now to think of the treasure. They came downstairs again slowly, fearful of what awaited them.

"Listen!"

From the kitchen came the sound of soft laughter—Miss Codling, all by herself, laughing. When they walked in, she seemed quite to have forgotten about the baggage still to be taken away. She invited them to "have a good look at the table." It was spread for tea. "There's something missing off the table," she said. "What is it?"

They stared not at the table, but at her.

"It's the bread!" cried Miss Codling. "Fetch it, David! The bread bin's in the larder."

David had already set off slowly, when she called him back. "No, I think, after all, Adam should go."

So Adam went, and David waited with Miss Codling, watching her. She stood with the teapot in her hand, apparently waiting for the kettle to come to the boil. There was an unnatural tenseness about her.

The kitchen seemed very quiet, except for the singing of the kettle. Adam's footsteps had died away down the stone passage that led to the larder. The kettle stopped singing, and began rattling with the fast boiling of its water. Miss Codling stood immobile.

Suddenly, from the larder came a cry and then the clatter of feet coming back along the passage, running. The door swung open; Adam ran in with something in his arms that was certainly not a loaf of bread. He dumped into the middle of the tea things on the table a familiar-shaped jar. It had the remains of a label across its lid.

"The label's torn," said David.

"The seal's broken," said Adam.

"Well, I think I'd better make the tea," said Miss Codling, and methodically did what she advised herself.

Adam took the lid off the jar. He and David peered into it. Inside was another container that seemed to be of old, worn leather.

"And that was sealed too," said Adam, "and the seal's broken."

Miss Codling put the teapot onto the table. "How slow you are!"

Adam opened the mouth of the leather bag. "There's another bag of some sort inside," he said, "sealed——"

"And that seal is not broken," said Miss Codling, so quietly that only David, who was at her elbow, heard her.

Adam, with David's help, lifted out a small but heavy package. The packaging—in some kind of transparent material—had evidently been old Mr. Codling's contribution toward the safety of the contents; the worn leather bag looked as if it dated from the days of Jonathan Codling himself.

Through the transparent wrapping the boys could see something that set their hearts beating fast—David had to sit down in a chair suddenly, while Adam broke the last seal, and tipped the bag gently so that its contents dropped out onto the tablecloth. A skein of delicately worked silver and gold, ensnaring precious stones, fell like a snake by the jam pot; a huge unpierced pearl rolled until it was brought to a stop by the butter dish; brooches and rings, chains and earrings came to rest where they could.

"Look!" whispered David, and held up a ring whose silver work, in the form of foliage, held a red stone. "It's Jonathan Codling's own thumb ring."

"And this," said Adam, touching a necklace with pendant pearls, "this must be Sarah Codling's own necklace."

" 'With pearls hanging thereby like tears,' " said Miss Codling, quoting Sarah's mother.

They were recalled from enchantment by Miss Codling's going on to say in a high, unnatural voice, "I wonder—" Her voice cracked, and she began again. "I wonder—" She let out a hoot of laughter that made them both jump. "I wonder," she gasped, "what Andrew Ashworthy-Smith will feel at having bought so entirely undesirable a property at so extortionate a price with the absence—the guaranteed absence—of any treasure whatever." But the last words were quite lost in the high, painful pealing of her laughter as Miss Codling indulged for the first and last time in all her life in a fit of hysterics.

26

Never Tell, David!

THERE THE TREASURE was at last, although how exactly it had come there seemed beyond any power of understanding.

"Mislaid" was the explanation upon which Miss Codling insisted. In spite of its unlikelihood, it was one that Adam accepted, then and forever, utterly without question. What did he care for question and explanation? He had gained what he had so desperately striven for—Codlings' still under the golden reign of Aunt Dinah, the Say, the *Minnow*, and all the adventures of the future he could share with David.

Only David still doubted, and might from the first have forced his doubts upon Miss Codling if he had not been so alarmed at her condition. Neither he nor Adam recognized her hysteria for what it was, and they applied none of the usual remedies. Miss Codling had to recover as best she could without any face slapping or cold douches.

David still regarded her anxiously. Her optimism had been fully justified—at least as far as the treasure went; yet her col-

241

lapse now was not reassuring. He resolved to keep to himself, for the time being, two especially odd features of his experiences that afternoon. He still felt a misty insecurity; only the treasure was substantial.

And how much was the treasure really theirs? What use was it to the Codlings, when Codlings' itself was now owned by Mr. Smith?

"Perhaps," said Adam, "we shall have to do an exchange—I mean, give him the treasure in exchange for his giving us the house back."

"Then you'd be no better off than at the beginning," David pointed out. "You'll have no money to live on if you just make an exchange."

"We shall make no such thing," said Miss Codling, recovering herself rapidly, as her business sense was challenged. "I think we shall find that Mr. Smith is only too relieved to cancel utterly the deed of sale when he knows what has happened. When that has been agreed—and not before—I shall want to discuss with him the question of the treasure. We shall need to sell it—or at least most of it—and I should propose doing that through the agency of Mr. Smith."

"But won't he cheat you, perhaps?"

"For the sake of his reputation as a dealer in two continents— no. This will be no hole-and-corner business of privately finding out an unknown treasure in some out-of-the-way English village; it'll be the public exhibiting and sale on the open market of the pieces of *our* collection."

Mr. Smith was fetched to Codlings'. He came with anxious haste, having had—ever since his being passed by the boys in so frantic a rush—a presentiment of startling events.

He was closeted with Miss Codling for some time, and then, the business details settled to Miss Codling's satisfaction, was brought into the kitchen. He appeared much subdued by his interview, but he was upheld by a feverish eagerness to see, at last, the treasure.

Adam and David watched him jealously as he wedged a jeweler's eyeglass into his eye, and examined each piece minutely. He began murmuring to himself—almost purring like a cat. When he had finished, he removed his eyeglass and said formally: "Madam, I consider it an honor to be put in charge of such a collection."

"We are not intending to sell quite all," said Miss Codling. "My nephew and I—my nephew, though still a minor, I consider joint owner with me—have decided to keep this." She picked out Jonathan Codling's ruby ring.

"And there's another thing," said Adam, to his aunt's surprise. He cleared his throat. "I know I haven't actually discussed this with you, Aunt Dinah, but I've been thinking of it for some time." (So he had, and had been trying in vain to put the repentant thought from him.) "This necklace with the pearls belonged to Sarah Codling. If it hadn't been hidden with the treasure, and lost with it, Sarah would have handed it down to her descendants. I think it belongs by a kind of right to Elizabeth—to Betsy, I mean." He held out the necklace to Mr. Smith. "I think my aunt and my friend David would like it to go to Betsy, with our very best wishes." He gave a little bow when he spoke of himself, as Miss Codling and David managed to do in dazed assent at the mention of their names. "And," he added—obscurely to all but David—"I'm sorry about her not going in the canoe."

Only Mr. Smith made any objection to the gift. "You can't give it, boy! The value of it! Why, it must be worth at least——"

"Please don't tell us!" said Adam hurriedly.

His aunt supported him and added, "Sarah Codling should have worn that necklace when she married A. Ashworthy of Cumberland, four hundred years ago; perhaps Betsy will wear it at her wedding, some day. She will look very beautiful in it."

"Yes, indeed," said Mr. Smith, touching the necklace.

"Although, of course, she is going to look very beautiful anyway, when she grows up. You can see that already."

"Do you think so? I must confess I haven't noticed Elizabeth's appearance."

Nor anything else about her, Miss Codling's expression said. She clearly meant to try to impress Mr. Smith with his duties as a father. "Really, Mr. Smith," she began, "you are very lucky. You should be grateful for what you have—take tender care——"

"Yes, indeed—indeed!" cried Mr. Smith, utterly misunderstanding her. "To handle such a treasure!" Miss Codling gave up her attempt; Mr. Smith had already turned away to pore again over the objects on the table.

The gift of the necklace somehow put beyond any doubt Mr. Smith's intention to do his financial best for the Codlings. "The business may take some time," he told Miss Codling, in parting. "But I do assure you that you shall have the best bargain that can be made in the world."

He took the treasure away with him. David went with him to the Smiths' front door to see that he was not robbed. On the way, they talked, and David found that when Mr. Smith's business in Barley was done he and his wife were going to move to London. It would be much more convenient for Mr. Smith's work—and, said Mr. Smith, as an afterthought, Betsy could live with them and still be near her grandmother, who was devoted to her. That plan was Mrs. Smith's. David felt glad for Betsy, and knew Miss Codling would be pleased.

When David left Mr. Smith, he tore home. He began shouting even before he was indoors. "Mother! Father! Becky! Guess! Guess!"

There was a startled clatter from the kitchen, and, at once, Mrs. Moss's voice: "Is it Dick? Is it Dick?"

"No!" David was inside by now. "It's the Codlings! Miss Codling and Adam! They——"

"David!" cried his mother as they met face to face. "What have you done to your eye?"

"Eye?"

"A finer black eye I never saw," said Mr. Moss appreciatively.

"I got it by—by mistake."

"Fighting hammer and tongs with Adam, no doubt!" Mr. Moss laughed at his fanciful joke, and even Mrs. Moss smiled as she fussed round the patient.

David was glad to divert interest by continuing his news. "Anyway, the Codlings are all right, after all. They've found the long-lost treasure, and they're going to sell it. So they're not leaving Barley. And Adam won't have to leave Castleford School, so we shall both be there together next term. Do you think Miss Codling could afford to buy him a bicycle now? Because then we could cycle in together!"

"A bicycle!" exclaimed Mr. Moss. "Why, that's nothing! They'll be rich if they've found a great treasure."

"Rich?" The news that David had brought had appeared of unmixed good. Now, he saw a cruel gulf opening between the Codlings and himself.

The next day, he said carelessly to Miss Codling, "Will you be having footmen and things?"

She positively jumped. "What on earth gave you that idea?"

"Well, won't you be rich?"

"It depends on what you call rich. Not footmen-rich, thank goodness! Rich compared with what we have been since my father died, and even before that—yes. More exactly we can't say, until we know what Mr. Smith can do for us. In fact, David, I have to keep telling myself that we must go carefully. For example—" She hesitated, and then went on sadly but with firmness. "It would be folly, for example, even to think of a greenhouse—extravagant folly." She shook her head resolutely. "But, of course, there are some little indulgences we ought to be able to allow ourselves. We used to have a dog."

"Toby."

"That's it, and I'd like another Toby—a dog seems right about the place."

"He could come with us in the *Minnow*," David suggested eagerly.

"Yes. I'd like to buy one as a surprise for Adam—nothing expensive like a pedigree dog, or the kind that eats like a wolf— a small, reliable, hardy, cheerful, sensible, nice dog. You know the kind I mean, David."

"Mr. Ellum's terrier bitch has just had puppies," said David. "They're a cross between wire-haired terrier and spaniel—Mr. Ellum's a bit disappointed at what they look like, but their mother was a wonderful rabbiter."

"Would one be expensive?"

"I'll ask Mr. Ellum."

They were all as busy with arrangements at Codlings' now as they had ever been in preparing for the move. There was a good deal of putting back to be done—although Miss Codling declared that she was heartily relieved to have got rid of so much junk to jumble sales and the rubbish heap. At the same time, there were Miss Codling's "little indulgences." An immediate plan was to hold a small party, with the Mosses as guests. The tea alone would be of a kind that Codlings' had not seen for a very long time. Miss Codling was going to buy peaches in Castleford, and real cream from Nunn's farm; there would be sandwiches with various fillings, including salmon; there would be chocolate biscuits; and Miss Codling was to try her hand, long unused to such things, at several kinds of cake, with ingredients—cherries, candied peel, almonds—that David felt sure she had not afforded for many years.

Surprisingly, there was an objection to Miss Codling's invitation, from Mrs. Moss. She remarked mournfully to her husband that she felt in her bones that Dick would choose to arrive that very afternoon.

"Now, Alice," remonstrated Mr. Moss, "is it likely? And anyway we can leave a message with the neighbors to say where we've gone. And Dick's got legs."

So the invitation was accepted for an afternoon just three days after the discovery of the treasure. Earlier that same afternoon Adam brought the *Minnow* down to pick up David and Becky;

they were all going up to Folly Mill. Mrs. Moss, having spent part of the previous day watching Adam demonstrate lifesaving, had consented to Becky's going in person to claim her kitten.

Adam brought the *Minnow* alongside the Mosses' dock, which he had not visited for some time. "Hello! What's that heap of stones for?" he asked.

"Nothing," said David gaily, and, to prove it, pushed them into the river.

It was a sun-golden afternoon, and this was the first voyage the boys had made on anything but business intent—or, at least, without the nagging consciousness of the passage of days and the pressure of circumstances. Now as they went upstream they did not hurry: they marked down places that would be good for swimming or for fishing; ancient willow trees whose fantastic bendings and twistings invited the climber; meadows that might bear mushrooms; reed beds that might hide the nests of moor hen. When they reached Folly Mill, Becky cried, "Oh! Look!" And there was a darting flight of turquoise blue as a kingfisher—the first that Adam and David had ever seen so close—flew out from its fishing haunt under the mill bridge, and past them.

At the mill, Mr. Tey welcomed them like royalty. He shook hands with each of them in turn, in a congratulatory manner. He said that he was delighted to hear the Codlings were not leaving Barley; and that Adam and David had been very astute in finding the treasure (no one had told anyone, yet both villages already knew the story in outline); and that Becky was the image of her late maternal grandmother. Mr. Tey was, in short, pleased with the whole state of affairs. "And even Squeak Wilson's on the mend," he concluded. "He sent word round today that he hopes to come to do odd jobs for me next week. It's my belief there was never anything seriously wrong with him—just something weighing on that queer mind of his."

They disengaged themselves from Mr. Tey's conversation at last. The kitten was put into its lidded basket, good-bys were said, and the expedition set off on the homeward trip. The afternoon was by now far advanced, but they did not care. David paddled dreamily, seeing in the bow, not Becky and her basket, but the head of Toby, with ears cocked forward and nose turning from side to side to take in delicious river smells. Adam was paddling lazily too, humming.

They tied the *Minnow* up at the Codlings' bank and made their way to the lawn, where they were all to have tea. There were two figures already there; Mrs. Moss, with a strange shimmering material round her shoulders, sat by the tea table; beside her stood a tall young man, dressed from head to foot in a dark-blue outfit that—even from a distance—did not look like an ordinary suit.

Adam was the first to realize the truth. "It's your brother Dick!" he cried. They all ran forward then, laughing and shouting. Dick was introduced to Adam; and Becky had to open her basket to show him the kitten; and Mrs. Moss had to show David the shawl Dick had brought her from his travels.

"I brought you something too, David," said Dick. "It's a real fishing rod, with line and float and hooks. I brought two, as a matter of fact, in case your friend would like one as well."

While the boys were examining their fishing rods, Miss Codling appeared round the corner of the house, in company with Mr. Moss. "Adam! David!" she called. They were too busy with their rods to listen, but Miss Codling, equally, was too excited to notice. "Mr. Moss thinks it would be quite practicable and not too expensive after all to build just a small greenhouse by the back door. It would be—" She turned to Mr. Moss.

"Section-built," he said. "I know the man over at Tidfield that puts 'em up cheaply. I could lend a hand, too, some evenings."

"Your husband is so kind!" cried Miss Codling to Mrs. Moss, almost curtsying to her.

Then they had tea, and talked—about greenhouses and king-fishers and the Panama Canal and kittens and fishing rods and a hundred other things.

"What are you going to do when you grow up?" Dick asked Adam.

"Go to sea."

"What!" exclaimed Mr. Moss, who overheard him. "All this fuss to find treasure so that you needn't leave Barley, and the next thing is you're going away to sea!"

Adam tried to explain. "You don't want the same things at different times. I want to stay here now, more than anything, and then I want to sail all over the world when I'm old enough."

"And I shall stay here forever," whispered Miss Codling happily, half to herself. Then, to change the subject a little, she asked what David was going to do.

"I'm going to America," he said, "to shoot rapids in canoes."

Adam looked envious for a moment, and the talk began again, of canoes and seagoing ships and the same delightful and inexhaustible subjects on which they had touched before. They talked until the sun began to redden and sink, and they had to move from the lawn to the porch, because the dew was rising. Mr. Moss carried Becky in his arms, where she had already fallen asleep.

Then Miss Codling remembered the fourth, unopened jar of wine. "We can celebrate a homecoming at last," she said. "Run and fetch the Flower Wine, Adam!" As he went she added, "And celebrate the end of the treasure search, too."

David knew suddenly that this was his opportunity—his last opportunity. Adam was already indoors; the others were busy teasing the kitten with Mrs. Moss's ball of knitting wool. David moved until he stood at Miss Codling's elbow.

"Miss Codling!"

She started, almost guiltily. "Yes, David?"

"The day we found the treasure there were two funny things I didn't understand."

"There were so many funny things—what a whirlwind of a day that was!"

"There were two specially funny things. You remember when

Adam was looking about outside—when he found the empty jar among the bushes?"

"Yes—oh, watch the kitten!"

But David would not watch the kitten. "While he was looking outside, I was looking inside. I went into the larder; there wasn't a wine jar behind the bread bin then."

"But, David, Adam certainly found one there when he went later for the bread. Doesn't that mean that you must have overlooked it earlier?"

David had an uncompromising "No" to give to that question, but he did not quite dare to utter it. Meanwhile, Miss Codling, taking advantage of his silence, had turned from him to fasten her closest attention upon the kitten. She seemed utterly without interest in what David, in his mind, called the Jar Mystery.

The Jar Mystery really concerned two jars: one jar had been emptied of wine and left in the bushes as mysteriously as the other, full of treasure, had appeared in the larder. David had pondered both mysteries for long. Now, he considered them yet again. The jar full of treasure in the larder . . . the jar emptied of wine, among the bushes. . . .

Adam had returned with the Flower Wine, and Miss Codling was preparing to serve it.

"I hope it won't go to the boys' heads?" Mrs. Moss said nervously.

"Not such a thimbleful as this will be."

"A whole jarful now . . ." said Mr. Moss.

A jarful of wine . . . David, for the first time, wondered where all the wine had gone from the jar found empty in the bushes—a whole jarful.

"A whole jarful of wine—now, that would make you tipsy," said Mr. Moss.

Thimbleful by thimbleful, the wine was dropping into the glasses. It was a reddish-brown color that the last of the sunlight illuminated to a deep gold. From it rose a scent heavy, sweet, delicious.

"No wonder they speak of the bouquet of wine," murmured Mr. Moss.

David, sniffing at his glass, tried to distinguish all the flowers of that summer bouquet: there was hawthorn, surely—and cowslips —mint—clary—roses, of course. . . . His nose twitched, trying to remember where it had known that particular mingling of scents before.

Then he remembered. A late, hot afternoon, and a song:

> *Heigh-ho!*
> *Heigh-ho!*

The singer came bearing with him, unmistakably, the scent of hawthorn and cowslips, apple mint and clary, honeysuckle and roses—all the flowers that go into the making of Flower Wine. Scented with summer, he zigzagged past on his tricycle, singing— lightheartedly, lightheadedly—yes, tipsily.

And the jar full of treasure?

Mr. Moss nudged David, thinking he was dropping into sleep. They were all raising their glasses to toast Dick and wish him many happy homecomings. The wine, sweet and strong, warmed David's throat, and warmed his memory and his wits.

> *Heigh-ho!*
> *Heigh-ho!*
> *Heigh-ho! Sweet summer!*

The voice still buzzed in his head, and he saw Squeak Wilson's tricycle, with Squeak caroling upon the saddle, and, fastened to the handle bars in front, a capacious—a *very* capacious basket.

David set down his glass. He wanted to tell Miss Codling that he was sure he knew how the treasure had been taken away— one could hardly say "stolen," for the thief had wanted wine, not treasure. What an appalling shock he must have had when he examined the swag closely!

"Miss Codling!" said David, but she was in conversation with the others. They were talking of the wine, marveling at its properties, for it certainly seemed to have done Squeak Wilson an amazing amount of good. Since Miss Codling had left him with a jar he had been getting steadily better.

David followed their conversation for a little, remembering Squeak as he had heard him described during his illness: hardly eating, hardly sleeping, crouching miserably all day in the basket chair in his back yard. David himself remembered seeing Squeak in that basket chair on the morning when he had interviewed Mrs. Perfect in the churchyard. Suddenly one incident of his visit came to his mind with new significance: he had been trying to bribe Squeak with two lengths of licorice. Squeak had taken the licorice, tilted back his basket chair, and thrown the lengths into the space beneath. "And mum's the word about *that* hidey-hole!" his wink had seemed to say.

"Miss Codling," whispered David, securing her attention at last, "the treasure was stolen—well, stolen by accident—and I know who stole it, and where it must have been kept."

"Nonsense, David! How can the treasure have been stolen? We found we had it safely after all."

"Somebody must have brought it back and put it in the larder."

Miss Codling was perversely inattentive, but David whispered on, now laying before her the second mystery of which he had spoken. "Miss Codling, you remember when I carried the jar of wine for you to give to Squeak?"

"In the Gladstone bag—yes."

"And you took it from me at Squeak's front gate, and you left me there, while you went round to him, and you gave it him and had a long talk with him?"

"Yes."

"You had a very long talk with him."

"We had private matters to discuss," said Miss Codling sharply, but keeping her voice lowered.

"Then we came back, but you carried the bag because it was empty." Miss Codling said nothing to this, so David went on.

"When we got back, you put the bag on a chair in the kitchen, and——"

"You were just going to pick it up," said Miss Codling quickly, "when I told you to help Adam with the trunk first."

"I did pick it up," David contradicted. "And it was heavy—just as heavy as when I carried it to Squeak's."

"How could it have been? We left the wine at Squeak's. How could the bag have felt heavy if it were empty?"

"It didn't feel empty."

"Oh!" breathed Miss Codling. "Oh, Davy!"

"So you see," said David eagerly, "I think I know everything: who stole the treasure, and where they hid it, and *who brought it back*. I think I know——"

"Then never tell, Davy, never tell."

"But, Miss Codling!" insisted David. In his excitement, he had slightly raised his voice. Idly curious, the others had turned their heads to listen. In the dusk, he could see the paleness of their faces turned toward him. Yet he must make one more attempt to speak, for he felt his opportunity—his last opportunity—slipping from him forever.

"Miss Codling!"

"Hush, David!" said Miss Codling. She shook her head at him, smiling, and laid a finger across his lips. "Hush—hush and listen: there's a nightingale singing in the trees by the river."

ABOUT THE AUTHOR

A. PHILIPPA PEARCE was born in Great Shelford, Cambridgeshire, England. She was two when her family moved into the King's Mill House on the tranquil River Cam. "My father's family," she writes, "seem always to have been milling or farming, or both, in the villages of south Cambridgeshire. My father and grandfather were flour-millers at the King's Mill [Folly Mill in *The* Minnow *Leads to Treasure*]. There has been a water mill on that site since at least the compilation of the Domesday Book." During her years at Girton College, Cambridge, and since then as script writer and producer for the B.B.C., she spent as much time there as possible, especially in summer, until the Mill and the Mill House were sold a few years ago. The Mill House itself and the names of all but the last of her ten nieces and nephews appear in this book, her first, which she calls "the acknowledgement of a happy childhood."